The Author and Me

Éric Chevillard

Translated by Jordan Stump

DALKEY ARCHIVE PRESS

Champaign / London / Dublin

Originally published in French as *L'Auteur et moi* by Les Éditions de Minuit, Paris, 2012

Copyright © 2012 by Les Éditions de Minuit

Translation copyright © by Jordan Stump

First edition, 2014

Library of Congress Cataloging-in-Publication Data

Chevillard, Éric
    [Auteur et moi. English]
    The author and me / Éric Chevillard ; translated by Jordan Stump. -- First edition

    pages cm
    Originally published in French as L'Auteur et moi.
    ISBN 978-1-62897-075-3 (pbk. : alk. paper)
    I. Stump, Jordan, 1959- II. Title.
    PQ2663.H432A9813 2014
    843'.914--dc23

                    2014016358

Partially funded by the Illinois Arts Council, a state agency

www.dalkeyarchive.com

Cover: design and composition by Mikhail Iliatov
Printed on permanent/durable acid-free paper

The Author and Me

My imagination is a font of glue, admitted Léon Bloy, and the author of these pages could well make the same confession. To give his tales direction and deviltry, he relies on the dizzying accelerations fomented by his taste for logical discourse driven to its most extreme conclusions and consequences, well beyond those at which, in its wisdom and prudence, in its tedious wisdom and niggling prudence, reason halts. But for this he needs a pretext, any pretext at all, the principal quality of a pretext being that it is immaterial. The author's tales generally affect a vaguely novelistic form, and so he must yield to at least some of the novel's reality principles; he must, for example, in some cases, name his characters—a preliminary ordeal for his sterile imagination, utterly hopeless at that task, incapable of conjuring up *ex nihilo* a plausible but original and euphonic surname. For which reason the author often resorts to identity theft—or, more modestly, since in the end it involves simply making use of a name, with no idea of despoiling anyone of his rank or privileges, to identity borrowing. And, so as not to give offense or create troublesome misunderstandings, his preference is to cull those names from tombstones.

The author is attached to the Ile d'Yeu by a thousand sensory and sentimental bonds, and although—O tempests! O maelstroms!—a not insignificant segment of its population perishes at sea, the Ile d'Yeu nevertheless has a cemetery, like anywhere else, in which he is fond of strolling. It would be a great shame if cemeteries were used only for resting in peace, perfectly suited as they are to undisturbed reflection. It was in fact at the front gate of this particular cemetery that, on July 15, 1994, at 2:30 in the afternoon, the author arranged to meet with a young female reader who wanted to make his acquaintance, and who would become—this encounter having been capped by a happy ending, as well as by a pretty frizzed topknot that may well have played its part—his stolid companion. That cemetery became, in 1951, the last resting place of Marshal Pétain, on whose grave, to this day, flowers are regularly laid by the traditionalist Catholic Church and a clutch of nostalgic old buzzards, whose flock nonetheless thins with each passing year, and who now lack the strength to raise the slab, hoist out the coffin, and conceal it in the hold of a boat for transport to Verdun, there to bury that moldering carcass, those metacarpals disgraced at Montoire, as they unsuccessfully sought to do in 1973.

For very obvious reasons, the author is reluctant to take the Marshal aboard in his turn, and dub one of his characters "Philippe Pétain." On the other hand, there is in that same cemetery one grave that irresistibly draws him, where his melancholy finds a charm that soothes it, pacifies it, transmutes it into a deeply tranquil sensation not far from serenity, a simple, modest grave, a grassy mound bordered in white, graced with a yellow rose bush, and in the center a marble slab bearing in gilt letters the names of its occupants and the dates between which they lived out their lives: *Dina Egger* and *Nino Egger*. The author has forgotten the years of their births and does not have that slab here in front of him (he can't very well spend his every waking moment in that cemetery), but he remembers the years of their deaths: 1985 for Dina, 1986 for Nino. Above all, he recalls that Dina's short life, contained within Nino's far longer existence, suggested that the one was the daughter of the other, and that Dina's premature demise had caused or at least hastened her broken-hearted father's. For some time, the author's deeply moved reveries revolved around that tragic tale and that grave, and he decided to mingle the two names Dina and Nino when he conceived the central character of his most recent book.

Thus was born Dino Egger, who was in fact never born, but that's precisely the subject of the novel of which that name is also the title, and which it would be somewhat excessive to reproduce here in its entirety. The curious reader need only peruse the volume in question; with a little diligence, it must still be possible to dig up a copy. Then writing takes over: that name proves extremely productive in the economy of the ensuing fiction. Observant critics note that the words "dinosaur" and "egg" resonate in the name Dino Egger—a most pertinent point, given the story's questioning of origins and speculation on beginnings. One of those wondrous workings of coincidence, well-known to all writers. No question about it, that cemetery is a very special place, rich in significant encounters for the author.

Then the book appears. Awaiting it are the customary critical acclaim, on which the author preens himself when nobody's looking, and the usual paltry sales, which he makes a show of scorning in public. None of that matters here. Because there now comes to pass something less predictable: two of his female readers—which makes three, let us note, so the author really has nothing to complain of; as for his readers of the masculine sex, they must all be resting in peace in various cemeteries, meaning that some of them still might make a name for themselves in literature one day—two of his female readers come forward to express their astonishment on discovering that book's title, *Dino Egger*, since, they tell him, they once knew a fascinating young woman with a very similar name: Dina Egger. Needless to say, they assume this is a matter of chance. A coincidence, actually, yet another. Alas, Dino Egger never existed, but Dina Egger did, and alas, she is dead. The author learns that she was a beautiful, fair-skinned young woman, German Swiss, an urban planner, funny, politically aware, a feminist, in love, and that a surging wave swept her away before her companion's eyes as they were strolling the island's rugged shoreline on the 31st of December, 1985. "The sea is not my friend," she had confided some months earlier, during a stay in Naples, to Elizabeth, who was (her friend). Because of her pale skin, she avoided the sun, which, it's true, she was unlikely to encounter on the Ile d'Yeu's rugged shoreline on a 31st of December. But you don't go strolling the Ile d'Yeu's rugged shoreline on a stormy winter day if you don't have a passionate heart and soul, and a taste for dramatic spectacles. Already ill, her father Nino did not long survive his daughter. Their mother and wife, Annemarie, known as Mouki, a former dancer, created this beautiful grave of grass and roses, which the author, knowing nothing of all this, so often visited to reflect, in his own fashion. Time went by, and Mouki died. The overgrown grave remains a splendid garden for dreams and meditations.

And so, in the end, a life blossomed from the inexistence of Dino Egger.

A few years earlier, on the occasion of a previous book, *Demolishing*

Nisard, the author had seen another of his characters rise from the dead, this time animated by a desire for vengeance and an itch to cross swords. A professor of nineteenth-century literature, enraged by the treatment dealt out in that novel to the figure—transformed though it be into a pure symbol—of the opportunistic old fart Désiré Nisard, not by the author, as it happens, but by the narrator, Albert Moindre, whom we will meet again later, notably in *Dino Egger*, and whose name was borrowed from a painter untrammeled by the asphyxiation of culture, Joseph-Albert-Alfred Moindre, nicknamed "the Egyptologist" (1888-1965), introduced to the wider world by Jean Dubuffet in fascicule 4 of the Compagnie de l'Art Brut, this professor, then, perhaps feeling, as if by metonymy, personally insulted—professors often bond body and soul with the object of their studies, specialists with their specialty, and biographers with their heroes, such that you can't tease a pig without incensing the *charcutier*, who nonetheless cuts that same pig into little slices every blessed day, but anyway—our scholar, on seeing the advance publicity for that book, wrote to its publisher in the following terms:

It has come to my attention that you intend to publish a book aiming to "demolish Nisard." Let me alert you to the tissue of inanities contained in that book's catalog copy:

1. Nisard is not a blinkered critic.

2. In no way was he harmful to mankind; the allegation is false and libelous.

3. The assertion that he never should have been born is an insult to the memory of a critic of great importance in our literary history, a critic who mattered, and who was not, as your author claims, utterly forgotten in 1888.

I write to advise you that this text betrays a profound misunderstanding of both the man and his work, which is my area of expertise. Let me add that he has descendants, with whom I am personally acquainted and whom I intend to inform of this publication; they may well take offense at these scurrilous claims.

Lashing out at a critic of the last century is a cowardly act, and a rather pitifully facile one.

I do hope you will bear this message in mind.

I am writing at once to Nisard's great-great-grandson.

Cordially,

"Sincere good wishes, sympathy," offers the Larousse as a definition for cordiality. What a curious sentiment! In any case, the great-great-grandson turned out to be a great-great-grandnephew of Désiré Nisard, whose ire this very cordial lady had thus sought to rouse in order to see him taken to court, the author and not Albert Moindre (protected from penal sanction thanks to his fictional-character immunity), thereby blithely wiping out a century of theoretical reflection on the notions of the author and the narrator. "Obviously," she added in another letter to the publisher, "you and your author have an ironclad defense: it's a novel! And so everything is possible because it is the narrator speaking, and not the author. I hope you do not assume we scholars of literature can be taken in by such sophistry."

Nisard's great-great-grandnephew, a retired doctor, a courtly nonagenarian with a keen literary sensibility, thereafter exchanged with the author a handful of letters, wry, entirely amicable, quite elegant, and left the matter there. He received another short note from that gentleman a few years later, when a critic from the *Figaro Magazine* sought in turn to "demollish" (sic) the author, on the appearance of *Dino Egger*. Still as sparkling as ever, the heir to the Nisard name wittily voiced his delight at seeing his ancestor thus avenged, even as he regretted that this churlish reviewer was so ill-informed as to refer to Nisard as an "imaginary old critic," which was indeed to deny him entirely, him and his work, something Albert Moindre would never have done, even in the full fury of his diatribe, Nisard becoming in that review Dino Egger's negative twin.

Everything was connecting up wonderfully.

One of those wondrous workings of coincidence, well-known to all writers.

The great-great-grandnephew, as irreconcilable to that fluke of genealogy as the lyrebird to the grim-beaked pterodactyl, lamenting that old age had left his handwriting so frail and unsteady, closed his letter with the perfectly legible words *no hard feelings*, which moved the author more than the most fulsome praise, for his heart is good, if often sorely tested.

These posthumous quarrels had in fact shaken him more than he can say. He is nonetheless in the habit of mocking—oh, the many things he mocks!—those novelists who claim that their characters suddenly spring to life and escape their control, as if their hairy, pencil-clutching hand sometimes bursts from the tunnel of their sleeve like a spider and runs off to chase flies. There is every reason to laugh. Rarely does irony find such sumptuous morsels to sink its fangs into. The real phenomenon, which does actually happen, is entirely different: it's rather the author who finds himself snatched up by his fiction, ripped away from his desk, swept off by the torrent of words gushing from his hairless hand, a dismembered, disarticulated babbler, clinging to his sentences like a shipwrecked wretch to his plank, and thereby irremediably confused with his character, even if this latter bears the name Albert Moindre.

This cannot go on. The author has his pride, and his autonomy. He stands before you determined to keep his distance from the narrator of his new book, to distinguish himself from him as sharply as he can, and thus to hold fast to his mastery. Which is why he will permit himself to intervene whenever circumstances require, coolly and firmly, so as to protect himself from any possible confusion. Better to consciously parasitize this story than to be its dupe and its patsy from one end to the other. And it is with iron in his soul that he now invites his reader to follow his lead, to cast off that past, to turn the page.

The Author and Me

A quick word, Mademoiselle, I don't mean to importune you, people are always importuning young ladies, and indeed what is there to do with young ladies if not importune them, what are young ladies for if not to be importuned, I ask you, Mademoiselle, you who are in an ideal position to answer, sitting quietly at this table, taking the sun on the terrace, sipping your strawberry juice, and finding yourself suddenly approached by a man who will thus very likely importune you, since if young ladies are to be importuned there has to be someone to take up the task, and for that, for importuning young ladies, nothing can rival and nothing will ever replace a good, red-blooded man, though in a great many other domains substitutes for him have been found—a strong woman, an animal, a machine, a robot—in this realm he's still number one, wouldn't you say, tell me, or rather no, later if you would, first I want you to listen, I won't be long, just a quick word, I need to talk and you're here, a young lady, all the better, and nicely put together if you don't mind my saying, but that's no more than a happy accident, I would just as readily have approached a portly gentleman had a portly gentleman been sitting in your place, modifying only my prefatory remarks, of course, deleting everything that concerns young ladies and man's unparalleled gift for importuning them, I wonder if you'd mind removing your purse from that chair, I'd like to sit down for a moment, thank you, you can listen much more comfortably this way, a big fat gentleman would have done perfectly well, I would have importuned a big fat gentleman just the same, I hope this will resolve any ambiguity in your mind, without giving rise to another, don't go suspecting me of some maniacal penchant for big fat men, my preference is for young ladies, which is what you appear to be, no one could be more astonished by that coincidence than I, in these circumstances so hostile to me, but once again, you or another, as long as she—or still another, as long as he—has ears to hear and is not overly mobile, I would have collared him just as I did you, so please don't assume—yes, hello, a large coffee, thanks—don't assume that I approach you as a result of some choice, some selection, this time your charms are entirely beside the point, sorry, but don't take it amiss, note that I don't dwell on your flaws either, which brings me to what brings me here, I've got to explain what has me so agitated, why I should be haranguing you so cavalierly, so rudely, when impatience and anger are entirely foreign to my true temperament. I am a level-headed man. Believe it or not, it takes a great deal to set me off. Perhaps I'm about as lovable as a prison door—I've been told so, in so many words—but that only means it's not in my nature to come unhinged. I deplore all excessive behavior. I'm not easily put out, it takes a good hard push, and a kick in the rear won't suffice.[1] But this morning, as I was leaving my house, summoned by the duties of my charge, I was promised in dulcet tones that my favorite dish would be awaiting me at lunchtime. As you may well imagine, I licked my chops all morning as I hammered away at my tasks, and at noon I sat down with the appetite of ten men, eagerly awaiting the trout amandine I so dearly love, when the kitchen door finally swung open and, brace yourself, I saw set down before me a dish of cauliflower gratin, whose sickly scent instantly turned my stomach. I can't stand the stuff, I cannot abide cauliflower gratin, I despise it, it's dreadful. You must agree, Mademoiselle, it is quite simply dreadful.

The look of it, for a start.

Then the smell. Putrid.[2]

---

1 It may well seem that this passage constitutes a relatively faithful self-portrait of the author, thus undermining the thesis laid out in his preamble and shattering his proudly proclaimed autonomy, as if, despite his stated intention, he has melded with his character from the very first moment of his appearance. Unlike that character, however, the author's reserve, and the phlegmatic temperament for which he is known, readily observable as they are, are nonetheless forced, are in fact wholly artificial. In his case, this constitutes a strategy for going unnoticed, inspired by the sort of social phobia that has troubled his relations with others ever since childhood. He thus feigns detachment, choking back his impatience. His fists clench in his pockets; often his feet make two more fists in his shoes. Bruxism has worn down his teeth. He suffers from a stage-four chronic gastritis, which may well degenerate into an ulcer. Nonetheless, he does not intend to distinguish himself from his character by systematically disparaging himself, nor by blurting out failings and flaws heretofore kept hidden at the price of constant effort. You'll see, he will gain the upper hand and prevail over his subject. He has his own qualities, which ask only to be expressed. He'll get a grip on himself yet.

2 The author isn't exactly wild about it himself. Still, he would avoid such excessive language. He would not make a cauliflower gratin on his own initiative (he's hopeless, in any case: able to go fry an egg and nothing more). Still, he will eat

And yet there she was beaming like the fairy godmother who's just granted your fondest wish! I disabused that witch in no uncertain terms. Hold on, I said, you're not seriously expecting me to put that in my mouth? Really, have you even looked at the stuff? I know of only one thing lumpier, and that's a chancre.

Where's my trout?

I was still thinking it might all be some sort of gag.

Very funny, but now where's my trout? You promised me a trout.

The joke dragged on and on, falling flatter and flatter. Oh, it's true, humor's so hard to pull off! You should never cling to a bit when the audience proves unreceptive. And here I lost my temper. You must understand, it was a pretty nasty blow. Hard to stomach, there's no better word. There you are licking your chops for a trout and you find yourself mired in cauliflower! The spangled trout, with its speckles of red, blue, and gold, swims nimbly upstream between two ranks of almond trees, heading straight for your stomach, and all of a sudden your delectable dream congeals into the warm sludge of a cauliflower gratin! If there was ever good reason for rage, can it be denied, can you deny it, Mademoiselle, that it was then and there? Can you even begin to picture the trap that had been set for me? And how naively, how trustingly I walked into it! It's the child promised a day at the beach and then roughly shoved into the cellar. It's the sweet, innocent fiancée prostituted in a dank alleyway, against a wall stinking of urine and decay, to the underworld's ugliest, most perverted mugs, she who was advancing toward the pink-and-white-petal-strewn bed of her wedding night, clad only in her hymen. It's the young donkey that thought itself a colt and gaily trotted off toward the meadow of tender grass, only to find itself brutally locked up in a thistle-choked paddock. Oh! the virtuoso's violin passed down by inheritance into the paws of a bear. The newborn hooked like a fish, ripped from his amniotic bliss and given a sharp clout just to hear him cry. Cauliflower gratin in the stead of a trout amandine! If that isn't a comedown! With that a whole world crumbles. Everything you believed in, all

---

cauliflower gratin if it's set before him, and would never make such a fuss. Will, however, politely refuse a second helping—let's not overdo it—claiming to be full, and even overwhelmed with delight.

your hopes and dreams, the few principles you still clung to, everything decays, cracks up, falls apart, crashes to earth. What good are flowers now, or butterflies? Sunshine? What's that?

Must I already remind you, Mademoiselle, of the facts, of the circumstances? I sit down with the idea—which is also a sensation, of the same order as a caress—of savoring a trout amandine, and I find myself being served cauliflower gratin. How can I make this clearer? You see the waiter, there? I order trout amandine, and I get back "One cauliflower gratin for table six!"

—I thought you said a large coffee?

—I did, I did, thanks … this will be fine, thanks.

(We could hear the traffic going by. The sighs of the articulated buses summoned up the ambience of the prehistoric plains, the last dinosaurs expelling the air from their lungs before toppling on their sides, but the buses soon started off again, once a number of men and women had alit, and others climbed aboard. We might have pondered the point and the import of this hostage swap; we didn't. We would have needed a bird's-eye view, perched high above the world, to fully understand the senselessness of this endless flux; but no, we were part of it, and therefore ill-placed; enclosed in the tumult of beings and things, our words added to it, no less than our chairs screeching against the tile floor.)[3]

Disappointment … despair … rage! The urge to kill then comes over you, Mademoiselle, and above all the secret temptations of torture. All at once you find yourself thinking of the many possible but overlooked uses of the most rudimentary tools. And this time your tongs won't undo your hammer's insistent labors. For once—how wonderful!—your tongs and your hammer will be working as one.

---

3 These intercalated observations record the to-do of the surrounding world such as the author's character perceives it, filtered through the sieve of his nerves, and thus inevitably skewed toward the sharp and the piercing. The author will most often find nothing to question in these lines, but it would be unjust to attribute these observations to him. He publishes his own every day on *L'autofictif*, his blog, a very awkward and unlovely term, for which, as he has already confessed, he feels no affection: "it sounds like popping bubble gum, unless it's an octopus blowing its nose or a frog gulping a mayfly" (*Libération*, March 17, 2011).

Something sublime may well be in the offing, exquisite in its inventiveness.

Have you ever longed to strangle someone, Mademoiselle? Besides me, I mean?

Your pursed lips say no—not even me? Really? Oh, but in that case you must never have endured so cruel and agonizing an experience. Just imagine, imagine a beautiful trout, still wriggling only the day before, as at one with the stream as the current, the muscle of the light, the intelligence of the water, its tender flesh perfumed with a little spray of lemon, sprinkled with finely slivered almonds, diaphanous hosts toasted golden brown in sizzling butter …

Just you take a whiff of that.

But what's this? What on earth can that be? That stench?

Unholy God!

They say disappointment is bitter—I find it more insipid than anything else.

It's cauliflower gratin!

But that's pulling the old bait-and-switch on the newborn babe extending his lips toward the breast of the Virgin and its fresh, wholesome milk! Better yet: it's beating that disarmed, trusting innocent senseless! How horrible! How ignoble! What a sham! Be so kind as to remove this thing from my sight, you seem to be forgetting that I left my boots on the doorstep. I'm not some swamp monster, I don't eat such muck! And to think, she'd promised me … But never mind, hear how it reeks! Like the laundry room of an army base the evening after maneuvers. Somewhere around here you'll find a gassy hyena with a caravan of two-humped cadavers in its gut, I just know it.

Oh, sooner that, yes! Much sooner that hyena!

Much sooner the putrefaction of blessed souls or some black rat vomiting up a plague-ridden microbe. She'd promised me a trout amandine, I didn't make that up. And what happens? What does she bring me, and pleased with herself to boot, more than a little proud? Cauliflower gratin! Pinch me, Mademoiselle, go on, don't be afraid, I'm beyond suffering. My entire body is such a wound that everything is a balm to it now, everything an unguent. A nettle would bring me only relief, or a blackjack, a dagger. Come on, pinch

>

>

harder—don't you have any strength in your hands at all? Sink those manicured nails into my flesh, let them serve some purpose for once!

And now do you see me throwing off some dire illusion, or waking from my nightmare?

You do not. That's a real live cauliflower gratin before me on the table. A dish that disgusts me, no less than a living toad, don't want it, never eat it. You'd have to force-feed me with a funnel, clamped to the wall … But could that sun move any slower? Will it never warm our corner of the terrace? Myself, I would never have chosen this table. Oh well, you're here, let's stay where we are.

All the same, odd place to sit.

Look, just ten yards to the right and we'd be basking in its rays.

Anyway.

(Pigeons were meandering between the tables. The custom was to consider them ugly, to compare them to rats. But were they in truth any more idiotic than the chickens of our merry countryside? They found their grain on the tile floor, we must thus have had more in our pockets and trouser cuffs, a spare supply betraying our rural childhoods, disowned to varying degrees. All that was missing was a few little urban cows lowing between our legs and under our skirts to remind us of our origins.)[4]

I didn't hold back, I let her have it right in the face, she went pale,

---

4 The author grew up in the country. He once saw a pig killed in the old-fashioned way, with one blow of a club to its head, the animal tied to a stake. The blow missed its mark, and the beast broke free, wild with fury and pain, spattering the courtyard with blood that would never see the inside of a sausage. Everyone take cover, till the fountain runs dry! Then the pig sinks to the ground; for some time its legs go on twitching, spasms rack its body. The farmer finishes it off with a cutlass. Then singes off the pink bristles, revealing a white nudity, the alabaster body of a Balzacian heroine: the author has discovered literature. The smell is unbearable. In those days, pig organs were not saved for reuse in road-accident victims. There was a rustic recipe for the preparation of each one; it was an innocent sort of cannibalism, nothing to be ashamed of. The author was only a little boy. It seems to him today that he once lived in a very distant past; he wonders if every childhood in fact belongs to the Middle Ages—if the Middle Ages might have the property of overflowing historical time to cover the age of childhood. Then the author ran off with a troupe of jesters and took up a wanderer's life.

stammering "But … but … but …" But what? You mesmerize me with the shiny silver of a trout and then you afflict me with a plateful of cauliflower gratin! I hope you're not expecting me to give thanks to God for inventing you? Or the tarantula, or the leech? Anyone would have hit the ceiling, don't you think, Mademoiselle? Do you not share my opinion? On that point our two minds are as one, our sensibilities conjoined. Can it really be mere chance that brought us together? With what portly gentleman could I have so quickly forged such a bond? For a big, fat gentleman, anything you can stuff your face with is just fine, he'd down the gratin in one gulp, along with its crust of earthenware or porcelain. He would have found my fury misplaced.

But you, I can't help but think, you at least understand me.

Isn't that so? You understand what I've been through. Hunger. Frustration. Nausea. I don't like cauliflower gratin, I never did like it, as far back as I can remember, even in the prenatal limbo I never touched it, or later when I was a lictor in Rome, or when I shod horses under Pépin the Short, and when I was a sea snail or a warbler, or a paramecium: I didn't like it then either—not even when I was a slug in the vegetable garden! That revulsion goes way back, it's written, it's rooted, it's the indelible hallmark of my very being.

That one trait sums me up entirely.

Yuck! Oh, God no, not that slop, anything but that!

For in all honesty, Mademoiselle, to you I can say this calmly, with you I can speak of it, there is nothing I loathe more in this world than cauliflower gratin.

Nothing.

And when I was a dung beetle? I DIDN'T EAT IT THEN EI-THER!

If all cauliflower and even all memory of cauliflower were abruptly to vanish from the face of this earth—O miracle!—then, I swear, I would don mourning clothes of red and gold, with a pointy hat and a party whistle unrolling from my lips with every breath. Oh, how good to be a man on earth without that psoriasis! I, who would be sincerely distraught at the extinction of the silverfish or the sea cucumber, I, who would perhaps weep for them—because that's the sort of man I am, Mademoiselle, I bare my soul to you without inhibition, sensitive as a lamb, like the skinless muscleman from a plate of an anatomy book, who fears the comb no less than the flail, the feather as much as the whip—well, in this one single case, if all cauliflower were suddenly to vanish from the face of this earth, I would dance, you would see me even dance a jig, that's right, Mademoiselle, a jig, knowing nothing of its steps, by instinct I would dance a jig on hearing the news of cauliflower's total and definitive eradication.

What sea-holly-loving nanny-goat will do me that favor? I would love her like a sister. She will inherit my fortune. Yes, yes, it's true: I will name her in my will as the recipient of all my worldly goods. What would she want with my Renaissance coffer? Let her chuck it out if she doesn't want it, let her sell it and spend the proceeds on salt licks.

Mind you, that coffer comes to me from my father,[5] it's been in the family for five generations at least. But she can use it for firewood if she likes, that nanny-goat, that beautiful beast, if it will bring her pleasure or profit. I'm so deeply in her debt! That rush of relief, my stomach like a lighter-than-air balloon ready to soar as never before, the beating wings of my heart—my memory once again a virginal white page on which to record the poem of this world.

But, no, Mademoiselle, we're dreaming, lost in your lovely eyes. The cauliflower is too well-named to disappear, its essence is communicable, its law takes hold, and, by contamination, contagion, gangrene, avalanche, it spreads: soon, have no doubt, we will be seeing the caulibutterfly, the cauliharp, the cauligirl: the cauliworld!

---

5 The author's father honorably and conscientiously earned his living in the widely disparaged profession of the *notaire*. He was buried on November 25, 2009 in the cemetery of Angers, more precisely—since cemeteries are in the habit of adopting a cartography better suited to an enchanted garden or a nursery, in the laudable but laughably vain ambition of lightening the family's grief—in *Sea-Holly Lane*. Further, if one knows that the author's honorable and conscientious sister herself became a *notaire*, this passage will seem to be chockablock with autobiographical allusions addressed to the happy few, that little handful of inconsolable mourners. The author does not deny it, he even proclaims it outright without anyone having asked, thus asserting his hold over his character, to whom he consents to lend a few of his own traits in order to underscore those that distinguish him from the other. For it is precisely because the marten and the weasel are so alike that they are in the end so very different.

And then where will we live, tell me?

In your lovely eyes?

Will there even be room enough for our feet?

You know, Mademoiselle, I like fairy tales, what I don't like is cauliflower. It's not good, and it's even worse in a gratin, where, beneath a dry crust—scurf or tartar—it becomes that translucent magma, as if already vomited up, urk! Simply speaking of the thing gives me palpitations, cold sweats, a sour stomach. I might pass out at any moment.

(Now and then an ambulance or a fire truck roared by, sirens howling: misfortune had struck again. We noted this only vaguely, forced to raise our voices to make ourselves heard. And yet a building had fallen victim to the flames, its occupants frantically waving from the windows. Or else two cars that had emerged gleaming from the factories of two manufacturers now formed a single model, intricate, unusable, as if the spies reciprocally planted in these competing firms had accidentally mixed up their stolen blueprints—now the doors wouldn't even close, and the bodywork was dripping blood.)

To fully understand how it was, when she appeared with her steaming dish—and the steam itself seemed to be blossoming, the monster duplicated by its ghost—to fully understand me, you must measure the distance between trout amandine and cauliflower gratin, you must sound that abyss: if we leave their shared nutritive properties aside, we will find no grounds on which to so much as compare them.

On the one hand, the loveliest fish of the rivers; on the other, the drabbest vegetable of the garden.

On the one hand, a dish of great elegance, worthy of the finest tables; on the other, something straight out of a lunchroom, the mortar ladled out by a fat paw between catechism and math class.

On the one hand, a thoughtful and attentive hostess's delectable offering; on the other, the botched improvisation of a dull-witted cookmaid.

On the one hand, a jaunty saunter through green fields, feet bathed in dew; on the other, an agonizing slog through bog and morass.

On the one hand, the vast openness of space, the loving moon, still more heavens beyond the heavens; on the other, a dull, leaden horizon, the collapsed roof, the flooded basement.

On the one hand, life in all its possibility, benign and, for a few moments—some ten mouthfuls—magnificent; on the other, the wretched gloom of day following endlessly upon day, a longing for death, death as rescue and release.

Because, Mademoiselle, I would so like you not to misunderstand the reasons for my ire. There's a whole world between cauliflower gratin and trout amandine, and that world is the one mankind has built, tirelessly toiling to make it a livable place, even painting bucolic scenes at the bottom of thimbles, with a brush made from a single bristle plucked at great personal risk from a billygoat's beard—civilization, if you like. And meanwhile the hominid was already ripping cruciferous vegetables from the ground and sinking his black teeth into them, grunting with pleasure.

With that dish I am reduced to a mere brute.

I am denied the enjoyment of art and science's noblest creations.

Think how cruelly I'm being dumped into the primordial pit of our origins! The humiliation she's visiting on me!

My chagrin was twofold—the creaking hinge of *not only* jointed it like the screw in a pair of pliers. *Not only* had I not been served the trout amandine I had every right to expect—had that promise not been made me, tacitly?—*but also* (there's the bolt on the screw) I was being deprived of my purest bliss, which is to enjoy the savor of things when they're wonderful and when we can nonetheless bite into them and thereby perhaps meld them with our own substance, perfume our own substance with them, leave it sunnier, more electric, more joyous: my trout was slipping through my fingers, I saw it diving back into the limpid waters, undulating, its flanks intact, twin mirrors of my unsatisfied hunger and rage.

And on the banks, the squirrels were stripping the almond trees bare.

(Later, a grubby little beggar girl made her rounds from table to table; the waiter shooed her away with a rag, like a bee. Others chose to

do their panhandling in dark corners, on backstreets. This seemed odd,
paradoxical. Were they ashamed of an activity into which poverty wel-
comed them with open arms? Or were they engaging in it as dilettantes,
lackadaisically, displaying the same nonchalance that had perhaps ended
up expelling them with no hope of return from the office, the workshop,
or the teller's window where they'd briefly found themselves imprisoned?
Or did this withdrawal perhaps obey a carefully considered strategy, an
intimate knowledge of the urban way of life, the rare passerby feeling for
once personally involved (that poor man has no one in the world but me)
rather than stepping over the alms bowl (more prosaically a cardboard
coffee cup) and vanishing into the unfeeling crowd?)

Then I was seized by a fear you can easily imagine ("a terror," you
mean! I believe the word is "dread"!): suppose she were to rub my
nose in that foul brew of hers, suppose she were somehow to make
me ingest a few mouthfuls, what consequences would ensue? Would
I myself not be digested? My body puffed and bubbling, and at the
same time flaccid and sunken, as if made up of successive gouts of
grease in the end forming a more or less human shape?

Never would I voluntarily have let myself be fed like that, you're
thinking!

And you're not wrong.

You're a pretty sharp tack, you know that, Mademoiselle?

But—suppose she force-fed me?

Suppose she clasped me in the vise of her enormous thighs, suppose she really did thrust a funnel between my lips?

Ah, it's all too clear you don't know her—and that ignorance puts
you at a grave disadvantage for grasping the danger I faced.[6]

---

6 Terror, dread: sensations well known to the author, occasioned of course by
very different causes—for he himself faces the menace of cauliflower gratin with
a rather extraordinary composure. But the prospect, for instance, of . . . actually, any prospect at all—because every prospect opens onto the future and the
unfathomable abyss, with no other guardrail than the line of the horizon, so thin,
so tenuous—any prospect at all fills him with that terror and that dread. An eager
revolutionary in theory, the author abhors the idea of any change to the order of
his days. He was perfectly comfortable in the uterus; ever since it's just been one
disturbance after another, one relocation after another. Here, then, is an obsessive

For my suspicion is that she'd long premeditated her crime. I suspect her of selecting the varieties of Salmonidae and the species of Rosaceae, of crossing them, breeding them, feeding them, to create the trout with its succulent flesh and the almond tree with its delicate fruit, then wedding them in her frying pan to give me a taste for them, all this simply for the sake of snatching that plate out from under my nose, simply for the sake of brutally depriving me of my pleasure. Can you conceive of the treachery of that scheme, the cold calculations that govern it, the ruthlessness required to see it through? For she would also, simultaneously, secretly, in some secluded plot, have had to conceive the cauliflower, tuck it into a bed of fertilizer, shape the monster with a pair of pruning shears, incubate it beneath a glass dome, and on top of all that devise the recipe that would realize its vile, gruesome potential, as one concocts a deadly poison that does not kill its victim outright but first stuns him with pain, then crushes his body beneath a freight-train of convulsions, and reduces him to despair.

Look at the state I'm in.

But the man sitting before you is not me. I am another man entirely, the warm, cordial friend to all those of my species, inclined to see beauty in the homeliest faces, I love everything, do you understand, I'm not the black vulture you hear croaking, nor the plaintive jackal, I love the ridiculous birth of the chestnut, the knit-browed timidity of the bachelor, the mauve webbed feet of the traditional grape-harvest goose, the unique shape of the cloud that fleetingly

more ritual-addicted than any monk, who is in fact very fond of cloisters, even if he grumbles that a twisted redbud in the center sometimes troubles their symmetry. He likes things to be in their place, in a case or a jewel box, neatly nestled into a little foam cushion. And if every living being henceforth moved from place to place on a rail, he would be greatly relieved. His vocation as a writer is thus easily explained. He finds in that exercise the opportunity to make an unholy mess without upsetting the order of things. Up to a point, he pretends to believe that literature is reality, and he works to deconstruct it, to shatter it in his disorderly fictions, knowing nonetheless that there is no blowback to be feared, that everything will still run perfectly smoothly, and that the space of dreams remains hermetically sealed.

justifies my existence, the red glasses of that lady now walking by, the tenacity of cousins who organize family reunions, the coming of winter, and also the fact that there's room for three heads of lettuce in my shopping basket, the fading of the petty tyrant's authority outside his realm, our uncertainty on the best way to proceed with anything that doesn't elude us entirely, the entomologist's disappointment on picking up an emerald from the grass, your rounded knees, Mademoiselle, stones that men somehow hoisted atop other stones, paper of no monetary value, a child's bright voice giving new life to a stale language, and your ears, the one I can see and the curtain of hair over the other, the bumpy ride of a perambulator or hearse conveying us through cobblestoned streets, the name Mouillefarine on a mailbox, public benches.[7]

---

7 The author could of course countersign this list, but he would add—after removing those very unbecoming red glasses from that passerby—the first names of his three adorable housemates, those of his friends, and he wouldn't forget his siblings, nor his brave, grieving mother, her strength drawn from the valiant blood of her father, who never wanted to die, and who died all the same without his consent at age 96, regretting that he would never know what his great-grandchildren would become nor who would win the French Open in 2050 (*What do you think I am, an old man!?* he would still grumble at 95, when someone tried to help him out of a car); and the author—who by the sound of it might just have been handed a literary prize—would not have failed to gratefully acknowledge his publishers, and all the writers who, one after another, meant something in his life, so much that he sometimes thought himself genuinely loved by them from the dim, distant past where often they lay in repose; and the Ile d'Yeu, from the Pointe du But to the Pointe des Corbeaux, but especially a flowered, mossy hollow known to him alone, facing the Vieux Château; and Nantes, where he felt the despair of the twenty-year-old thanks to a Nantaise whose letters he still rereads now and then, more and more rarely, it's true, magnificent letters written with the pink cushion of her finger and then with the sharp edge of her fingernail (as for the ones he sent her, those he has of course completely forgotten, no doubt they strove very diligently to be charming, all pointless byplay and stylistic affectation, though she did tell him, after the third one: *I never thought I would so soon be putting our correspondence on the top shelf of the big polished oak armoire, like jars of jam in our childhood, forbidden lemon delight, very, very hard to reach*)—whatever became of her? And how is it that literature has never heard her name? Is she dead? She never wanted to turn forty, she perched over the abyss like a poet or an acrobat, just to feel the dizzying pull, and alas, now we know that rogue waves sometimes come and carry off daring young women who never asked for such a thing, even when they ventured out onto coastal paths—and Sienna, where for once he felt himself

But let's get to the murder.

(Occasionally we found an appointment book under a table. We leafed through it. Inevitably, it seemed to have fallen from the pocket of an obsessive maniac tormented by chronic dental and digestive disorders, exclusively preoccupied with trivialities, who maintained an assiduous telephone relationship with his banker, an on-again off-again liaison with his barber, and forever deferred the apparently utopian project of buying batteries. The man who finally returned to claim it displayed, at this reunion, a joy that might well have been deemed excessive, given its contents.)

Although I dispute that term "murder." I reject it.

We owe it to the police currently on my tail. That's their primitive jargon.

It bespeaks a total lack of understanding of human affairs. An impoverished insect language.

Murder!? The healthy response of a body recoiling before an atrocity!?

Remember, I was about to be stuffed full of cauliflower—or have I not told you about that? If that's not a mitigating circumstance!

If that's not a mitigating circumstance, it's a justifiable motive. Do we punish people for biting the foot that kicks them in the teeth? Shouldn't people know they're not supposed to tickle a tiger's nostrils

---

living without the meddlesome intrusions of sorrow, and Koulikoro, in Mali, the riotous company of Rokiatou and her sisters, and the volcanic-sand beaches of Basse-Terre, Guadeloupe, where he gathers sea urchin tests, then Dvorak's *Slavonic Dance* in E minor, which rends his heart, the smell of February daphne, the smell of the fig tree on the road to the secret cove of La Garoupe, near Antibes, and the elephant, always with the same excess whether irascible or easygoing, and the butterfly—less the dusty-winged flying caterpillar than its description by Vladimir Nabokov—and coffee, which he drinks as if he were a lion and it blood, and the circle of sunlight when he's swimming up from the depths, and the lighter-colored cowlick on Ludovic's head, which he places between these pages as if in a locket, for Ludovic is no more, and pianos weep to have lost his brilliant, hypotonic touch, and he would gingerly add the egg, of whatever sort, which, for as long as it can, in the tightest embrace, holds in disappointment.

with a feather? Forgive me, Mademoiselle, I don't know with what words to combat that insect language, which begins with an insect thought and then sets about disseminating it—that *bzzz* from flower to flower. I don't know how to make an understanding of human affairs possible again.

Say "murder" because you don't know the word "jujube."

Because in your mouth "hurrah" is a belch.

Say "murder" as you would say *bzzz*, in your insect language.

But why not say "desire," why not say "pyjamas," why not say "lilac," "aria," "mechanics," or "azure"?

Why not say, one last time, "bicycle"?

I was promised a trout amandine, and that promise was not honored! No, it was cruelly mocked, like joy by the seagull's moronic laugh. Where was the enameled tin dish, or even the oval porcelain dish, with its blue garlands and fine border of gold? Where the companiable creature, offering its flanks to the teeth of my fork? Where the almond, the thrall of the almond, the thrill of it all? And who was it that cancelled these festivities? Who is she, she who gratinées her cauliflower in mid-stream to hold back the current, who erects her cauliflower dam before the oncoming trout—that trout launched from the stream's very source, speeding like a knife straight for my stomach!? Aiming for my stomach, the trout ended up in the muck. All the trout's ardor in the muck, all its silver. And her with her bear-paw hands, draining the trout basin for her cauliflower seedlings! Can you imagine that, Mademoiselle, are you getting the picture?

That dull smear over our whole world?

Left by a brush plunged deep into the paint. And the color! You call that a color? That raw, murky beige, thick, claylike, that grim goo—you wouldn't be at all surprised to find a dinosaur's footprint in that mud. Although for that you'd have to lean in for a closer inspection. No thanks! Put my delicate sensory organs anywhere near that dish? My eye, my nose—why not my mouth, while we're at it? My perversion is not that polymorphous. My ear, too, will hear none of it: it's sizzling, that dinner of yours, is there a fly in there on top of everything else?

Poor creature.

And yet such is the fate you had in store for me. You wanted to smother my protests in cauliflower, I can read your mind, you wanted to plug up the mouth voicing my justified recriminations, as the dead man's last scream is buried along with him. It was ignoble, but it was cunning, I'll give you that. The protest smothered by the cause of the protest—I would have seemed quite a fool at the police station. How well advised I was not to touch the stuff.

Touch the stuff!

Can you imagine such a thing, Mademoiselle? That crust, rough as a heel's underside, the touch of that dead, tanned skin—better to sleep with the mummy of an Egyptian slattern! My hands would have instinctively retracted, like a cat's claws, the distal phalanx into the intermediate, the intermediate into the proximal—and if I could only retreat still further! Complete self-involution, invagination! Disappearance by self-absorption—oh, how insufficient are our reflexes before certain horrors! As if fire were all we had to fear!

(The accordionist was as annoying as any jackhammering workman. It wasn't anything like the ambiance he was after, and his face—anxious, glum, or indifferent—didn't help. We couldn't imagine who that music was meant for, those ripples and flourishes designed to accompany the gambols of seamstresses and coppersmiths on the banks of the Marne in 1910. The nightingale's trills at least aim to signal his presence to his mate, with her hot, tight cloaca. But the accordion's joy struck us as misplaced, insulting—like a string of sausages offered to a starving vegan. We kept the tinkling music of our coins in our pockets. Failing to earn a sou, the man shambled off with his diseased lung.)

Because I could see through her plans. She was hoping I'd lose myself in the vertiginous contemplation of fractals and end up passed out in my plate, my nose in the slop, in spite of myself—for it is a fact that cauliflower is equivalent to itself at every level of its structure, each part identical to the whole, meaning that a cauliflower's every tiny efflorescence is still another cauliflower! The hell of infinite repetition, the labyrinth closing on me, my pointlessly keen nose crashing down that spiral staircase, step after step, and me, ever smaller and sadder, tumbling unstoppably down that tunnel of mirrors, with no hope of escape—as far as the eye can see, and even beyond the horizon, still more cauliflower!

Help!

Mademoiselle!

Imagine!

Still more cauliflower!

When I was expecting to follow the trout upstream to the origin of all things, to discover the soul of all things, the seed, the delicate heart—for that was indeed what the promised feast would offer, that was indeed what I longed to taste, what I yearned to dig into, and so to become a part of this world, undismayed by its ways. Did she take me for some mindless chowhound? Did she see a snout on me, and an appetite for any sludge that might wind up between my paws? Did she seriously believe I was going to wolf down her gratin—because how can you eat that dish in any civilized way? It's soup to the fork, macaroni to the spoon! Where had she got the idea that I so loved this world I was willing to kiss its leprous face?

Murder!? That reflexive revolt of my disgust and indignation!?

Will the wretch shoulder-deep in quicksand be judged so severely because he shoots a dirty look at the brute bashing his skull with an oar?

After all, I was the one being killed, Mademoiselle. Oh yes! And what a horrible way to go! After such terrible suffering! Has anyone ever imagined a crueler death, slower in coming?[8] Allow me to gaze with envy on the agony of the man on the cross—a vinegar-soaked sponge, how I would have loved that fruit! And then her, prodding

---

8 People have, of course, but this is a fairly good example of the humor of excess so dear to the author. He believes that by giving free rein to the logic of the discourse that founds our reality, a reality entirely created by language—such at least is his impression, often confirmed by experience—he will reveal the imposture reality constitutes, precisely because it is a fact or an effect of language. Only death can do without words—is death perhaps the only reality, and all the rest a fiction of which we are at once author and character? Quite possibly, muses the author, who also senses that it doesn't do you much good to understand the mechanics of the trap when its teeth are sunk into your ankle: yet another leg you can't stand on, which you'll have to cut off in order to be free.

me with her pieties—I was supposed to say a prayer before masticating her cauliflower, I was supposed to give thanks to God! And also for the roof caving in and the ground giving way beneath my feet, I suppose?

Thank you God for the torrent of lava, the backed-up sewer, for all that decomposes, for the thick pall of smoke hanging over blackened countrysides.

Because she herself who had promised me a trout amandine had set before me a dish of cauliflower gratin, and it was the saddest substitution anyone could have imagined, fomented, hatched, the direst conceivable metamorphosis, mutation, degeneration—conceivable only by a vile, twisted imagination, the kind that begets nitroglycerin and brass knuckles. Rather than the ever-so-slightly pink trout, cooked just so, that mangrove where the vilest species of snakes and octopi would thrive—can't you almost see them writhing around in there, twisting through the stalks and florets? Blind, white monsters, their movements sluggish, almost imperceptible, but we know that their lethargy is a subterfuge, a ruse, a free-floating trap, we know that all at once they awake, all at once they uncoil and strike, and snatch, and absorb you in the sticky folds of their intestines: once thoroughly softened, your bleached skeleton melds in every way with the inescapable, cream-and-cheese smothered vegetable, in which the world's foundation, its cornerstone, is a warm mortar of potatoes where the dinosaur's second foot would also have left a print, had the creature made it that far—but here, then, is the cause of its demise, revealed at last: oh, what a horrible death! I've felt the first shudders of that death, I know what I'm talking about.

For yes, Mademoiselle, perhaps you already knew, I hereby confirm it, there is also potato in cauliflower gratin, even if its name prefers to keep that a secret.

Surprise!

(The police presence in the city, visible and profuse, created a sense of security that fueled our unease, our visceral terror of everything around us. In the same way, the child strikes his sister for the pleasure of consoling her, of pressing to him her trembling little form, her warm, tear-soaked face.)[9]

---

9 This might, in fact, resemble one of the author's personal memories. What

Another disappointment.

Cauliflower gratin is chock full of them—they must be folded in prior to cooking—just as it is of disenchantment fatigue. Quite a feat, really, making of despair itself, once the disillusion's behind you, yet another letdown. Only cauliflower gratin can offer us these rare pleasures.

The potato, that's all that was missing.

All that was missing was the potato.

The recurrent potato, always there when misery comes crashing down on a family or a people. And which on top of that passes itself off as the last ally, the ultimate comestible. But does that inevitable presence in misfortune, at the very heart of torment, not seem to you slightly suspect? Does it not seem a little too regular? Is the fireman who spews the most water not often the pyromaniacal dragon? I've studied this matter carefully, Mademoiselle, and I repeat: it's sinister. Listen to me closely: *j'accuse*, Mademoiselle, I accuse the potato of causing all this world's sorrows. Buried in the furrow like a stone, it spoils the soil for any other crop: the generous stalk of wheat, the mellow asparagus, the juicy orange, the perfumed fennel bulb, they all perish beneath that relentless bombardment. There, soon, is the only fossil, the sole vestige of all human activity!

The potato, and the many varied forms of boredom growing in that stifling egg—how many sad little sculptures in there, stunted and rotund!

Colorado beetle, my friend!

Comrade!

Colorado beetle, attack!

Why were you not at her side when she was bringing her plans to fruition? What a glorious mission for your mandibles, what great work to be done! Now, there's an insect language I understand, although, alas, I don't speak it, for if I did I would take that Colorado beetle aside, and I would say: Colorado beetle, have you really no

---

perversity! Shame be upon him! Must he then dissociate himself not only from his character, but also from himself, from the person he once was, and perhaps still is? And then what will remain of his being, his entirety, once that operation is complete? What dust, which will rest in peace only on calm, windless days?

beef with cauliflower?

Man's dearest friend, his most noble conquest: the Colorado beetle! The ideal stone for a wedding ring: so much future unpleasantness avoided had it only had been thought of in time, every potato simultaneously peeled and devoured, never that godawful slop on the table.

Quite the reverse: a tender idyll that never ends, love eternally untarnished, evergreen, as if freshly emerged from the mandolin even twenty years on; it is the Colorado beetle that watches over the harmony of the hearth, the friendly bug in the kitchen. It takes a Colorado beetle to make a house a home.

My God, it's better than all the bichons frisés in the world!

A Colorado beetle!

Ah, Mademoiselle, if only we could start everything over!

Because, you see, before that plateful of food I suddenly sensed that the unceasing labors of my energies, engaged since childhood in the struggle for my survival, for the advancement of my mind and the harmonious development of my body, rather than finally receiving their just reward, than gathering the fruits of their success, their moment of well-deserved triumph and recognition, were being punished as might be a criminal career. A cruel misjudgment. Nothing in my existence justified so draconian a sanction.[10]

(A group of mental patients strolled past, out for a walk with two escorts, the latter easily distinguished by their clothes, suited to their measurements. For, in that age, congenital imbeciles could be spotted by their dress: incongruous getups, down coats with rolls of blue flab, red wool caps with pompoms or cloche-like beach hats, ridiculously short trousers for

---

10 The author is no stranger to bitterness and resentment. Unlike his character, however, he also knows self-satisfaction and smugness. Indeed, he finds it no easy task to juggle, in the confines of his fractured soul, those two unlovely emotions— which in certain happy moments opportunely cancel each other out—and so he achieves a very respectable stoicism, ordinarily attained, if we are to believe the philosophers, by a less twisted discipline. Not so much an athlete as a bodybuilder, but so what, you can't argue with results, and in any case, isn't being good company what matters most? Who knows, perhaps this tortuous path will one day lead him to sainthood?

the tall fat ones, ridiculously voluminous trousers for the short slight ones, tennis shoes with mismatched laces. No one dressed like that. You could tell at a glance they weren't normal.)

My father wore a putty jacket. He wore that putty jacket in every season. From as far back as I can remember to my last sight of him alive, he was clad—or coated, it seemed—in that putty jacket. And when I say putty, I mean not just the color, which was indeed a drab gray, paler in spots (the elbows, the collar) but also its fabric, which wasn't exactly putty, of course, but mimicked its appearance and, how to put this, its consistency more than it did leather, despite the manufacturer's likely intentions, unless that manufacturer, cynical capitalist scum that he was, did indeed mean to humiliate the worker by rubbing his nose in his life's lot (oil, grease, putty)?

Was it leatherette? Plastic? Rubber?

Sea lion?

Whatever it was, my father was encased in it, in that limp, thick, clinging substance, which squeaked feebly whenever he moved and, no matter how often worn, how worn out, never acquired the slightest suppleness or fluidity, remaining irreducibly alien to the body that so faithfully inhabited it.

The reverse was not true, for my father identified in every way with his jacket. My father without the jacket was scarcely conceivable. The few times I saw him denuded—through the half-open bathroom door or on a Northern beach—he frightened me, like a man skinned alive, peeled, I thought he must be in pain.

Their relationship was that of the turtle and its shell.

The jacket wrinkled pitifully (or perhaps comically, for that turd of a manufacturer), catching the light and dulling it. It was like patches of dirty water, puddles. And inside it my father's movements were cramped, making it squeak like a mouse, or crackle like a burning log, or creak like an armoire, according to his humor. He was a man of few words. You had to make do with those uncertain sounds to guess at his mood. There wasn't much to answer. He liked me, I think, but his affection was clumsily expressed. Sometimes he pulled me to him; I was then absorbed by the jacket, which stuck to me slightly, smelling of erasers or burned tires. Those embraces left me nauseous. I was twelve years old when he died, mysteriously.[11]

A workplace accident, that was the official explanation. Nevertheless, I saw strange glances exchanged, heard the conversation suddenly go quiet when I approached the visitors come for a last long look at the departed, parted at long last from his jacket. Someone had tied a broad, gray cravat around his neck, a kerchief actually, once used by my mother to cover her hair on windy days.

(A man at the next table interrupted us, thinking himself authorized to join in the conversation. Either he made out a word or sentence and tried

11 Forty-five, in the case of the author, who was nonetheless left a feeble orphan when his own was carried off by cancer, more octopus than crab, taking advantage of the patient's weakness in the wake of his so-called therapy to spread, to progress, and then, as they say, to generalize, hugging the arborescences of the skeleton and the blood, of everything that supported the powerful fatherly body, the magnificent fatherly body, sapping it with a cruel precision that one might have thought meticulously planned, like a military operation: every target hit and destroyed. Where does one find the commander in chief? The author would like to congratulate him. He vaguely recalls a leather jacket, mustard or caramel, that his father wore with great elegance at some point in his life, when he was still young. This would also be the place to describe the handsome, serious, frugal face of a man who observed the Christian commandments with rigor and modesty—quick, before that austere picture congeals, tie his black Judo belt around his waist, put the oars of the little rowboat back into his hands, the Jimmy Connors racket, the gardener's scythe, and especially the Spanish guitar that was stolen from him and consequently knows nothing of his death, for he is indeed dead, for he did indeed die, in order to teach the author one last lesson, to teach him death after teaching him life, to teach him that people die, which the author thought he already knew, which he often wrote of, and which was nonetheless revealed to him when his father died, revealed as if he'd had no idea, a revelation as astonishing as the discovery of life on the moon, a staggering, agonizing revelation, because it's also the son who dies when the father dies, all the time they shared suddenly racing off to join a past now over and done with, prehistory, it's the life of the son that cracks up, suddenly no longer enclosed within that of his father, now inscribed in the void—there was once a road, now there is only a wire beneath the son's feet. Cancer carried off the father, and the father carried off his son. There remains only his son as an adult, as if by some deliberate act newly become a father himself, as if he'd become a father because the father's place had been vacated, and because he would henceforth find the place of the son too thankless, and who today anxiously wonders if he should give his daughters such good reasons to one day mourn his death.

to continue in the same vein, or else he brazenly broke in to talk to us of other things. Either way, his intervention was not welcome. Yes, we were sitting on the same terrace, but that didn't make us a group, or a club, or a family! Who could still believe in such things? Who couldn't feel the invisible walls separating us one from the next, so firm you might almost have knocked on them? We repelled the invader with our resolute silence, our unsociable air. His face fell. Society was a mercantile setup. Everyone could easily supply himself with bread, soap, and aspirin, without having to walk too far. We wanted nothing more from it than that.)

The jacket disappeared.
I later found it hanging in the closet.

(Nevertheless, the café had its regulars. They nodded on spotting each other. Some swapped banalities and information on the meteorological conditions. About as useful as reminding each other what they were wearing that day. Empty words, more an avoidance strategy than anything else. Thus did the regulars keep each other at a distance. The clouds served as a buffer.)[12]

Now I know, Mademoiselle, there are some who will say—and their smug, knowing looks fairly cry out to be wiped off their faces— that my phobia of cauliflower gratin originates in the paternal figure confused in my mind with that jacket, so similar in appearance to the hated slop, that this is all therefore an ignoble renunciation of my father, his laconic, hard-working tenacity, my humble origins, as if I had since been granted some diploma in higher humanity, qualifying

---

12 This is also the reason for the screen of politesse that the author unfolds between himself and others. He even adds a certain unctuousness, to prevent any friction. Can harmony exist without distance? Obeying an impersonal code, we efface anything that makes us stand out. We become any man in the street. In the end, it's as if we weren't there at all—and such is indeed the author's most constant desire: to be somewhere else, far from here. What to do with the hyper-presence of those boors who refuse to fade into the background, or at least suck in their stomachs a little? Civility is a game of capes and passes by which we dodge the bull, which is more often a talkative neighbor than a savage beast blowing steam from its nostrils.

me to feel that shame. And, let me guess, I'll be accused of ingratitude at the same time as arrogance—admit it, Mademoiselle!

But nothing could be more unjust. I am not so addled as to reduce my father to his jacket, and then to allow an analogy, and a rather vague one at that, to so cloud my judgment that I can no longer distinguish a jacket from cauliflower gratin! If we are to believe your magisterial elucidation—oh yes, Mademoiselle, I know what you're thinking—then I should feel precisely the same horror for white asparagus, custard, and goose-fat jelly.

But no.

But no: allow me to inform you that I have a great weakness for white asparagus, I swallow the spears whole, all the while chewing their fibers.

I am fond of white asparagus beyond all reason.

The only thing I like better is custard.

And better than that, goose-fat jelly.

Had someone not one day come up with the idea of garnishing trout with almonds, my favorite food would be goose-fat jelly.

That's right, goose-fat jelly. Too bad for you if your grandmother never made it.

But that glorious day did indeed dawn—Lord, how glorious days could be, in spite of all this! how glorious every one of them would be, if some such simple idea could fill each with its magic, if day after day we could so happily marry a fish and a nut—that day, then, when someone—but who? how? by what chance, what intuition, what calculation?—came up with that idea, slicing almonds over the trout recumbent in its pan, and with that, obviously, goose-fat jelly's wings were clipped just a little.

In any case, you must concede, you were barking up the wrong tree. No trauma here. My dislike for cauliflower gratin is founded intellectually, esthetically, sensorially, and I'm proud to say that I found a firm footing for it in that muck. It wasn't easy. I had to feel around a bit with the tip of my toe.

But I believe I have successfully overcome my instinctive repulsion and attained the most perfect objectivity in this regard, my reason's coolly assured judgment concurring perfectly with my instinct, though I can't decide whether to preen myself on the sagacity of the latter or the infallibility of the former. They coincide. Their conclusions are one and the same. Nothing conflicted about me, at least. I am a straightforward man, all of a piece, uncomplicated. My body and mind have recognized each other: they agree on what matters most.[13]

So what's next?

Next he's going to tell me about his mother and exonerate her in her turn, that's what you're thinking, and there you're not quite so sharp a tack as I, I who can penetrate your every thought! I can read you like an open book, a perceptiveness that as it happens I got from my late mother, from whom I could keep nothing secret, especially not what she wanted to find in me: all the vices rolled up in one, the most sordid fantasies and a whole encyclopedia of pornography she invented when she thought she was untangling my daydreams, which were nonetheless wholly innocent, but starting from a foot I'd glimpsed through a shop window as it tried to choose between three slippers, my mother—the paleontologist resuscitates a hominid in much the same way, embroidering a dream around a single malleolus extracted from a crust of clay and calcite—concocted for me a lubricity worthy of a Dutch sailor trawling the red-light district: by a foul-smelling corridor I made my way into the back rooms of a brothel—my choice was made—and a moment later one of those

---

13 And here the author is once again obliged to intervene. As we'll see, his character is prone to boasting; he'll be sorry. The author is not such a braggart. He must confess that his body is a disagreeable right-winger, selfish, protectionist, and grasping, repelled by the tender kiss of a homosexual couple, put off by the foreigner's sonorous, incomprehensible language—and if it doesn't agitate for the return of the death penalty, it's only for fear of having to stick its neck out. That obscurantist cretin had to be brought to heel. Had to be taught a lesson. That job falls to the author's mind, less obtuse, closed to mathematics alone. Thank goodness, its cranial cap keeps a lid on that cranky, anxious body, which seems to encounter life only as a threat. The author's mind is more spirited, bolder, and even more sensitive. Which is no doubt why he finds fulfillment in literature, his one true domain: brilliantly or otherwise, that's for others to judge. The overall impression will always be confused, muddled, untidy. Only written expression can be precise (but the author naively entrusts his written expressions to a printing press, to impressions upon a page, which is why everything always has to be started over again, why everything must be continually rewritten).

ladies was drawing her curtain on the street.

And here I received a preliminary slap.

Then I threw the whore onto her bed, pulled up her skirts, unhooked her underthings. My avid, rough, grasping hands clutched at her thighs, her buttocks, clawed at her breasts, I was a filthy, depraved little brute, my bestiality revealed through these scenes discovered in my soul by my mother's eagle eye.

A second slap sent my head spinning.

From which we can see that my mother's hand was no less nimble than mine.

My fingers found the damp fleshy creases, the constricting orifices, and got busy, none too tactfully, while I punctuated that onslaught with lewd cries; her ear as sharp as her eye, my mother didn't miss a single one.

… take that … bitch! … you like it, you know you like it …![14]

That sort of punctuation, I imagine.

Now the blows were raining down on me. Pulling a truncheon from her sleeve, my mother pummeled my shoulders, my back, which I protected as best I could with my head.

All the while taking refuge in the sugary fairy tales conjured up by my imagination, the princesses all dressed in high-necked gowns

---

14 Never would the author have written such a thing. Never did his mother attribute to him such ideas, nor did she once raise a hand to him, save to brush his unruly hair. Pornography inspires him to contradictory reactions and reflections. In literary terms, he finds it uncompelling, because necessarily realistic, always clinging close to its subject, without distance, leaving no room for humor or irony, precisely like scripture—as with the latter, the goal is to create an illusion, and allow the reader to place his faith in it, or better yet place himself in it. And that very obviously goes against all the author's literary ideologies. With pictures, on the other hand, he cannot repress a certain fascination. Having very late lost his innocence—just look at the archaic euphemisms he uses even now to evoke his recent defloration—he so long saw the pleasures of the flesh—oh, listen to that!—as a total mystery and a rare bolt from the blue that he can only look on in astonishment at so complete a lack of inhibition among those women (women in particular, for his own erection, more solid than that of his character, another noteworthy difference, was no secret to him) exhibiting themselves so overtly, so freely. This is a new mystery for him: what for centuries was kept hidden (centuries that overlapped his own life, that he felt he belonged to) is now the thing most openly exposed, to the point of dismemberment, or colonoscopy.

ly torn by the conflicting forces of emotion and desire. She noted my discomfiture and smiled at me.

At long last, an event.

(As a general rule, however, the most talkative were those sitting alone. Telecommunications had made spectacular progress. Everyone was compulsively fingering his mobile phone—the term was accurate, if slightly deceptive. What had become mobile were the house, the workplace, the solid block formed of family, friends, and acquaintances. Mobile, but heavy as ever, and people's backs bent accordingly under the weight. Sitting at café tables or walking down the street, hunchbacks everywhere. All that scoliosis, all those soliloquies betrayed the imposture and untruth of lives risen up from the void, written on the wind. The deluge's great wave was sweeping those drowned souls away, no one knew where.)[15]

---

15 It's finally come to pass, at long last we have in our power—or almost—the magic wand of fairy tales: those multifunction telephones that know everything and work all manner of wonders, soon to include teleportation. Of course, by this short-circuiting of all distance (which once mapped out human space) and delay (which once structured human time) we're also remaking our bodies and minds. We're mutating, flocking toward the future, sheep that we are. Paradoxically transformed into dumb beasts, stripped of the power of concentration, motivated by impatience alone, by immediate necessities, by imperious, rudimentary instincts. And so we see the rise, in the flesh, of the man so long dreamt of by science fiction:

/39

Now, Mademoiselle, you're gazing compassionately at the poor battered child turned impotent adult, and you're trying to find some connection with the cauliflower gratin I was served in place of the heralded trout amandine.

There is, of course, baseness and depravity.

Yes.

That's a start.

As you see, I don't reject all your suggestions out of hand. I'm struggling to understand all this myself. I have no taste for cauliflower, nor for enigmas, and I'm tired of being such a mystery to my own mind. Just imagine, I don't even know if I'm the victim or the culprit here. I believe I've often displayed courage. For example, I once came to the rescue of a poor fellow who was being mugged by three young louts. They'd taken his cap, and they were tossing it back and forth over his head, laughing at his cries of protest. Then one of them sent him sprawling on the ground with a slap to the back. The man fell face first. His nose burst open and began to spew blood. The three cretins laughed all the harder, kicking him mercilessly.

Finally I found the strength to stand up and intervene, repelling my aggressors with a fury and violence I didn't know I had in me. So much darkness inside me, even then. My repulsion for cauliflower gratin is the one fixed, stable point of my being—that and, I feel obligated to mention it lest you think me nothing more than a carping wet blanket, my taste for trout amandine, a gastronomical synecdoche for my broader affection for streams, nut trees, riverbanks, poppies, tree frogs or dragonflies, siestas in the grass, the sight of my crossed

---

savage, uncultured, and coarse, but at the same time endowed with the most sophisticated technology—allowing us at long last to abandon the task of furthering civilization, in which we'd been engaged since the start of the adventure. Here, consequently, is man entirely under the thumb of those technologies' inventors—themselves still capable of the concentration necessary for their creations' refinement, for all those micro-calibrations—and the interests they serve. And here is that flock herded into virtual space, from which there is no escape, here is the sheep shorn by invisible hands as soon as one hair grows back, says the author, proud of his resistance. For he does not own a mobile phone. For the first time, it seems to him that his inertia makes of him a colossus: Michelangelo's David, that's him. No one will ever shear that fine white marble, bare and immovable. When nobody's looking, he stretches his limbs a little to relieve his cramps.

ankles and feet against the horizon, the thunderstorm's first raindrop
on my forehead, waking me, and the pleasure of discovering my mistake, of realizing it's actually a drop of snot from the nostril of the bull
trampling me underfoot, and also the suspended globe formed by
the willow and its reflection in the water, no telling which of the two
hemispheres is the more fragile, and the dream this gives rise to, of a
peaceable world, where the minnow will lie down with the sparrow.

That much I can tell you of my vague, blurry person, in spite of it
all; that much I've been able to grasp. My hatred of cauliflower gratin
remains its firmest foundation, the least likely to crumble, no surprise
that I cling to it. It's a matter of fidelity to what I am, it's my duty to
cling, lest I lose myself entirely in the labyrinth of my past. That at
least I know, and it is confirmed with every passing moment: cauliflower gratin is a horrible thing, and if I were forced to partake of it,
I would take out my lighter, heat the blade of my knife till it glowed,
and apply it to my tongue to cauterize my tender taste buds and
spare them the painful acquisition of that useless, utterly unforget-
table knowledge. My hatred of cauliflower gratin describes me: I'm
not far from thinking that it would suffice to define me—or perhaps,
at least, to delineate me, for let us not heedlessly omit my passion for
trout amandine: I do indeed often forget to mention the latter when
I speak of myself, and so might be mistaken for a monomaniacal mal-
content obsessed by his folly, at every moment interposing between
the world and himself the curtain of noisome steam that billows from
the gratinée pan, unable to see beyond it to the changing landscape or
the showering nymph.

When in fact no.

I rarely think of cauliflower unprovoked. I am far more likely to
let my thoughts drift along the banks of the trout-filled brook. As if of
its own accord, that fish opens up head to tail, like that rare thing—
a book, whose second half is as compelling as its first, whose interest holds up unflagging from one end to the other; a book, what's
more—that exceptional thing—that you would reopen with pleasure,
not after a few years but the very next day, nibbling almonds all the
while, torn between the desire to endlessly prolong your reading and
the urge to hurry voraciously to the end, a book—that extraordinary

thing—thus wedding the qualities of the thriller, whose pleasures lie entirely on the surface, a surface you skim over, breathless and panting, with those of the metaphysical poem that can only be appreciated by diving deep into it, straight to the depths, and most certainly not panting, as in a hunter's blind where it is vitally important not to stir up the grass or the leaves, for behind them lurks the skittish elephant.[16]

(The squirrels were coming back, even in the urban green spaces. They had long been so scarce that children took them for the sprites and trolls of enchanted forests. Their return seemed to disprove the alarmist prophecies of those who day after day recorded nature's gradual decline—or were they in fact multiplying on the ruins of this world, habituated by atavistic reflex to creating little emergency stashes in every nook and cranny?)

So you begin, of course, by cleaning the trout, through the gills if you know what you're doing, or more simply by making an inch-long incision in its belly, starting from the anus, taking care not to puncture the bile sac, lest you impregnate the fish's pink, delicate flesh with a bitterness it succeeded in containing better than I, I must confess, Mademoiselle, but I have my reasons. Now rinse your trout, with care once again: there are sometimes little clots of blood still clinging to the spine. Cut off the fins, slash the end of the tail to prevent it from curling up in the frying pan like a scorpion's, which would introduce into your lunch a note of aggression that will sooner or later be sounded by one of your tablemates anyway—whereupon you will lower your nose to your plate to find the exquisite tenderness your

---

16 The author's books enter into neither of the two simplistic categories here laid out by his character. They follow a digressive and troublesome path. The reader can't skip a word without losing the thread, but neither must he linger too long, lest he become entangled. Whereupon a big, fat spider will creep out from one corner of the page, pierce him with its fangs, and suck out all his soft tissues, starting with his frontal lobe. All proper reading is a question of speed. It's all about finding the right one. There is an appropriate speed for each writer, and it will be fatal for the reader if he doesn't shift gears when he starts into a new book. Thus is it ill-advised, according to the author, to claim to make one's way through all of literature in a golf cart.

fellows deny you. Next, melt a tablespoon and a half of butter in a frying pan and, in another, dry roast a half cup of sliced almonds, stirring them gently with a wooden spatula. In your enthusiasm, you will have grown a third hand for snipping the parsley. Lower the heat under the first pan and, while in the other the almonds turn golden, brown your trouts (I put in two: I'd like one myself), dusted with flour and perhaps stuffed with a sprig of thyme. After eight minutes—men will have been born by the thousands, men will have died, that will give you a sense of those minutes' import—turn the fish, salt and pepper the browned side, and add the parsley along with half the almonds. Let a few more minutes go by, turn the fish once again, scatter over the reserved almonds, drizzle the whole thing with the remaining butter and a little spray of lemon.

What do you think?

How much we'd have to say, if it weren't rude to talk with your mouth full!

Whereas.

Whereas that woman.

Whereas, quite to the contrary, that woman.

Whereas, quite to the contrary, that woman began by dividing a cauliflower into little florets!

How's that for single-minded! How's that for cold-hearted!

Each of those little florets, let me remind you, being itself a whole cauliflower—tiny, yes, but complete.

This part of my account may prove disturbing in its smallest details. Plug up your ears if you like, Mademoiselle, or rather pinch your nose so you won't have to hear, I won't take it amiss. I believe my esteem for you would even soar to new heights.

Because then she dumped that sickening hash into a pot of boiling water.

In a second pot, meanwhile, she brought milk to the boil.

I call that premeditation.

Malice aforethought—whereas my own act was spontaneous, unthinking, motivated by fury alone.

She melted some butter with a pinch of nutmeg, measured out a half cup of flour, stirred it into the butter—then let the whole thing go cold.

She was making béchamel sauce!

Stonily, like the mechanism of death lurching into motion, utterly untinged by humanity, she drained her cauliflower and mingled the branches with sliced rounds of potato in a gratinée pan.

For she owned a gratinée pan—should you require any further proof of premeditation.

Off heat, she poured the boiling milk over the cold roux. For five minutes she stirred up that brew with a whip, over a cruel little flame that was already consuming me. She salted and peppered, added grated emmental.

Then she daubed—you heard me right, she daubed, daubed as one would daub a piece of toast with honey or a vacherin cheese with currant coulis—she daubed the cauliflower and potato with that béchamel!

And what's more, sprinkled the whole thing with a mixture of breadcrumbs and parmesan.

Then she put me into the oven and left me for twenty minutes in that blistering heat, where my last illusions withered.

(The children were jumping and hopping, the little girls especially. The girls on the square punctuated their mad dashes with exceptionally graceful entrechats, uniquely their own, apparently natural, innate. No boy had ever managed that. To what festivities did those sweet little angels think themselves invited? Aspiring ballerinas, every one of them. Their skirts were light, and life full of promises. We trembled for them, nonetheless, just as the hunter, moved by the sight of the doe's silken lashes, trembles as he takes aim.)

Indifferent and fatalistic, my parents conceived me amid a host of other children. How many I can't say, for on the one hand their brood sometimes grew by a brother or sister, never seeming to reach a conclusion, and on the other some of them also died, through accident or illness. Two additional circumstances complicated the matter still further.

First, less out of cynicism or anguished refusal to face reality than for lack of imagination, my parents gave their newborn children the first names of those who had died. I'm the second Blaise. There were also two Jeannes, and, if memory serves, three Alberts. The affection and attentions they bestowed on us were diluted accordingly. The second Blaise was not given the care lavished on the first, and had to consider already behind him everything learned by the first before he was cut down by a meningitis epidemic or a Renault R16. Each new birth was a regression to which my parents adjusted with great difficulty.

Wasn't Albert walking last year?

I'll say he was! He even threw himself under a car!

What a little worm he's turned back into! Look at him, he can't even find his thumb!

We'll have to start all over again … you think it'll come back to him?

Let him figure it out for himself!

What's more—if you're following me, Mademoiselle, you will have understood that I am now embarking on the second point of my demonstration, I promised you two points, and unlike some I could mention I think myself duty-bound to honor my promises—what's more, our clothes were stored in a single enormous chest, stuffed in higgledy-piggledy, and we shared their use catch as catch can. Some mornings I found myself clad in the jacket and pants worn by one of my brothers the day before. That day Blaise would be called Albert, and before long we all came running when my mother bellowed any of her offspring's names, even, for my part, when that name was Jeanne or Emilie. We reflexively jumped on hearing any of those well-worn cognomens; my mother soon came to appreciate the efficiency of this system, and took to calling out only Albert, even after the third Albert was fatally struck down by a Renault R18, unless it was the Spanish flu. We all answered to Albert, and Albert was dressed in clothes now too tight, now too loose, and now, furthermore, the sleeves of his sweater stopped at his elbows while he had to hitch his pants up to his armpits so as not to tread on the cuffs. And it was the same for his shoes, which slid off with every step when they weren't painfully pinching his feet, when, that is, he'd had the good fortune to dredge up a matching pair from under a bed or a sideboard—often one under the bed, the other under the sideboard—for if not, his right shoe would slip off with every step until evening while, until evening, the left would painfully pinch his foot. Whether by mischievous chance or the workings of Providence, it seems there was never among us one single Albert who fit into the clothes at our disposal.[17]

(Our eye was regularly caught by the headline of a newspaper left behind on a table. A natural disaster had struck a country on the other side of the world. An incredible number of casualties. Tens of thousands dead. It was quite simply unimaginable. The only way to grasp it would be to see all the inhabitants of the city teeming around us lying motionless in the street. An earthquake, a tidal wave, a volcanic eruption—the blind violence of a police raid. No heart could be moved by so many dead. And so we went back to our depression-racked lives, on solid ground and calm seas, at the foot of a quaint little mountain.)

Yet more grist to the mill of your interpretation mania, Mademoiselle, am I wrong? The very structure of the cauliflower—that close-knit little clan of identical units making a single fat head—the very structure of the cauliflower brings his own family to mind, that's what you're thinking, those indistinguishable brothers and sisters

---

17 Well, that's not how it was at all for the author, nothing of the sort. If in his childhood he could often be seen rather grotesquely attired, it was due not to parental negligence or indigence but to the particularly uninspired fashion of the time, which compressed young torsos in nylon turtlenecks, often red, sometimes even rust, from which the fingernails could produce sparks and the teeth learn what it means to be set on edge, whereas you had to feel around for the little boy's scrawny legs—even today the author has a modest thigh, a rooster's calf, and the slim ankle of an agile rhetorician—in his vast flared corduroy pants, frequently brown, whose wales, worn down by the edge of the school desk, revealed the weave here and there. Elder to a sister and a brother, he maintained with them a relationship akin to that of cats and dogs that torment each other all day and curl up in the same basket at night. If he sometimes misused the strength that comes with primogeniture, he has happily overcome that proclivity, his brother having practiced karate and his sister Pilates, and today their rapport is sunny. He did give some thought to embittering his sibling relationships for the present volume, with an eye to spicing up his anecdotes, but he soon gave up on that idea, judging such facile ploys unworthy of his art.

bound up, furthermore, in the gratin by a mortar of potatoes and thick béchamel sauce, it's more than he can bear, it's the indigestible madeleine of his past lying heavy in his stomach!

You're starting to get on my nerves.

Your naïve intuitions. You find a dead mouse and immediately picture a cat.

Have you ever thought of setting up shop as an analyst, or a clairvoyant?

Everything can be explained, can't it, by people's tastes and distastes? Everything has its roots in experience. It's because you pinched your finger in a door when you were two and a half that you now don't dare go in or out.

Poppycock. There's an amnesiac goldfish swimming in your crystal ball. Don't expect much recapturing of things past out of him.

Let me tell you the story instead.

Once upon a time there was a man who didn't like cauliflower gratin. The roots of that repugnance dug deep into the dish itself, where they intertwined, drawing strength from the dull white sauce, more vigorous with each passing day. That loathing was sturdy as an oak, and, like that oak, age-old and full of dark shadows. No point seeking its origins or motivations elsewhere. It fed exclusively and sufficiently on that gratin—stuffed itself with it, gorged on it, couldn't have managed a bite of anything else.

Suppose you upended your little system of causes and effects, just to see?

Suppose the existence of cauliflower gratin truly were the origin of all my woes?

Did I not expose myself to its depredations at every step and turn? Any open window constituted a threat. From it might suddenly gust the dreaded miasma that would impregnate me until evening, as if permeating not only the weave of my clothing but the very tissue of my skin. That evening, in the shower, out came the loofah, the currycomb.

I wouldn't have said no to dialysis.

Cauliflower gratin was watching for me on the rooftops, its rifle fitted with a telescopic sight and a silencer. It was watching for me alone. I was its chosen target, its whipping boy. It kept me forever on guard, my simplest pleasures spoiled by its threats. At every moment, I knew, in some kitchen somewhere, cauliflower and potato were grati-néeing. It could be far away, or could just as well be on my own street, and sometimes, manifestly, in my very house! No place was safe. There was no shelter, subterranean or aerial, to protect me from cauliflower gratin, no waiting refuge to dash into should danger rear its ugly head.

How to live, in such conditions? What projects to conceive, knowing that peril might defeat or despoil them at any moment? An evening among friends that opened with a cordial round of aperitifs suddenly degenerated into catastrophe. Of a lovely trip into the distant provinces, I recalled only my discomfort in an inn.

(Most of the conversations we could make out might well have been snatches of a dialogue scripted long before, spoken and acted with varying degrees of talent and conviction. A and B had decided the roles with the flip of a coin. Every statement called up its response. That wasn't talking, it was rustling. The wind had come from afar to shake those leafy branches. People could have, no doubt should have, made do with nods, grimaces, and sighs. But in silence nothing grew but discomfort, anguish, and incomprehension.)

But at the same time, you will say to me, for I hear you, Mad-emoiselle, even if I'm not listening to you, and you were wanting to say to me, you were going to shoot back at me, in the naïve hope of shutting my mouth, that there also exists at every moment the pos-sibility of trout amandine. That miracle too can occur: radiant, un-mingled joy, caught from the spring's pool of clear water, pulled out flipping and flopping, then prepared just the way I like it to make of my life a triumph or at least an untroubled haven for felicity, all my senses suddenly attuned to the phenomena around me, my nerves like guitar strings beneath the wild beasts' talons and claws, my soul at rest, lulled by that music. Why forever fear the worst, why not be sustained by that hope?

You're saying to yourself.

But, Mademoiselle, open, if not your porcelain eyes, concerned above all with being seen, then at least your nostrils, and tell me: how many trout amandines are cooked for every cauliflower gratin? What's the ratio, the differential? Any idea? Well, then, I'll tell you: that ratio is one to a hundred, one to a thousand, one to ten thousand, a hundred thousand perhaps! The odds of stumbling upon a trout amandine around some street corner—or at least its aroma, or the sputtering of the pan—are so slim that we must call them essentially nonexistent, whereas ... whereas crashing into a cauliflower gratin, sinking into it, not only around some street corner but on your own straightforward path, or under your very own roof, is a twist of fate so common as to belong to the realm of the non-event. That's the fact of the matter. There's no way to weigh the risk against the reward—the first always infinitely greater and more likely than the second.

And worst of all ...

For the worst is an added flourish that can always be counted on.

It can come along, for example, at the same time as that exquisitely rare, exquisitely exceptional reward: the scent of trout amandine wafts from a half-open window, and then all at once, from the wide-open window across the way, belches the stench of cauliflower gratin, filling the street like fog, you could have bet your life on it, it was a sure thing.

And the stench drowns out the scent, just as the drum silences the fife.

What good does it do to sing when your neighbor is bellowing?

Here, then, is the truth, and a bitter truth it is: trout amandine can't compete. Against cauliflower gratin, trout amandine can't compete. All its subtlety and finesse are wiped out by that platter of cauliflower, by the energizing self-evidence of cauliflower, and the quick-setting, gut-plugging plaster of cauliflower, which freezes the world on its foundation, in its trivial, disappointing reality, and prevents the trout from piercing through it with its silvery dart. Were the poor fish alive, it would die in that magma. Three desperate thrashes of the tail and everything would be over: it would suffocate quicker than in the gentle heat of the frying pan. The world is now a gigantic cauliflower, gratinéed, and the elegant creatures of the waters lie agonizing in the béchamel.

Oh! Let's get to the murder!

(The schools were populated by mute, terrified children. The joyous cries that came our way at recess actually burst from the lips of their sadistic minders and wardens, expressing their delight in that grim spectacle. How could the adults on the other side of the wall have been taken in? How could they have forgotten?)[18]

But I myself have already been there, long before that sinister day, blessed among all others.

I endured everything childhood has to offer, the whole panoply of humiliations and misfortunes for a man who's just starting out, little aware of the ways of this world, and ready to swallow anything.[19]

---

18 After three warnings you got a demerit; after three demerits you were suspended for a week; after three suspensions you were expelled from the school forever. That will tell you how distant was the exit and how unreachable freedom for a docile, timorous boy like the author, who couldn't even manage to snag his first warning. His junior high school diploma, oh yes, with flying colors, but his first warning? Not even close!

19 For there's no reason why the author shouldn't sometimes make use of his character as a marionette, to take his gift for ventriloquism out for a little exercise. Lucid and perceptive, children—even when the conditions imposed on them seem wholly enviable—come to know humiliation all the more quickly in that they are humiliated by the very fact of their childhood. The child is small and weak, his word has no force. He experiences his immaturity as a powerlessness, a painful deficiency. Some children, at least, the author among them. The uncle who patted his head as he struggled to recall his first name—and who ended up calling him *chief* or *little man*—humiliated him unwittingly, thinking himself genial and benevolent. The high-hanging apple humiliated him. His clumsiness, his ignorance, ever flagrant, humiliated him. Even his continual progress, rather than filling him with pride, humiliated the boy he had been only the day before, left him ashamed of the drawing he'd done that morning. It was a very sad sort of existence, which nevertheless, he'll come back to this, might have played a part in the birth of his vocation as a writer. As a child, he felt like a belittled, diminished, almost vanquished adult. People laughed at him openly, and with his imprecisions, his ignorance, his incapacities, his incompetence in every domain, he continually gave them good reason. He rebuked himself for holding out the stick with which to be beaten—to be crushed, to be flattened. He would show them. He would take his revenge. He would be vindicated. There ensued many tedious pages of poetry

Yes, you're right, my dear young lady, I complain a great deal, I complain all the time. One of these days I'm going to get fed up with myself! In short, I know all the words of the plaint, I keep them at the ready in my mouth, don't expect me to hold my tongue.

And yet I was once so full of good will.

Just imagine: I was naked. I had a little pink body and two eyes that never blinked, not even in the most blinding sunlight.

Could anyone be more trusting?

As if there were no pointy pebbles or crabs or thorny chestnut hulls or hot embers.

I might as well have been offering myself up as a sacrifice. I naively invited the pinch and the punch, the slap and the slug. I was just asking to be bitten and clawed. People salivated when they saw me, out of hunger or cruelty. They couldn't wait for the fun to begin.

That's how we are when we're born. And must we become the opposite of all that in order to be called men, must we renounce all our innocence and our nudity?

Imagine. The baby giraffe staggers to its wobbling feet. They tell him: if you want to be a giraffe, pull those legs up into your flanks and that neck down into your shoulders, throw off that short, spotted coat, cover yourself with thick brown fur.

And so the baby bear is born.

But since, meanwhile, the bear's real son finds himself urged, if he would be a bear, to remake himself head to toe; since, meanwhile, he casts off his fleece, stands as tall as he can on his four legs, and cranes his neck till his vertebrae crack, there are still baby bears and baby giraffes in this world, but the former are the offspring of the

---

that, paradoxically, displayed above all whatever naiveté he had left, that, in short, showed his paralyzed, spiteful childhood at play, even if his obvious lack of talent multiplied his rage tenfold. Such sentiments are perhaps incomprehensible today, the author tells himself, perhaps they belong to another age. Children have since learned to exercise their rights; they've taken control. They've figured out how to put their capricious stubbornness to good use. They've become monstrous domestic tyrants, authoritarian, intolerable, impressed by nothing, never again. And now it's the adult who feels humiliated before them, for being so overripe, so flabby, so stiff, still so wanting even at the very peak of his power and command, but this time with no hope that things might one day be otherwise: no vengeance is possible now.

giraffe and the latter those of the bear.

And why shouldn't it work the same way with the sons of men? Whence man becomes that unfeeling, bellicose lout who will survive only if he soon develops enough violence and duplicity to fit in with the pack and live the life he was meant for.

I long remained the naïf of those very first days.

I never saw what was coming. It's true, of course, that the enemy's skilled at concealing itself.

Take, for instance, that woman on her way home from the market.

(A woman was on her way home from the market, a bundle of leeks poking out of her basket.)

There's a bundle of leeks poking out of her basket. All very open and aboveboard. Maybe you don't like leeks; and so, seeing her approach, you have plenty of time to flee. But how to be sure there's not also a cauliflower in the depths of that basket? Cauliflower is given to huddling deep inside baskets; even before it's put in, it's already curled into a ball, like the slyest snake. It will later unfurl, and spread—oh, how it will spread!—and go on spreading till there's nowhere left to spread. Seeing it so curled up, so coiled, so compact, you'd never guess it could spread as it does, until it covers everything, or nearly, and not with some thin varnish, not some delicate coating! Layers and layers, it will be endless, it will be bottomless.

Under the cauliflower, still more cauliflower!

And a mere newborn babe is supposed to see through that ruse? How can you expect such a thing? How is he to suspect that one fine morning he'll be abruptly cut off, that the font of fresh, wholesome milk will go dry, that he'll then find himself sitting before a plateful of cauliflower gratin? And there real life begins, little man, such will be your regular rations from here on, your daily fare, you'll never be free of it again.

The cauliflower suddenly blows up in your face like a bomb, it fragments, and everything shatters along with it, the world you once thought so solid, which can thus at any instant explode, fly apart, disperse, and your confidence in yourself takes a serious blow as well; could it be that the soundness of your being is no less a lie, are you yourself made of nothing more than identical bouquets of fibers clinging together to give themselves some heft and significance, while the tiniest has already said all there is to say of you, the last word—to which there is nothing more to add, and which you endlessly, absurdly reiterate, twig of a girl or stalky young man, a continually proliferating metonymy, invading the world like tentacular seaweed; where are you, in that infinite reduplication of echoes, reflections, and shadows? You exist no more than the cauliflower, which has no core, no heart, no brain, even if it vaguely assumes the look of the latter, in actual fact its circumvolutions are only circumlocutions, a mad spiral, a vicious circle producing only a stutter—me me me, the cauliflower repeats, and you'll get nothing more out of it; and that's all it wants to convince you of, that's all it would have you swallow, that's what's supposed to put food on your table!

But the cauliflower eats itself, just as Russian dolls devour one another. It leaves you with your hunger and desire unsated, lost in the regret of your wasted days.

(Some people seemed to devote all their time and attention to perfecting and dramatizing their inborn status as men or women—exercise regimens for the men, beauty regimens for the women, putting on muscle for the former, makeup for the latter—as if gender alone were not enough and each was obliged to exploit vague, uncertain virtualities to become a full-blown man or woman. The results were sometimes impressive, but most often this extreme specialization was punished by caricature. Muscle pumped up the eyelid; lipstick adorned the teeth.)[20]

---

20 This observation, attributed to the character—or to his agitated state, as he captures the bustle of the city, its daily course, on the margins of his obsessive monologue—can be found word for word in the author's journal, under the date of December 17, 2010. This can't be a coincidence; it would be simply too extraordinary. The author has a certain tendency—it's the nature of his job, he claims—to theorize his pet peeves. In so doing, he naively seeks to withdraw from the game, to distance himself, to look down on the world from on high and so remedy his many sufferings, even if it means being thought a pretentious prat perched in the heavens like an arrogant god, little concerned with human affairs and shaking his head as if before a dispiriting spectacle whenever they cross his mind, usually engrossed in more exhilarating speculations: creating a new star,

My life interests you, Mademoiselle, of course it does, it's a life of sorrow and decline. Don't forget, it drove me to murder, I'll get to that. For the moment I'm still on the schoolboy's lament. I did not excel as a pupil. Mathematics taught me only to distrust history. They said to me, "Louis XIV, 1638–1715." I did the subtraction. I got -77. That king did not live for seventy-seven years. I found it highly unlikely that in the course of that long non-existence he could have built a palace as imposing as Versailles, which, quite logically, I suspected of being just one more fantastical delusion, a house of cards that held up only in our dreaming or hallucinating imaginations. Was there not good reason to believe that Molière never wrote the plays performed before that king who did not live, and who reigned even less (1643–1715 = -72)? It all fit together. As for me, I wondered what I was doing there. This lesson confirmed what my senses had already told me: that reality was elusive, hollow, fake, a torture our injured nerves inflict on themselves. Our awkward, spasmodic gestures armed us with the ax and the saw we carried into a forest of soft-barked columns to cut out sharp-angled furniture with wobbling legs, squeaking doors, stuck drawers. Everything was made up. Everything was our fault. Everything was false.

The teachers took a dim view of that skeptical, apathetic pupil. I should have applied myself more, pretended better; perhaps, with a little persistence, I might have ended up believing in it all. The Château de Versailles was a beautiful illusion all the same, what did I get from the lucidity that burned holes in its cardboard walls? I was furthermore a lonely revolutionary, timid and taciturn, powerless, and at the same time guilty of an absurd sentimentality that, foreshadowing the perverse passions of my adolescence, focused on the baby bird

---

conceiving an incombustible body, reflecting on the consequences of the expansion of the universe and wondering if the amplitude of the flea's jump should be increased accordingly. The author half-heartedly denies these accusations. It does seem to him that the writer lives simultaneously on two planes of reality: that is at the same time his great good fortune—he can hurriedly flee the one for the other whenever things get messy here or there—and his curse—he has no idea of the plenitude of presence: at the height of emotion or passion, two of his fingers are still feeling around for a pencil. Then he comes back to earth and observes that reality is never anything more than a flattening-out of his own metaphors.

and the tender young flower, and lulled itself with old-fashioned romantic verse, with fits of nostalgia borrowed from those tear-stained alexandrines, which I soon learned to churn out myself with a certain facility;[21] and it might well have seemed, from my writings, that my adored, still-virgin lover had died at age twenty of an excess of pallor. But as it happens the only girls I knew were my sisters, irascible harpies, volatile, capricious, exasperating, themselves experts in little cross-rhymed quatrains—claw / tattle / gnaw / the paddle—of which I was the dazed and contused dedicatee.

Whatever became of them?

I have no idea.

I do have a suspicion: they're gratinéeing cauliflower in big Pyrex baking dishes, so the horror will be complete, exhaustive, so no one will miss a thing, or as little as possible, so that everyone will get an eyeful of its edges, its entire depth, through the glass—and that's not being open and aboveboard like the woman with the leeks, not at all, not at all, it's aiming to torture my eyes in advance with the dregs of that chalice, so that from the start I'll abandon all hope of finding something better under the surface, if I dig into it, if I sink into it, perhaps merciful deliverance, perhaps the treasure such travails must surely lead to, at least a comforting beam of light—but no.

Because cauliflower gratin is also a sight, a hell of a sight.

A wound for the eye.

Was it to gaze on such monstrosities that we were born into this world?

It really is just plain ugly. As though everything inside it were dismembered, broken, ground, reduced to debris, to detritus, to rubbish. We see here a ruined world's last load of garbage, its scraps, its leavings, its ruins. The color is indefinable, the scene depicted as

---

21 Here it is the character who coincides with the author, not the other way around, the very character who claims to weight himself with authenticity and experience to take on some semblance of life. He robs the author, rifles through his pockets, ransacks his existence. Poor guy, he deserves a break; the author lets him take what he wants, unburdens himself of his excess baggage. He torches his own barn for the insurance money. Up in flames go the meager harvest, the emaciated cattle, the broken-down combine. He'll rebuild it all where it stood, with renewed ambition. He will, he will …

muddled and disharmonious as can be. You'd think it was furiously stamping feet that made the stuff. Because only feet, only big yellow feet with gray toenails could have trampled out that swill.

(The more Western man yearned for comfort and safety, the more he asked his jeans to express the opposite. A cynicism no less radiant than innocence. There were grimy jeans, faded jeans, fraying jeans; there were outsize jeans that sagged down to the hips in imitation of the emaciated prisoner at hard labor, forbidden to own a belt; finally, as an apotheosis, there were jeans sold with holes and tears already in place, a make-believe pauper's garb gracing our gilded youth, informing us with no small precision of the sensitivity of our consciences.)

The only appetite such an abomination can whip up is an appetite for destruction—but that one's insatiable. You want to lay waste to the world, since everything's screwed from the start: since man has so desperately failed, has so thoroughly ruined all his chances, let's cut loose, let's at least share in the joys of destruction, so we won't be only its dupes, its victims and martyrs—that's the idea that comes to us—let's hack out a stone of our own from the foundering edifice, let's chop everything that once held together into little tiny pieces. Cauliflower's not the only thing in this world that can crumble! Isn't everything prone to cracking up and falling apart?

And then, nothing prevents us from gratinéeing anything at all.

In the end, everything can be gratinéed—potentially, everything can be gratinéed.

Like all those without power, I first turned that urge to destroy on myself. I dreamed of my own suicide with a sort of spiteful jubilation, like a conspirator plotting a coup. I thought of stabbing myself in the back. I was the first and very possibly the last target of a terrorist campaign that I nonetheless hoped, with a naiveté bespeaking the integrity of my intentions, would rend the fabric of society forever.

I would leap from my window and land like a bomb on the city. If I threw myself into the river, my body would poison its waters; hung from a roofbeam, it would swing back and forth like a flail. My death would be contagious.

I proceeded by stages. Before giving myself the coup de grâce, I tasted of the rare delights of torture. My body became the plaything of elaborate nervous tics whose eloquence more than made up for my taciturnity, for in those days I could go nearly a year without speaking a word. All this world's allergies fought for a little patch of my skin, gaudy as Harlequin's motley, and often, for lack of space, superimposed their eruptions, scabs, and scales one on the other. I had to scratch long and hard at my eczema to relieve the itch of the fungal infection beneath it.

Since I bit my nails, that relief was slow in coming, and accompanied by excruciating pains in my fingertips. Such was the therapy I came up with: inflicting for and on myself the wounds that had not been gouged into my flesh when the blows were raining down. A skilled torturer can wield his pincers without scarring the victim's body, without drawing blood—cauliflower gratin being an example: it works you over and leaves you for dead with no visible trace of its savagery. And then just try and find someone who will hear your complaint! No one takes you seriously. The chief of police laughs in your face; sometimes his dog pees on your boots. People show you amputees stripped of all four limbs to reawaken your sense of decency. But there is no sorrow worse than the sorrow you're denied. It only grows stronger from that refusal. And then there are those who delight in the very cause of your misery, who find comfort and joy in it, so true is it that the worm and the fox do not have the same idea of the hen.

That was a painful discovery, Mademoiselle. I nevertheless had to concede that cauliflower gratin had its devotees. Some of them basked in it like an alligator in a mangrove. Some seemed eager to spend their whole life camped out amid that vegetation, and even, why not, to multiply, their brats begging for no other treat. They're perfectly at home with cauliflower gratin; once they've emptied the dish, they lick the bottom, they even scrape the sides!

Could anyone possibly be more unlike me?

What was this world—and who these creatures nonetheless so like me that they should have instinctively shared my disgust?

(We heard radio advertisements coming from inside the café; more ads were posted on the buses, whose shelters were in fact even crueler traps. All equally moronic. All equally mindless. Mindless and grotesque, and oppressive. They twisted and perverted the image of happiness: the women were lures, the false cleverness of the slogans dulled our minds, suddenly we were ashamed of our intelligence; the language of poetry and emotion was relentlessly humiliated. Nevertheless, this was accepted, considered normal; it appalled only a few pests who refused to see that commerce was the only glue still holding society together, our last remaining reason to talk to each other.)

Finally came the end of school, and of childhood, which are one and the same.

I'd learned something else—which makes two things, if we include the revelation I just mentioned: that pathological fondness some people feel for cauliflower gratin, utterly incomprehensible to me, and which even today feeds my anguish till it chokes; that second thing was the following, no less staggering, no less devastating … the very words rip out my tongue and my teeth, one by one … there were some who didn't like trout amandine!

Some people, given a choice between trout amandine and cauliflower gratin, will, without the slightest hesitation, choose the gratin! Such people exist. I know a few myself. Try living in peace and harmony with your contemporaries once you've realized that! When from the very beginning there are such grounds for discord and conflict! When we're sitting at a table facing each other like the garter snake and the mongoose!

And so the scales fell from my eyes, Mademoiselle: suddenly I understood. I understood that men were bound together by false compromises and tenuous circumstances. Peace could never be anything more than a lull in the fighting. The threat smoldered on. At any moment that inextinguishable discord might burst out into the light of day and two armies lurch irrevocably into motion. We were fundamentally irreconcilable, perpetually, truth be told, about to pounce on each other.

Imagine the torment of my heightened sensitivity, as pained by our similarities as by our differences. We were *almost alike*, and the two terms of that truth dismayed me equally. How to tolerate oneself in the other's eye? And our own so perfectly reflects that other that this exchange of glances proves utterly empty, and we share only the horrified realization of our sameness, of that unity pointlessly doubled. And yet our difference asserts itself—the *almost* that disastrously unites us also divides us, but *just barely*, and we experience that minuscule divergence as something monstrous, immediately making the other intolerable, as if we were suddenly forced to live a few inches away from our own fractured body. Were the resemblance less perfect, we would surely not suffer in our flesh as we do. An outright otherness would have been preferable; the otherness of the animal, for instance, places us in a solitude where we can flourish and grow, melding as we do with those of our own species, where the graft is instantaneous, the incompatibility of tissues and humors revealing itself only later, once the fusion has taken hold; and the rejection that inevitably ensues rips us apart as if our limbs were tied to four charging horses.

Given all that, what love is possible?

Can an embrace be anything other than a prelude to that future rift? I came to congratulate myself for counting so little in the eyes of women.[22] It must be recognized, my lovely young lady, that they never importuned me with their advances. Your sisters' indifference to me was such that I sometimes thought I was living in distant Mongolia, and I would have been sure I was, were I not, after twenty years of that exile, as ignorant as ever of its people's language and customs.

I lacked confidence: when the sight of a woman stirred me, my

---

22 The author long felt a jealousy toward ladies' men, the many varied minds, laughs, and skins they knew intimately, that multiplicitous experience of life and delight. But looking at them today, immutably identical to themselves, flush with their success, the author finds himself thinking that in all those adventures they find nothing more than one endlessly reiterated occasion for an egocentric and even onanistic ecstasy, and that those minds, those laughs, those skins, of no more consequence to them than the changing weather, in the end affect only the clothes they pick out and then later doff so as to bring themselves off without wetting their pants. In short, the author has matured, and very wisely prefers today to mock what he is not rather than to bemoan his fate from morning to evening as he watches the pretty passersby passing him by.

gaze clouded, my thoughts grew muddy, my face grimaced just as it would have done on the surface of a pool of murky water.

And my entire person exuded an odor of silt.

As you see, Mademoiselle, I am capable of something other than boasting.

It was the sweat oozing out of me, it was my bowels squirming in agonized timidity.

But the beauty of women left me reeling. It confounded me, it demolished me. It cudgeled my skull, my shoulders, it viciously kicked my legs out from under me, tendons ripping as I fell. It was a violence directed against me personally, with a viciousness not far from frenzy. So much beauty—not to exalt and delight me; so much beauty to make of my life a misery. So much beauty to lay me low, to humiliate my body and pain my heart. No ugliness, no monstrous facial injury could have shaken me so, could have split me open from top to bottom that way. I writhed in pain, I howled, I did. All at once, only to vanish a moment later, there had appeared in my gaze the one good reason for being alive, but which I would have had to physically restrain and lash to my body, and whose disappearance each time meant my annihilation.

(Sometimes, even now, a young man sat down on the terrace with a book. He was generally a pathetic loser, or at least seemed a pathetic loser, which is to say someone on whom life had clearly not smiled. Ugly or sad, a little pudgy, with something gloomy, tired, cold, and dead about him. When you got a good look at the guys who still read books, you couldn't even begin to imagine what those who wrote them must look like.)[23]

---

23 The author can only agree. A touchy subject, of course, to be broached with tact and certain precautions. It would be a mistake to insult the reader of good will and inform him too brutally that he belongs to a community of pitiful nobodies. The author hastens to include himself in their number. And thus immediately softens his assertion. Literature is intimately bound up with humiliation. Those on whom life smiles (with its slightly empty-headed smile) waste no time with books, neither writing nor reading them. This at least is an undeniable fact, confirmed all around us every day. Like every law, it allows a number of exceptions, among which the author hopes to include his reader; nevertheless, on the whole it holds absolutely true. The audience at public readings is made up mostly of bored middle-aged ladies. Those women are highly respectable and graced with

Who will ever believe that the Buddha's detachment and supe-
riority are not undermined just a bit by his pot belly? As soon as I
seemed to be pulling myself up, life took it upon itself to strike down
my pretentions and thrust my nose back into that elemental magma
of which you now know the recipe.

I took to frequenting museums. Standing before the paintings, I
strove to fill myself with their power and harmony. The greatest men
had imbued them with all their force, all their passion, served by
the nimble intelligence of their fingers, expressing its boundlessness
with minute precision. Here, at last, the execution obeyed the idea,
never betraying it. It seemed possible—in a limited, modest space, of
course—to master the imponderable torrent of incidents and chances
on which we ceaselessly sail, struggling not to capsize, and thereby ex-
hausting our resistance, our courage, all the resources of our imagination. And yet those works left me cold. The painter alone, I thought,
had found in that act a brief and sterile gratification. I might almost
have thought it an ejaculation only a little more self-aware than the
other kind.

And before the work of the sculptor, too, I might as well have
been made of stone.

Or bronze.[24]

---

as many human qualities as the sharp-elbowed, downy-cheeked nymphet or the
devoted father, but they have time to kill, a time not filled with the occupations
of an existence exciting enough to satisfy them. When the reader happens to be a
young man, you can be sure that his psychological profile presents certain doleful
peculiarities: that boy has no friends, his aggrieved, endless virginity torments his
clenched body from the tips of his hair to the yellow nail digging painfully into his
big toe, he has no sense of style, he moves without grace or agility; his gestures and
walk are self-conscious, his words sparse or hurried, and most often profoundly
confused; his bookish learning, unreal and disordered, creates an unwholesome
monster, ill-adapted, antisocial, possibly perverse. Writers are no more appealing
a sight. Is it by chance that Michel Houellebecq has become the hero of our literary microcosm? His visible, flagrant, triumphant wretchedness is the symptom
of a lamentable state of affairs to which a thousand other signs bear witness. No
misunderstanding is possible. The victor had to be a victim. Literature is a misery.

24 The author sometimes catches himself yawning in boredom as he stands at his
bookshelf. Suddenly, he can't imagine what book he might implore for his rescue.
At such times, he can't help thinking that writers are snakes that humanity nurtures in its breast, that their only gift is to make our plight even more painful by

ÉRIC CHEVILLARD

And yet, to be sure, man could not have done better.

But if they thought they were working for me, those artists had gone to a great deal of trouble for nothing. I then turned my attention to the other museum-goers. All but a handful looked deeply beleaguered, eager to put this ordeal behind them. It was like witnessing some obligatory ritual, such as walking on a bed of hot coals. The end of the agony brought such relief that they must have concluded they'd had a lovely time. But the fact is they couldn't care less about art, no more than I, and they vaguely resented artists for forcing them to endure such torment. Good taste requiring that they revere the great masters of the past, they took their vengeance on those still alive, crushing them with their mockery and indifference. But the old masters too inspired a secret loathing, all the more tenacious in that it was thought appropriate to feign a sort of passion for their works. I wondered how that hypocrisy had come to be, how it was that artists, universally abhorred, were nonetheless bathed in such prestige that lines formed before museums, made up of people who considered them good-for-nothings and parasites, who yawned before their canvases, heaving a weary sigh when the door they took for the exit opened only onto the interminable prospect of still more galleries, the walls so uniformly covered with paint that it would have been quicker to put it on with a roller—the unanimous temptation was then to take a running start and zoom straight through the mu-

deepening our awareness of it, by describing it so clearly that we're robbed of all life-saving illusion, all restful insouciance, that a tragic lucidity ruins our happiest hours, that time runs through us like a blade. Only laughable fools have sung of the joys of existence. Writers have devoted all their efforts to disabusing the naïf, throwing acid in the beauty queen's face, weaving a shroud for the newborn babe. He accuses himself of belonging to this malevolent, sadistic crowd of killjoys, all the less forgivable in that by taking refuge in language the writer finds a private solution to the disaster, a survival tactic that works only for him. The poisonous exhalations of his flowers of evil so intoxicate him that he thinks himself invincible, indestructible, even immortal. But his readers, cruelly abandoned to their bewilderment, will seek in vain the *mystical nourishment that would bring them vigor in his pages.* Rather, they will be pierced from all sides, bombarded with unstoppable, devastating revelations (for example, oysters have been deceiving us all along, their pearls are artificial!), and in the end, more tormented than ever, flayed alive—while the ungrateful volume is now bound in fine leather, clad in their cold skin.

/62

seum with one vigorous slide over its gleaming parquet floors. That at least would be an entertainment of some possible value, but only children let themselves indulge in it, and they were immediately rebuked, caught by their hoods and forced back to the creeping procession, back to their initiation into the hatred of art and artists in excruciating detail, down to the very folds of their sumptuous drapery.

But if mankind could feign such enthusiasm for what in fact he most despised, art, which rubbed his nose in his own incompetence, his own impotence, was it absurd to hypothesize a similar imposture in his bewildering taste for cauliflower gratin?

For is there anything so dull in this world? Honestly? Does cauliflower gratin not exude the most colossal boredom, along with that suffocating steam? It's boring to look at: I ask you, what is there to see? It's the worst of the daubs we've just been talking about. Worse yet, it's boring to eat. Your fork slogs through it, your knife sinks in up to the elbow. Nothing to cling to. Nor any heaven above. The vegetation unrelentingly monotonous. The Transsiberian Railway, its entire route one narrow path between two ranks of birches, at least offers the vigilant eye an occasional sweeping view of the steppe. Not so cauliflower gratin: you have to clean your plate to discover the clearing. No labor could be more draining, more sterile. You'd like, at least, to be able to think of something else as you toil, but cauliflower gratin never gives you the chance. All your anxieties of the moment parade through your mind as you eat, summoned up by the atmosphere. So this is your life, that steaming ruin, that dreary mess—that's where you stand, everything you've built lies there in pieces.

And my faith was restored, Mademoiselle, yes.

My faith was restored by that idea.

My faith in mankind was restored.

Which is to say in my fellows.

Which is to say, too, in myself.

For if it was indeed deplorable to cover your eyes like this, if it was scarcely to mankind's credit that they deceived themselves in this way, out of cowardice or weakness or vanity, that they couldn't bring themselves to openly affirm that art and cauliflower gratin disgusted them to the highest degree, such insincerity was still better than a genuine liking for such things, a fondness I alone could not share. Better cowardice than perversion. I wasn't a monster. In their heart of hearts, everyone agreed with me. I could fraternize with others, as soon as they stopped lying to themselves.

(Rarely, very rarely, but now and then all the same, a pretty girl also sat down to read, but then it was a bad book.)

Perhaps I had only to appeal to the virtues still nonetheless lingering in the hearts of men to revive the passion for truth that none of us ever loses entirely, no matter how solid the illusions we thought it wise to take shelter in so as to endure our reality; and to be sure reality is very painful and hard, but is lucidity not preferable to the lie that degrades our intelligence? Maybe there was still time to extricate ourselves.

Suppose that mission fell to me?

Suppose I was the angel of disillusionment?

Don't laugh, Mademoiselle. Although I can see you're not laughing. And it's true, there's nothing to laugh about. I didn't feel like laughing either when I was visited by that idea. Don't misunderstand me. Although I know you're not misunderstanding me. I myself was not so naïve as to believe I'd been chosen by God, or one of his chimerical avatars. That idea had simply come to me, to me of all people, it had landed on me as a fly lands on my nose and not yours, the secret reason for that choice forever beyond our grasp.

Very likely there is no reason.

Just one of chance's little tricks.

I happened to be standing at the intersection of its random trajectories. And was thus designated, off-handedly and without to-do.

You there, step forward.

Lucidity dazzled me. To me, now, fell the task of informing the world, of opening its eyes, sobering it up, and inspiring in it a horror of cauliflower gratin.[25]

---

25 And here, once again, we must note that it is the character who is blindly following the author *(see note 21)*. The character is merely an ape, with a parrot on his shoulder. An analogy that the author believes he might already have used at

And then, immediately, doubt and anxiety.

Were my powers of persuasion up to the task?

Because prejudice is a stubborn and deep-rooted thing. Cannibalism too wasn't wiped out in a day—if it had been, what would they have done with the leftovers? People liked other people's meaty calves, their thighs, their buttocks, they found them tasty, they helped themselves to seconds (calf, thigh, buttock—there were indeed two of each); the viscera too, served on the side, had their aficionados. Not all of them were mere gluttons; true gourmets could be found at their table as well, delighting only in earlobes—and who can blame them?

It must be said, earlobes look perfectly delicious.

I would nibble yours with great pleasure, Mademoiselle, had I not learned to stifle that craving, to choke it back. I swallow hard. I clutch the arms of my chair and hold on with all the force of my will, struggling to distract my thoughts and my appetite from that temptation.

And here we run into the stumbling block of every comparison, and particularly of this one, for which I had such high hopes, between

---

some point, no doubt in one of his other tales, but which one? He doesn't hold them long in his memory, as if, on finishing a book, he pronounced the case closed, sent the file to storage. He retains only a vague idea of it, fairly similar on the whole to the presentiment that preceded its creation. All that work for nothing. The original muddle reestablished, as if it were order itself. And perhaps that's exactly how it is. Perhaps it is the story organized, mastered, and immobilized that constitutes the real disruption; perhaps fog is the normal context of a human existence, or at least of thought, of consciousness, blurred, imprecise, fumbling, alien to all sharp-honed conceptions, on which it cuts itself, and to all stable ideas, which paralyze it as well, as if instantly congealing the brain in the skull. Eventually the consciousness produces a book, waste in its most perfect form, which it expels in order to finally regain a perfect openness and freedom; its attention must remain wavering, its grasp lax and flabby. Vagueness is its element, daydreaming its way of knowing and understanding. Elucidation, and every manner of resolution, encumber it—like making your way through the trembling forest with a long board under your arm. Nevertheless, the author is sometimes aggrieved that he cannot make a solid foundation of the work he has done, that he must forever try to advance over shifting sands, as at the very beginning. Everything has to be started over—but no matter how doggedly he persists, he will always have before him only the void, and oblivion behind.

cannibalism and the barbaric practice of ingesting cauliflower gratin. There's a very real difference between the respective delights of the two foods in question. To the same degree that cauliflower gratin is objectively repellent—on that point at least I like to think we can all agree—earlobes, especially those we call free, attached high up and making a lovely plump curve, are incontestably mouthwatering. If there's one thing that everyone would happily bite off with his incisors, then roll around in his mouth with his tongue, then suck at great length and chew at great length, it is beyond question that tender pink or brown earlobe, prettily rimmed, with that little bulge of flesh and blood that you can imagine unencumbered by any skeleton, cartilage, even nerves, like a melt-in-your-mouth mousse or a delicate *calisson.*

To be sure, the eradication of cannibalism is a matter of public order—eating each other being apt to occasional disputes—more than a purely gastronomical concern, and therein lies its difference with respect to the question before us, even if I would argue that the mindless consumption of cauliflower gratin is one of the least known and hence most pernicious causes of societal breakdown and the violence that comes with it. You can't feed on so uncohesive a dish without fragmenting yourself. First you crack open, then your rupture propagates all around you like a wave; everything you touch falls to pieces, the sentiments of friendship or love you once felt so sure of now pitifully crumble, the solid mass of your thoughts disintegrates in your skull, your vision dims, everything that's soft is abraded by everything that's hard, everything that's hard is swallowed by everything that's soft, the ground opens up, the firmest foundation blows away like sand, that's what we get for so carelessly wielding our forks. That's why everything's so uncertain, so vague, and why we can no longer find our donkey in the cloud of flour. Our hands grasp only shadows rubbed with black soap, the eel is the most affectionate of our daughters, it's a torment.[26]

---

26 Surely there can be no better way for the author to ensure his mastery and stand up to his character than to drag him out of his soliloquy by one ear and cast him without warning into another fiction, where his puppet-like doings will illustrate some of these same themes, but in a different context, since the context

matters no more than the pretext. Why should it be forbidden to write a novel at the foot of the page? Paper is paper: is the author's vocation not to fill it with ink? Will he allow his angst, so carefully repressed, so scrupulously sidelined, to regain the upper hand in the lower margin? Given the limited space, though, he thinks it wise to miniaturize himself to serve as a foil for his invasive character, to teach him a lesson, to show him what's what and lead him where he will. Here he very openly offers his reader a hint, a trail to follow—if some insist that he incarnate himself in his story, then he will do so as little as possible: why not as an insect? Here, then, is what this book could just as well have been, no longer entitled *The Author and Me* but, more accurately, *My Ant:*

Little did I suspect where I would be led, through how many twists and turns, when, out of boredom, as a game, and for another reason I'll explain later, I began to follow that ant! I was something of a drifter back then, without obligations, and I sensed that this ant was bound for some goal, resolute, urged on by a vital necessity; thus, having nothing better to do, simply to kill a few minutes of a decidedly interminable existence, and just a bit curious, all the same, to know the path she—for the rules of gender in my native tongue make of every ant a she, and who am I to disagree?—the path she was taking and where it would lead, when I saw her there on the public square where I was loitering, I decided to follow her. An impulse, if you like, nothing thought through. But that ant was quite clearly obeying an inflexible destiny, and this was enough to intrigue me, alien as it was to my own random course, subject to the whims of the wind and the clock. I believe I was wondering what could so entirely occupy the energy and will of a being living here and now, where I myself happened to be, when I could have so easily been somewhere else, and where I was with no justification, unable even to recall where I'd come from and what had brought me there; whereas, I repeat, that ant seemed compelled by some duty, a mission perhaps—how extraordinary—and one could guess, seeing her hasten along on her tiny legs, that her path was set once and for all, that nothing would turn her aside, that she never even asked herself if some other life might be possible, some other fate more enviable; no, that minuscule ant—unlike me, a man of some heft—knew what she had to do and abandoned herself body and soul to the task, without fuss, without hesitation. Myself, you understand, I was vaguely awaiting some order or injunction to get going, to put my strength to some use, to act, and that order never came. Time passed, the days went by one after the other, and nothing took hold of me, no cause, no desire. I was even thinking of turning myself in to the police, so that I might be taken firmly in hand and guided down a path marked out by the stations of the inquiry, and then the trial, and so on up to the verdict, when my fate would finally be decided. But I couldn't in truth imagine delivering myself up to the judgment of my peers, who had always condemned me, even in my days of innocence, when my soul was like clear water, when no one had been throttled by my hands, assuming …

Then that ant crossed my path. Not quite the sign I was waiting for: I wanted an illumination, a bolt of lightning, the finger of God. But by then I'd lost all faith in such things. And at least that ant, however tiny, was quite real, irrefutable, and full of vigor. Her tenacity fascinated me at once, and I hitched my wagon to hers.

She was a little brown ant, of the most common design, of a sort so widespread that when you see one you most often see others as well, the entire contents of the overturned ant vat, you might think, but not this one, no, this one was alone, at least I saw no other, and I didn't bother looking around to be sure, this one would do nicely, just the thing. Besides, once again, none of this was premeditated, I was obeying something like inspiration, an unthinking reflex, nonbinding, at any moment I could wash my hands of the whole affair, let her go on her way, instantly forget her as I had until that day systematically forgotten every ant I'd come across, every one without exception, and mind you there'd been more than a few, I could forget this one too if my attention was suddenly captured by something else, some important or even gratuitous task, so long as I found in it something to occupy me.

When I first see her, bent double to tie my shoelace, she has wandered into the thin crack between two paving stones on the square, a thin, shallow slot, but for her a ravine lined with sheer cliffs. I hesitate to step forward: one false move and I'll break my ant's back. Perhaps lend her a hand? Even my little finger is too fat to fit into that gap. There's nothing I can do for her, I'd like to think she'll get out of this on her own—and if, on the other hand, she were to stay there and die of exhaustion in the maze of paving stones, I'd get over it. I wasn't yet fully committed to this adventure. I was granting myself a little moment of distraction. I had no intention of throwing myself into this affair to the exclusion of all other things; I was a long way from suspecting that my life was about to take a new turn, that this time, at long last, I was off.

The ant was saved by a tiny pebble stuck in the groove: she had only to scale it to climb back to the surface, with no sign of haste or relief. I think it important to note that she'd never given me the impression—even in the very depths of the abyss—of succumbing to panic. I didn't see her turn back or freeze in despair. It was as if she knew just what she was doing, where she stood, even why she had to go through this ordeal. I myself didn't cut so fine a figure—I was all too aware of the rut I found myself in. And now, on top of everything else, an ant was teaching me a lesson!

People must be wondering what I'm up to here, where I'm headed. How should I know? And indeed, for reasons I will explain, that universal ignorance suited me nicely, I myself never even posed the question. Not yet. I was tailing that ant as another might have stalked a pretty passerby. It was a jaunt at that point, a stroll, whose direction I left up to an insect so as to give myself some momentum without having to make any decisions, and without pushing myself too hard either (I could just as well have run after a bus), or so at least it seemed to me; I was still up to following an ant, I told myself, despite my little appetite for effort, my natural inertia, my sad lack of aptitude for track and field: I was quick to lose my breath, I never declined a bench's invitation to sit down, and then to stretch out (you come for dinner, you end up staying over).

My ant—so little mine, in truth, that I doubted she'd even noticed my presence—

had thus regained a more amenable terrain, a smooth paving stone whose vast expanse, relative to her tininess, did not seem to frighten or disorient her. She never strayed from her path. Now, as if wiser from her experience, when she came to the intersection of two stones, she didn't head into the gap but walked alongside it until she came to a natural bridge, the pebble or wad of gum plugging it, or better yet, the bus ticket, receipt, or handbill that would offer her effortless passage from one stone to the next. Then she confidently resumed her course, as if obeying a compass's imperious needle. My curiosity was now mingled with admiration, even, dare I say it, with envy. Ordinarily, that cruel emotion was more apt to visit me when I saw a man pass by arm in arm with a charming and desirable woman. Never would I have thought myself likely to feel it on the sight of an ant—and a little brown ant, of the most common design—going about her business. Clearly, I'd fallen very low.

The men passing by arm in arm with charming and desirable women made my solitude all the more painful. I hated their lightheartedness, their assurance, their aplomb: evidently they thought it perfectly normal, the boors, to be strolling along arm in arm with a charming and desirable woman. Some even seemed a bit weary of the whole thing. Some dragged their charming and desirable woman along with a certain brusqueness, others let themselves be dragged. There must have come a moment, I concluded, secretly exulting, when charm and desire went stale, and from then on each was for the other as burdensome as a full suitcase.

At least following my ant, eyes glued to the ground, spared me those dispiriting sights as well as those ignoble thoughts. Quickly, to be sure I wouldn't lose sight of her, I squatted on my haunches. For from my lofty perch I descried her movements all the more indistinctly in that I suffer from a fairly severe case of nearsightedness—and I like to think that the women arm in arm with those guys are neither so charming nor so desirable in reality as they are in the mist through which I perceive them, a nimbus of mystery produced solely by my myopia. But one way or another, I was already finding in the observation of my ant a welcome change from my daily travails. It brought into my life a subtle change for the better, even if I wasn't yet fully aware of the improvement, at least not enough to rejoice in it or think myself cured. Its effect was discreet; for once the gnawing anxiety of my life left me in peace, my mind free, and despite the discomfort of my position and the cramps now beginning to paralyze me, I felt an undeniable relief, a new lightness. And with that, the little surge of spite I'd felt on catching sight of that ant, so sure of herself, so determined, dissipated entirely.

And I dropped the idea of crushing her with one thumb as I'd more or less been intending, to escape humiliation for once, since for once it was in my power to escape it, and to regain my advantage in the most decisive of ways. I've known humiliation all too well. I grew up with it, or it grew with me, standing taller with every inch I gained. The uncle who pats you on the head and calls you "chief" because he's forgotten your first name: humiliation. I remember every one of the humiliations of childhood. I remember that childhood itself is humiliation, it's being humiliated day after day. Or calls you "big boy," or calls you "little man." And all those longings with no way to fulfill them, humiliation again. You're too little: humiliation. And you're too little for everything, even simply to sit in a chair. You're too little for chairs. You're too little for love. Women are already charming and desirable, but you're too little for love. You're a child, a kid, a tot—those humiliating words—you're a little nobody, that's what you are. Evidently others forget on reaching the requisite height, they forget those many humiliations. Not me. Me, they still make me blush and rage. Besides, it would seem that I'm still too little for love—not for chairs, but who cares about chairs—too little for charming and desirable women, they cling to arms other than mine; mine never interest them, closing their long fingers over my biceps never enters their minds, and so my arms hang limp at my sides, inert, my arms remain virgin, the arms of a child, the arms of a little worm.

And so that ant—what a stroke of luck, that ant smaller than me, that ant I towered over, which I'd chosen not to crush all the same, when it was in my power to do so, a power I relinquished out of compassion, because I'd forgotten nothing of the humiliation, of the wretched condition of all tiny creatures, without name or identity, whose existence remains hypothetical, lost in the crowd, however stubbornly they force their way through it—my ant alone seemed unimpressed by the world around her, the avuncular world, just as I was at her age, if I can put it that way, you see what I mean, or rather no, you don't see, I'm used to that, my Chinese is too bookish, and as I still am, impressed that is, come to that, because people have fearsome eyes and mad gestures; but that ant, I know, inhabits a reality of another order entirely, she doesn't give a damn about men and women, and no doubt the other ants, her sisters, do not have fearsome eyes and mad gestures, and truly do resemble her just as they all look alike to our eye, and so she never feels at fault, unwelcome, inferior, inapt, inept, but rather always just where she belongs among the others, in the flow, wholly accepted, recognized: her legitimacy is beyond dispute.

Why, then, was she so alone? What mission was keeping her so far from her anthill? Was she lost? Was she going ahead to blaze a trail for her tribe? I might not have realized it, but now I needed answers to those questions. That ant's destiny suddenly seemed to me a most extraordinary thing. And I wasn't far from thinking, even then, that her adventure was my own. And I was thinking, too, that it was an adventure not without interest. Yes, I was swept up in an affair that was worth the living. What exaltation all of a sudden! Mind you, I wasn't naively identifying with that ant. I knew what was what. Certain differences caught the eye at once. Our builds, for instance, could scarcely have been more unalike. Beyond that superficial distinction, the ant was clearly better at dealing with solitude than I. No sign of the panicked air that is mine in a crowd, and which stops me in my tracks whenever I glimpse it in a shop window: who is that old lunatic?

Whereas my ant, my little ant, my teeny tiny little ant, no doubt more alone than I from being so small (whereas I've got some meat on my bones) in the big wide world, went about her work undismayed by the complete absence of support or encouragement, on her own and perfectly aware of it. And perfectly at peace with it, asking nothing more. How doughty she is! how bold! and so full of initiative! That must be what I've always lacked: initiative, tenacity. I tend to abandon things very quickly. Even walking, even words, there are days when I regress to a time before all that, when I lack the strength or the know-how to walk and to talk, when I can't see the point: to go where, to say what? Besides, he who never stops walking, if he wants to keep talking as well, will soon have to learn other languages, and he who never stops talking, if he wants to find new people to talk to, will soon have to move on, and walk a bit further. You soon realize there's no end to it, and you've got to seize happiness on the move, the happiness of moving, of effort, and that seems to me a very cruel thing, the joy of the wind in your hair, a very abstract thing; and in any case I don't have much hair, none at all, blown away on the wind, that too, like happiness, if I understand myself properly, but I've answered that question already, and the answer is no. I was bald young. I remember a few strokes with a comb. Then my mother saw her baby reappear. I wasn't wished-for the first time, I'll let you imagine her dismay. No doubt my baldness reminded her of the torments of childbirth, and when my last hair fell—I was only sixteen—she once again hustled me out.

My ant's none too hirsute herself, I'd like to point out, having insisted perhaps more than is reasonable on our differences. The sunlight gleams on her skull as on mine. Two of us together holding up the heavenly vault. At last I've got a little help. Of a negligible sort, it might seem, but an ant can lift sixty times her own weight; I wasn't going to turn down that unexpected support. Henceforth we were two. I was two. I wasn't far from feeling, for the first time in my life, the euphoria of the soul that suddenly realizes it's no longer alone. Nonetheless, the ant had not yet taken note of my presence, and very likely my emotion was still to some degree rooted in erotomania. I've learned to be wary of myself on that score, as on every other, and I am never without my knife.

No doubt this would be the moment to speak of the crime of which I had allegedly made myself guilty a few weeks before, but I fear such a confession might turn the reader against me. For the moment, then, he need only know that I was on the run when chance opportunely placed that ant in my path. Not knowing which way to flee, where to hide, unsure even if the detectives were actively seeking me or had no idea of the killer's identity and were thus merely gathering statements and clues, I made the decision to hand over my destiny to that ant, to entrust myself to her entirely: she would decide everything, as much the direction of my flight as its destination. I made of that ant my accomplice, without seeking her opinion on the matter. But what had she to fear from the human legal system? Even if her good faith were doubted, the penalties exacted for harboring a fugitive would surely not apply in so atypical a case. All the same, let me repeat, just to be sure, that I never informed her of the suspicions hanging over me, and that I had all the outward appearance of an ordinary passerby, or at worst a slightly cracked amateur entomologist.

Now I had an objective, or at least an agenda, and I found my serenity coming back. If the police were on my tail, my strategy would not fail to hinder their crude, simplistic machinations. Rather than try to outrun them, rather than make for a train station, an airport, a seaport, where men furnished with my photograph were no doubt keeping watch, I slowed down so radically—even a hurried ant moves very slowly, relative at least to our mile-devouring stride—that the brigade's finest sleuths would inevitably race past me unseeing, caught up in their velocity, in their bloodthirsty fervor, certain that speed was their only hope of catching up to me, ever more, ever faster. On the run at a crawl, I would be throwing their every instinct into disarray.

A little modesty might be in order for one as lowly as I. Though I might seem to boast of this tactical flair, no one could be more surprised than I to find myself graced with it. In truth, it was nothing more than a happy, unpredictable consequence of my pursuit of the ant, a pursuit undertaken, must I already repeat, not to elude the police, but out of idleness, boredom, and curiosity. All the same, it was the best thing I could have done—and at the same time the most improbable—and a certain sense of the situation, rooted in intuition, must surely have played a part.

Godspeed to the police. Having set off on my heels, they already have a solid lead on me. I'm going nowhere, but it would be untrue to say that my ant has been idling. To be sure, she was sometimes slowed by an obstacle. Now she had to circle around a long flowerless planter. She did so with no sign of impatience. Then she was off again. At the risk of losing sight of her, I looked up for a moment. Enclosed on three sides by buildings, the square stretched out before us to the street beyond. In the middle was a fountain, a round basin with a triton spewing water from its mouth. The usual little crowd was going about its business—all the roles had been cast, and the disorder itself seemed studied, so thoroughly that for a brief moment I feared a trap laid by the lawmen: women hitched to their strollers, children irresistibly drawn to the spray, a group of Japanese tourists relentlessly photographing each other, passersby far less solitary than they seemed, one ear suction-cupped to their telephones, the inevitable grandmother unleashing a torrent of injunctions and recriminations on a very undissolute poodle, a delivery man loading crates of bottles onto a dolly; any second now they would throw off their disguises, freeing their imprisoned bodies, even the German shepherd huddled inside the poodle, and descend on me like a thunderbolt, armed with assault rifles, handguns, handcuffs, throw me to the ground, neutralize me. I kept a discreet eye on a child equipped with a whistle: perhaps it was from him that the signal would come. Then I thought better of it, and the imaginary SWAT team instantly dissolved, its crestfallen members fanning out into the city. The pigeons too seemed to be obeying the direction of a not very inventive filmmaker: reality is in good hands—it diminishes the incongruity even of the elephant or the manatee, its boldest creations, by confining them to their natural milieu, never parading them around the world at large for the wonder and amazement of all. But a fat lot of good it did to fit a limp trunk to the hulking monster only to strand it in some distant savannah, where it's most often a mere dot on the horizon! No larger than an ant, as it happens. But to conclude thereby that I might have been mistaken, thinking myself closely eyeing a hymenopteran when I was in fact following a pachyderm from a great distance, there would be so much ground to cover, and so quickly, that my legs, even before my imagination, give out at the very thought.

There now passed by a man arm in arm with a charming and desirable woman, proving decisively that we were indeed still trapped in the old unchanging reality. I lowered my eyes; the ant had not taken advantage of my distraction to disappear. I even had the unmistakable feeling—and it touched me to the core—that she was waiting for me, slowing the rhythm of her racing feet though not drawing to a full stop, in a sense finding a compromise between the urgency of her mission and her consideration for my needs. Had she spotted me? Might she have grown attached to me? Before pondering that second hypothesis, I thought of the first with a certain unease. After all, if a simple ant, occupied what's more with her own affairs, which seemed to allow her no rest, if, then, that overworked, hurried ant had noted my presence behind her back, how to imagine that the forces of order pursuing me, well used to dissimulation in all its many forms, had not also perceived it, that they were not even now imperceptibly tightening the dragnet in which I was innocently quivering like a hapless young carp?

Then I chided myself for that thought and that fear. Was my ant not far foxier than any policeman? Caught up in their momentum, obeying the primitive logic of the hunt, the forces of order were now so far ahead that they were probably searching for me at the borders, amid the dotted lines, and in this, let me observe, they gravely misjudged me. I would never take my chances in a foreign land; this foray into the world of the ant was already quite a departure for me. I knew my abilities and talents would be of no help to me in that world, of no use, and yet I threw myself into it with no small confidence. I was even beginning to delight in those joys I'd always found dubious in travelers' tales: lost bearings, discomfort, complications, even repulsion or terror, I finally realized that these disagreeable experiences could be accompanied by a new intoxication, a liberation that freed you above all from the slavery of habit, the dull satisfaction of a restful existence. I'd let go. I was finally following the curve of the earth. My broken moorings trailed behind me like puppy dogs' tails. I'd left the old world and its toppled columns behind. So this is the thing they call speed! Flames at my temples! Before, I was stuck on the goat path, arduous and twisting, and it climbed so very slowly; but now here I am already on the gentle slope of the hill, in the falling wave: I've slipped over to the other side. So this is what they call immensity. And that's my heel making that galloping sound! My lungs swell—what a frigate I am! Mine is the open sea, the heaving main, a cordillera my horizon.

Do ants sometimes pause en route for a few hours' sleep? Because now the sun is setting, visibility declining, and I fear that there may be no way to follow so diminutive a creature by the parsimonious glow of the streetlights, particularly because my myopia grows more acute with the dusk, and I have to take the astronomers' word for it when they claim that a satellite known as the moon daily describes a complete revolution around our globe. Take their word for it, that is, on the assumption that a certain skepticism is not out of the question.

Before setting off from the cottage by the canal, I'd hurriedly filled a bag with a few effects and objects, the essentials. How essential I hadn't quite realized: from that knapsack I extract a bowl and invert it over the ant. No gap between its rim and the paving stone, that ant won't be going anywhere, and I'd like to think she'll have oxygen enough for the night. We needed some rest. As for myself, a barren planter made a sufficient sarcophagus. I had only to extend one arm to touch the bowl and thus mark it as my property should some passing pedestrian or pedestrianess—there are fiancées with no trousseau—attempt to make off with it on the grounds that it had been abandoned on a public roadway. *Hands off, you! That bowl is mine, and all the fauna it houses! Back away from the bowl! I've killed before!* And here the ingénue would beat a hasty retreat, with no choice but to quaff the waters of love from her cupped hands (obviously, it will all slip straight through her fingers).

A beautiful night, now that the cast of thousands has gone on its way. A welcome break, the self set down on the ground like a heavy burden. Nor would I be found prancing about in some dream. Adventure had entered my life itself, I could devote to rest those hours of sleep once given over to the confection of overwrought extravaganzas that left me exhausted the next day. We've got places to go in the morning.

I awoke with an eagerness I might have felt in childhood's golden dawn, and never since. I had ants in my training pants, even then. And now, by the tortuous route of a lengthy existence, I was finally growing young. I bounded to my feet—to think of my hand writing such a sentence! I went off to refresh myself at the fountain. A little spurt as meager as a pee, but for one making his morning ablutions any running water is a mountain torrent—another sentence written by my hand! Let the police track me all they liked, I had only to slip my face beneath that water to become unrecognizable. Who will pull that limpid mask from my face? And they'd still have to catch hold of the slippery eel beneath it!

Come on, my beauty, we've got places to go. And I lifted the bowl: oh no! All at once my age caught up with me, then swept me along further still, into an apocalyptic era of moss-covered ruins and derelict factories. I was overcome with despair. The ant wasn't under the bowl. How had she fled, and where? What tunnel, what exit had she discovered or dug? I'd made quite sure that the rim of my bowl adhered perfectly to the ground, without gap or interstice. The opacity of that mystery recalled certain detective stories whose final elucidation always left me disappointed, relying as it did on chronological trickery or tedious doubletalk, but this time the enigma was flawless. My captive had escaped with no sign of a breakout, without the collusion of a member of the prison staff or the complicity of her lawyer: she'd vanished, I might even say vanished into thin air—a third sentence in so few lines that I never thought I might one day so spontaneously write, as if it had written itself, in the current of this endless prose that duplicates my days—she'd vanished into thin air, I might even *say she had simply vanished into thin air*—may I be forgiven this brazen repetition, may I be pardoned for reveling in my wrist's great leap forward on the heels of that ant, and the prospects that suddenly seemed to lie open before me: could I not already imagine the day when, with perfect serenity, I could write, "she offered me her trembling lips," that sentence streaming naturally from my pen in the endless current of prose that duplicates my days, and then, with the same insouciance, this one: "she let the silk negligee still draping her body slip to her feet," my hand dancing over the paper, lithe, light, laying down curled little words, passionate words, quivering, a thread of ink drawing the movements of arm and leg: "her four limbs enlaced me and we rolled over the rug like one single body," etc.. I concede that these examples betray effort and artifice, I wasn't yet ready to put together such sentences, the adventure of my emancipation was only beginning: all the more urgent that I locate my ant, now vanished (but that one word I'd already thoroughly mastered).

Then I thought of inspecting the bowl itself, and of course the ant was inside, walking circles over the inner wall as she must have been doing from the moment of her imprisonment, never abandoning her quest, not even in the vertigo of that never-ending spiral—held captive in the most airtight of jails, she had not for one second forgotten her goal, intent on that goal with her entire being, now reduced to immobility—awaiting the opening, the opportunity, and seeking them in constant movement; and now all at once the way was clear, there was the light at the end of the tunnel—she raced toward it, as if propelled by the momentum of her rotation, like a stone from a sling. I followed her into that opening, close on her heels. It took us some time to cross the first two paving stones she encountered, zigzagging a bit, somewhat the worse for wear after all, having spent the night vainly making her rounds. Unless, I said to myself, this is precisely her mission, and she's dutifully scouring the area to scout out potential threats or determine the most practicable trail for her sisters. I assumed she was marking the terrain with odiferous reference points, imperceptible to me, to be sure (afflicted as I'd been with a stubborn headcold since my stay in that damp canal-side cottage), but easily spotted by her kind.

Toward morning's end, an unpleasant encounter justified this marking out of the way. Advancing in the direction opposite ours, and thus approaching, but as if materializing out of nowhere and in an entirely unwelcome and unhelpful manner, there suddenly appeared, as we were beginning the assault on the third paving stone, a red ant, slightly larger than mine, looking for a fight. My ant paused to consider her next move. Her duty was to preserve herself for the good of her mission, but, in order to pursue that mission and see it through to the end, and perhaps, I like to think, possessed of a natural, spontaneous valor that compelled her never to back down, and so finding a balance between the demands of her task and those of her self-respect, she agreed to do battle, and a merciless battle it was.

It was one straining against the other, one straddling the other, toppling the other, rolling in the dust, bloodthirsty eyes fixed on the fragile joint between body and head, that thread that is a neck: cut here to open. I would have liked to see my ant a bit more full of cunning, as she was clearly dealing with a far mightier foe, but I suppose any ruse would have been cowardice in her mind. She thus

ÉRIC CHEVILLARD

fought with her will alone, and if her more modest size put her at a disadvantage
in an out-and-out brawl, it granted her a greater vivacity, which in the end proved
decisive. At one moment, however, she found herself on her back, the other pum-
meling her mercilessly, and I wondered if I should intervene. But how to untangle
those interlocking parts with my fat fingers and not put my ally in danger? Might
I also admit to a twinge of fear that I might take a nasty blow from their wildly
thrashing limbs? Because they really were going at it pretty viciously. It was a bru-
tal confrontation, with no quarter given. We've all seen referees roll in the dust,
never to rise again. I thus chose to remain prudently on the sidelines. This neutral-
ity suited me nicely. I must further add that an inglorious thought briefly flashed
through my mind—will I perhaps be absolved by the present confession? I imagined, then, that should the red ant emerge victorious, I might turn to following
that one, choke back my shame, join the other side. After all, the one or the other,
what matter? Why prefer the little brown one to the little red one—more caramel
or pinecone colored, in point of fact? I needed an occupation, a discipline, and
an itinerary for a flight unseen by the police, and the red one offered me all that
no less than the brown one. One thing troubled me, though: should it turn out
that I would henceforth be following the red one, I'd have to turn around, which
is to say retrace my steps, perhaps all the way back to the scene of my putative
crime, where some staked-out inspector would have only to scoop me up. A bad
idea, then. And besides—what strange shame keeps me from confessing it?—I
had already developed a real attachment to my ant, difficult to situate, of course,
on the scale of shared human emotions, but which engaged my heart and made
loyalty a duty in my mind.
    The brown one nimbly slipped out of the red one's crushing grip. I seized the
moment to eject the intruder from our territory with a flick of my finger. The
intervention seemed to leave my new companion bemused. This was no way to
settle a dispute, nothing was resolved or decided, the question of territorial dominance remained up in the air, not to mention how was she going to recount this
adventure to her sisters? I believed those uncertainties were jostling for space in
her pinpoint head; she turned right, she turned left, struggling to reestablish a little order and logic in a situation inopportunely perturbed by Providence. I vowed
to mind my own business in future. I'd entrusted my fate to this ant, it wasn't my
place to play the hero.
    She soon recovered her senses, seemed even to instantly forget that regrettable
episode, which evidently hadn't left her too battered, all her legs were working
perfectly (I counted six), nimble and limber, and as best I could judge, her head
on one end and her abdomen on the other displayed neither wounds nor lumps,
but but but it is also true this superficial auscultation was unlikely to reveal internal injuries or more profound traumas. On this occasion, for the first time, I
sensed her smallness as an irreducible separation in itself, a distance that founded
our relationship, and so doomed it to failure. On my knees, squatting or bending
down over my ant, I nonetheless did everything in my power to close that gap, to
initiate a rapprochement that she might have yearned for as well, but which was

still compromised by our essential difference: my vision blurred when I looked at her too closely, my eyes welled with tears, well-deserved, let it be said, cursed soul that I am.

Nonetheless, I was not displeased to lay my hand on that shard of glass—or rather I was, at first, more than a little, when the blood began to flow from my punctured palm, I was even venting my spleen in fairly brisk terms against a hostile fate that seemed bent on bedeviling me in every way possible, as if life hadn't tormented me enough already, ever since it distinguished me from among the misty children of the prenatal limbo, perhaps because I was the most chubby-cheeked, to make of me its long-suffering plaything. I knotted my handkerchief around my hand as best I could; then and only then did I take an interest in that shard, the broken-off bottom of a clear glass bottle, and cautiously picked it up to deposit it in a nearby trash can—for, despite the crime imputed to me, I wish for the death of no one, not so much as a scratch, and I was eager to purge the square of that danger even if it might have been sound strategy to leave it where it lay, in hopes it might wound my pursuers, and perhaps, why not, with a bit of luck, rip their dogs' all-seeing snouts. But some innocent bystander might have trod on it, a child might lose a finger, and that was a risk I preferred not to take: better to endure the shame of public arrest and the years of imprisonment that would follow. That's simply the kind of man I am.

I thus clasped the shard, still dripping blood, between thumb and index finger, and as I lifted it from the ground I suddenly spied a horrific creature—I leapt back, I believe I put my arm in front of my face to ward off a possible attack— which was thus my little ant, my teeny tiny little ant, monstrously enlarged by the magnifying effect of the bottle glass, which must often have been confused, the wine swilled to the dregs, with an attack of delirium tremens; perhaps, I said to myself, that syndrome was in fact nothing other than this optical illusion. I broke off the sharp edges against the pavement, then polished that crude lens on my sleeve, which had seen worse in my many wanderings. Now I was equipped to follow my ant's movements more closely; I could thus observe her at her toilet and spy on her in every circumstance of her life. My indiscretion caused me a certain shame, which I quickly shooed away: there's no harm in looking, and I wanted to serve as my ant's bodyguard, her guardian angel—the clearer my vision, the surer her way.

I smiled as I adjusted that monocle. Did I not hold in my hand the magnifying glass of the detectives now on my tail, fallen from one of their pockets, without which they had no hope of finding me? I've left few and very slight traces of my passage on this earth: my trail might just as well have led to me as to a scarab or sparrow. How to sort out our footprints without this glass? And now it was mine, and with that I became imperceptible, almost as much an ant as my ant, almost as little, almost invisible to the naked eye.

The first thing revealed by that lens was the laughable, despicable falsity of our metaphors. Human society seen as an anthill, with the underlying idea of the in-terchangeability of its swarming denizens, engaged in activities as vain as they are frenzied: that hoary old simile couldn't stand up to scrutiny, not, at least, if I could believe what my ant was showing me of herself, what a profoundly individualized creature she was, isolated from her kind, what's more, and not one to be taken for another. The question, of course, was whether my ant was an exception—a thorny problem indeed, since if not, if all ants, that is, were exceptional, if every ant was, then none of them were, and the metaphor of the human anthill was thus justified; my magnifying glass became superfluous, good for little more than pointing out the sad banality of our serial destinies. I too lay exposed, on the other side of that pitiless glass, every bit as insignificant as my ant despite the alleged horror of my crime, a representative of humanity as a whole, a perfect specimen informing ants of the sorry lot that we were, telling them all they needed to know of our behaviors and tricks. Did this information hold even the slightest interest for ants? That was less certain. Animals' incuriosity with respect to us is a constant vexation. Whatever we build, they will at best only piss against it—the most engaged will piss the most copiously. Our cruelty alone can move them; as for our gentleness, our finesse, our esthetic sense of the realities of this world, they don't give a damn about such things, they'd prefer a bone or an apple. On the other hand, I may well be exaggerating the significance of these revelations; my ant would have seen of me only a single bulging myopic eye, the simplicity of my soul, and nothing more.

Then the sky went dark and I found love. It was presaged by the sound of tap-dancing, high heels striking the ground with such precipitation that I first thought it would take no fewer than six legs to produce that rat-a-tat, and I briefly concluded that my shard's magnifying effect also worked for sound, that it was my ant trotting along I was hearing. But just then the pointed toe of a high-heeled shoe entered my field of vision, into my little friend's theater of operations, over which I myself was advancing, now squatting, now crawling, mindful to stick close behind her. That shoe, I said to myself—and let it be noted with what speed my usually sluggish mind was working, spurred on by the urgency and the danger of the situation—would inevitably be followed by a second, which might well land inopportunely on the ant, perhaps unthinkingly crush her, despite the resilience of her chitinous armor. I interposed myself between them. Without a moment's hesitation, I launched myself into the fray. I blindly threw out one hand and closed my fingers over the menacing brute's ankle, an ankle so fine that my fingers nearly encircled it, and so soft that I was transported—my first sexual experience was thus not the usual disaster. It was a woman's ankle, a woman's foot, a woman's leg, and, higher up, a woman's piercing shriek. She jumped, and I leapt to my feet. Coiffed with her skirt, my head crashed into her chin, and we staggered under the effect of our mutual ardor, clasping each other so as not to fall, already feeling the solidity of our union amid trials and upheavals, even performing a few steps of a wild, heedless dance on the ruins of this world, thus sealing the triumph of love over adversity, and then she began to call for help, proving the disorienting depth of her emotion, I thought, since I was right there, offering her all the aid she could wish for. Nevertheless, I was gripped by the fear that her cries might alert and alarm the policemen deployed throughout the area, and I loosened my grasp. She fell, rather heavily, but she didn't make a peep. I trembled. Clearly, misfortune was not about to desert me. No sooner had I found love than I had to come up with some way to get rid of the body.

Luckily, the fall hadn't killed her, and she soon emerged from her stupor. She stood up, pulled down her skirt, tossed back her hair, and skewered me with a glowering eye. I stammered out an apology, though I could well have considered myself the victim here. You might at least have the nerve to look me in the face, she said. It's that ant, I said. Ant? she shot back. And there we were. Yet another who didn't understand me. I'd grown accustomed to these incredulous faces, it was to them that I owed my tenacious bachelorhood and my timid, fearful virginity. I would usually have let the matter drop there, cut my losses and run. This time, though—why?—I made an effort. Well yes, that's right, the ant, my ant, I specified. She seemed to have progressed no further into the understanding of the mysteries of my soul. I even thought I spied a glimmer of terror mingling with her incomprehension. Why did I always have to run into the halfwits? Oh, cruel fate! What had I said that was so obscure? Was the unvarnished truth so painful to hear? I must have had a rather pitiful air; in any case, her gaze softened. What ant? she asked. This ant, I answered, and I suited the gesture to the word, pointing toward the paving stone where an instant before the ant could be seen, but . . . I don't see any ant, she said. And I didn't see any ant either, not on that paving stone, nor on the next, nor further on still. I fell to my knees, clapped the shard to my eye, explored the surroundings, the slots between the stones, feeling around, kicking up the dust, all in vain. Scarcely a few seconds had I taken my eyes off her, fascinated by the pretty, pointed-chinned face now dissolving into a perplexed scowl, slightly sarcastic, perhaps just a little compassionate too, and that ant had seized the moment to slip away, farewell Blaise, what you need is a woman, I've led you to her, now I'm off, I have things to do in the world of ants, it would never have worked out between us, my sisters are waiting for my report on the mission, be happy, don't forget me completely, I too will think of you now and then, and who knows, maybe one day we'll meet again, maybe our paths will cross ... then my hand, brushing away those meanderings of my mind, as if slipping free of my grasp to spread its wing and fly off, leaving me stranded where I stood, lost, crushed, one-handed, soared through space and gripped the bare calf of the beautiful stranger, my lover, closing its five fingers around it, even the pinky, more grasping than one might have thought, its first phalange flexing Hercules' biceps as it tenses ... Hey! You're not going to start that again! she cried. Hold still, don't you feel something? I asked, not relaxing my grip. Of course I do, I feel your fingernails digging into my calf, it's extremely unpleasant, Monsieur, please be so kind as to remove your hand at once! But don't you feel something else, don't you feel something tickling you? Look, there she is!

For my ant had undertaken to climb up her tibia, and it was hard to believe that in so doing she was following the straight and narrow path of her civic-minded mission. And, I added, I've vowed to follow her wherever she goes, you must understand my dilemma. I then heard, for the first time, the laughter of my longtime mistress—we could still surprise each other, struggling successfully against soul-crushing routine. Don't laugh at me, I said, I've never been more serious, I have to catch her without hurting her.

The ant had now reached her knee, and was already starting onto her thigh. It was high time that I intervened. An incongruous, dilatory thought then crossed my mind; if it was imaginable to detach the ant from the girl, it was on the other hand utterly inconceivable—though this would have been the ideal solution, the least fraught with danger—to detach the girl from the ant, carefully detach the girl from the ant, the former being after all more resistant to rough handling than the latter, less likely to be bent out of shape, she'd get over it, or would have got over it, for the operation, theoretically simple to envisage and even, up to a point, to undertake, had no chance of success—I gave it a try all the same, with no great confidence, just to be sure, pulling back the leg I still held in a firm grasp, that calf no less firm, a lovely oblong muscle that rolled beneath my fingers. The ant too clung to it, without the slightest effort, seeming to appreciate no less than I that skin's silken elasticity, a nice change for us both from the cold paving stones of the square, as if her feet—a boon multiplied by six—were endowed with sensitive feelers and she were genuinely in ecstasy at this state of affairs, shamelessly neglecting her duty, aiming higher, beneath the bell of the skirt, sensing new pleasures to be found, and her antennae sprung up taut, vibrating, while I received their signals on my own internal radio, obscured by the static of my pounding heart, but still sufficiently loud and clear to stir the bachelor in me, and his skin around me as well, every hair standing on end.

You're hurting me, she said. I loosened my grip. I'd like to try something else, if you'll allow it, Mademoiselle, together we're going to set a trap for her, and I laid out my plan: I'll put my hand flat across the ant's path, I know her, rather than turn aside, she'll want to head straight over the obstacle, and then we'll have her. Clever, she conceded. All right, then, go ahead. But I was in no hurry. First I rolled up my sleeve—meanwhile the ant was climbing ever higher, and I wasn't sorry to see it, I must confess, I even exhorted her *in petto* to pick up the pace: all the more ground won for me. I put on the professional air of the termite exterminator who looks at the Medieval Virgin of painted wood and sees only the hole left by the burrowing insect, a clinical dispassion unmoved by the stirrings of the flesh, a perfect indifference to the mysteries of the origin of the world, and I slipped my hand beneath her skirt—please be so kind as to allow me to repeat that sentence "I slipped my hand beneath her skirt," which I have so rarely had the opportunity to formulate *in situ* without it turning into a prison sentence, lengthened by repeated offenses, that I want to take full advantage of it—I slipped my hand beneath her skirt with her consent and—for goodness' sake, what could I do about it, a man's hand is broad, especially with its fingers spread as wide as possible—my thumb touched the elastic band, girdled with a fine lace of satin or silk, of what my ardent quest for the truth in all things and behind all disguises obligates me to call a pair of panties, a term that does not figure in my lexicon, which I didn't even realize

I knew, but which suddenly surfaces here, no doubt bubbling up from long-ago and less long-ago readings, as obsessive as they were compulsive, a pair of panties, my thumb was touching a pair of panties which in this case was not hanging from a clothesline in the dim light of a moonbeam, but well and truly—oh so well and truly—engaged to the hilt in its function as panties, very seriously and without provocation, most discreetly in fact, beneath the cover of a skirt—the circumstances that now brought us together eluded all probability and had been neither foreseen nor anticipated: those panties were perfectly innocent, perhaps even a little prim and goody-goody (and possibly black!), which only compounded my turmoil (or possibly red!). Silk or satin, it was in any case a fabric that conducted heat and emotion. I believe I even got one or two electric shocks. A most agreeable sensation, and now I better understood why from childhood on we're warned not to stick our fingers into electrical outlets: just try and go through life afterward without that tingle! No way to disconnect, and consequently it's the whole system that falls apart. A man will grow old there, sitting on the ground, index and middle finger plugged in, quivering gently, in the grips of a circular, infinite frisson. What economy could accommodate that unproductive debauchery?

A bare thigh beneath the hand of lonely Blaise, a soft thigh, a firm thigh, beneath the bare hand of lonely Blaise, beneath his callused hand, his inexpert hand, a thigh—so what now? I'd taken things far enough for a first meeting, I'd made a good start, I'd progressed further than ever before in my life as a serial groper. I'm slandering myself out of vanity. I hadn't lived as much or as well as I claim, too awkward for that, too shy, I caressed those glorious dreams with my fists clenched in my pockets, fingernails digging into my palms. So, have you got her? asked a voice from above. Got what? I answered, to buy myself a little more time. The ant. What ant? You know, the ant, your ant. My ant? Yes, your ant, have you got her? Oh, do I have my ant? Yes, have you got her?

I had her. Or was it her who had me? As expected, she'd clambered onto the obstacle that was my hand and was now making for my wrist. I withdrew. The young lady wanted to see—did she suspect me of not being entirely truthful? I thrust the ant in her face, thereby recovering all the moral dignity she'd had the gall to doubt, and my blood regained its composure as well, having been set aflame by my hand's brief contact with the soft swelling of her privates when, retreating from her thigh, it had grazed the panel of her clinging underthings, most unfortunately but not without precision or audacity. Here's my ant, I said, now what about you?

—Me?

—Will you tell me who you are?

—Pimoe.

—No one's named Pimoe, Pimoe.

—Well, I am, my name is Pimoe.

—Your name's really Pimoe?

—Really Pimoe.

For yes, there comes that moment, as inevitable as it is tedious, when newly-minted lovers, overwhelmed by the irresistible force of their spontaneous, sublime passion, moved and teary (those stars in their eyes are a little hard on their epithelia), their hearts rebounding like squash balls off the four corners of their ribcage, mutate into a couple of punctilious bureaucrats from the Office of Vital Statistics: Fauvel, Pimoe, 28, unmarried, tourist guide. Blaise, 42, unmarried, lockkeeper, currently on the run from the law, wanted for murder. That last quip earned me a smile.

—And you're not afraid I'll turn you in?

—A little, yes, and I haven't ruled out cutting short your existence to forestall that danger.

And so we bantered, Pimoe and I, Blaise was bantering with Pimoe, would perversion really be polymorphous if it didn't reserve a place of honor for emotion?

And of course, I sincerely hoped I wouldn't have to do her in.

I set my ant back on course. From now on Pimoe would be with me. There were two of us walking in the ant's footsteps, forming a group more easily spotted, to be sure, but also more innocuous. Couples are reassuring; everyone knows those two lovebirds save their cruelest blows for each other. Besides, the police were looking for a lone man, not the happy husband of a young woman with a pointed chin, publicly displaying his unashamed felicity right there in the middle of the city, openly engaging in some rather bold acts of foreplay—far more intense than the most triumphal apotheoses known to this day by my senses, which is saying a great deal, for I once glimpsed, through the gap in her blouse, the breast of a little waitress who'd bent down to pick up my money (another coffee, please, Mademoiselle, but when she came back she'd buttoned up).

Far be it from me to dream of blindly reproducing the old marital set-up— the man out on the road, the woman at home—but it was nonetheless true that Pimoe had come along just when I needed someone to help sort out my problems of provisionment, questions I'd completely neglected, now beginning to make their urgency felt: hunger, thirst, hygiene, and other natural needs I couldn't hope to meet without losing track of my ant, which was simply unthinkable. I had, it's true, considered taking the ant away with me, imprisoned in a box, after making a mark on the pavement so we could set off on the right foot when we returned, so we wouldn't lose an inch of ground in our absence, but with that solution came multiple complications whose consequences could easily prove fatal. How would my ant have borne these interruptions? Her mission was perhaps of an urgent nature for her sisters. The slightest setback could spell their doom. Or perhaps, diverted in mid-journey, my ant would lose her grip on her task, unable to orient herself on a path that had vanished from beneath her feet, cast forever adrift. As for me, I would have put myself at great risk in these comings and goings, abandoning the discreet itinerary of my getaway, that invisible ant tunnel, and diving back into the stream of passersby, constantly filtered by the harrows, nets, and sieves of the police.

—Pimoe, would you mind going and getting me a sandwich?

She happily went off, and also brought back a pastry and a can of beer. She lived fairly close by, and she agreed to take over for a few hours each evening so that I might refresh myself, not to mention take a dump and get some shuteye, making my way to her apartment under cover of darkness, when the vigilance of the gendarmes wanes. She had opportunely and on her own initiative equipped us with a flashlight, which we turned on intermittently to avoid attracting attention and which allowed us to follow the ant's progress by night, the urban illumination being too dim—sometimes you have to wonder what we pay taxes for! My ant, our ant, also allowed herself a bit of rest during those hours of darkness; the flashlight's beam did not seem to disturb the rhythm inscribed in her genes, which, by a slow process of habituation, became ours as well.

Not without some misgivings had I made Pimoe my accomplice. If I were arrested, that would inevitably spell trouble for her too, and an accusation of aiding and abetting a killer. She was taking a great risk. To think of that flower of youth sent off to languish in prison through my fault, there to fade, to wither, for having generously come to my assistance and perhaps fallen for me, moved by my despair and my solitude and because there's always a touch of compassion in a woman's love for a man—good thing too, let me say in passing: if you had to be loveable to find love, the human race would never proliferate so freely ... Did Pimoe fully grasp the danger? I sometimes suspected she didn't take my project quite seriously. Perhaps she saw in me only a slightly cracked amateur entomologist. In her defense, I must acknowledge that I'd only vaguely alluded to the circumstances that had left me a wanted man, a desperate fugitive, zigzagging and careering over the square in hopes of throwing off my pursuers. No doubt the time had come to go into the details. As it happened, the ant had slowed to examine a cigarette butt—might there be something beneficial for her community to be gleaned from that wad of fiber and ash? I decided to make use of that respite to confide in Pimoe.

I was a drifter back then. I lived on apples and anything I could scavenge. Now and then I adjoined my footfalls to those of a chance companion, and we went on for some time side by side. Thus it was that I fell in with a sort of vagabond who was walking along the canal. I offered him an apple, he passed me his canteen, friendship requires no more elaborate ritual. He told me these miles we were walking together would be his last as a wanderer. His destiny had taken shape. After many hesitations, he had at long last found his way: he would be a lockkeeper. He wished for no other life. Circumstances had smiled on him, and he had in his possession the address of a lockhouse where, he'd been assured, he would be welcomed and educated in the rules of river traffic. Soon we were within sight of the cottage. My companion bent down over the water to check his appearance. It took only the tiniest shove—one of those hearty claps on the back by which a firm friendship is maintained. He splashed me a little as he fell—for there is such a thing as justice, and so he was avenged after all. Then he sank like a stone. The incident had been witnessed only by three or four water bugs, whose silence I bought with a single menacing glance. The circles spread ever wider around the site of his fall, until they enclosed the entire indifferent world; men die, and then they're forgotten.

For three days I hid beneath a willow; then I rose to my feet, newly invigorated, and walked the last few yards separating me from my journey's end. Paul and Marthe Moindre welcomed me like a son. They asked me no questions when I appeared on their front step one bright summer morning. I knocked on the door of their canal-side cottage. A slightly stout woman, her hair gray, permed, and sprayed, showed me in and covered my face with wet kisses. I attributed this expansive familiarity to the legendary hospitality of bargemen, and I allowed myself to be embraced, and then fed, without protest. I'm looking for work, I finally confessed as she brought me a cup of coffee. She laughed. We knew you'd come sooner or later, she said, good seed makes a good crop! I attributed this certainty to the legendary clairvoyance of bargemen. Just wait till Papa comes home, she added, how happy he'll be!

Clearly, this was all going to work out very nicely. And indeed, the lockkeeper in turn flattened me against his breast. I even thought I felt him sobbing. I attributed those tears to the legendary emotionalism of bargemen. They immediately assigned me a room, in which I was invited to observe that nothing had changed. It was indeed a little run-down, but it would do. At dinner, between two slurps of a succulent pumpkin soup, I summoned the courage to confide in Paul Moindre concerning my desire to learn the lockkeeper's trade. Nothing could make me happier, son! he cried. I attributed that interjection to the legendary family feeling of bargemen: already they saw me as one of their own.

The next morning my initiation began. I learned to communicate with barges by means of signals, to gently but firmly manipulate the levers of the lock. What exaltation! I commanded the tides! The river's flow had to go through me: it was in my power to shut the door. I who had always had difficulty rowing my boat gently down the stream—a sadly deficient oarsman, and what a swamp!—I here experienced an omnipotence that filled me with joy, an exhilarating sensation, no doubt more or less that of a surfer on his wave. Paul Moindre had to rein in my ardor—sometimes, reveling in my newfound powers, I stranded the sand-and-supply-laden barges awaited with some impatience downstream, letting them sit there for hours, far longer than necessary. He was good enough to attribute this to the legendary enthusiasm of the eager neophyte. His lessons bore fruit; observe, Pimoe, with what care I tend to my ant's unhindered circulation. Sometimes I clear the way for her, I pick up a pebble, a piece of trash, I hold the doors open for her, she makes her way over an impeccably maintained trail, a forest bridle path, like a queen out for a trot.

I took all my meals with the Moindres. No other arrangement was even considered. From the first evening, my place at the table was laid. Marthe saw to my laundry as well. After a few moments of understandable modesty—the bachelor does not entrust his underthings to the laundress without placing his impure soul in her hands—I agreed to let her look after me. The easy life was mine. I was gaining weight before my eyes. My mirror now reflected the image of a flourishing, plump-cheeked quadragenarian, his shirt well ironed (before: skin stretched tight over his bones and a wrinkled shirt, how people can change!). My hair was still sparse, but it shone with a newfound luster, and when the wind kicked it up,

I thought myself a celestial body suspended from a ray of light. I'm only exaggerating a little. In the evening, we chatted as we sipped a vintage plum brandy that plunged me into a happy torpor. Open the sluicegates, Paul would say as he filled my glass, and we smiled at that ritual jape, which you can't fully appreciate, Pimoe: it was all in the repetition. In a word, I was living the good life, coddled by my hosts, performing a task better suited than any other to my nature, sedentary but in love with movement—the flight of birds, the wheeling of the stars, and every other sort of motion that doesn't obligate me to bestir myself in any way.

(It was in fact not by chance that I had chosen to follow an ant, which went on pushing valiantly ahead as I recounted my life to Pimoe, forcing me to move on a little myself lest I lose sight of her, but at a pace I could keep up without effort—never would I have followed a gazelle, for example. But let us not too hastily accuse me of indolence: although a yard's lead is enough for an ant to vanish into the distance while a large mammal requires two hundred, it must nonetheless be acknowledged that the result is the same in both cases, and thus that their respective pursuers are identically obliged to close a gap that can only be similar; one of those pursuers will be panting heavily, he has no one to blame but himself.)

The misunderstanding came to light after a few weeks of this dream existence. As Paul and I were setting out on the three-yard commute to our workplace, Marthe, waving good-bye with one hand (the other one pressed to her cheek in the guise of a megaphone), promised to make me my favorite dish for lunch. I licked my chops in anticipation all morning long, and at noon sharp I took my seat with the appetite of ten men, awaiting the fine trout amandine I so dearly love, when I saw my hostess set down before me a cauliflower gratin whose billows of insipid steam instantly turned my stomach. I loathe cauliflower gratin, I detest it. Let's leave literature aside for one moment and be serious: cauliflower gratin is quite simply revolting. The look of it, for a start. Then the smell. Putrid. And yet there was Marthe beaming like a fairy godmother who's just granted your fondest wish. I rid her of that illusion, taking no pains to spare her. Hold on, you're not seriously expecting me to put that in my mouth? Just look at it! I know of only one thing lumpier and spongier, and that's a chancre. Where's my trout? You promised me a trout! I lost my temper. You must understand, it was a pretty cruel blow. You're licking your chops for a trout and you end up mired in cauliflower! The silvery trout with its red and blue-spangled sides nimbly speeds up the stream of your rushing blood, between two ranks of almond trees, heading straight for your stomach, when all of a sudden that delectable dream congeals into the warm slop of a cauliflower gratin! If ever rage was put to good use, can it be denied, can you deny, Pimoe, that it was then and there? Can you picture the cruel trap that had been laid for me? And how innocently, how trustingly I walked into it! Like a child who's been promised a day at the beach roughly shoved into the cellar. Like a sweet, naïve fiancée prostituted in a dark alleyway, against a wall oozing decay, to the ugliest lowlifes of the underworld, as she was advancing, heart pounding, toward the petal-strewn bed of her wedding night. Like the young donkey that thought itself a colt suddenly finding itself locked away in a thistle-choked paddock.

Oh! the fly preparing for the treat of a jar of jam, cut down by the rag of a vicious little tailor. The virtuoso's violin passed down by inheritance into the paws of a bear. A cauliflower gratin in the stead of a trout amandine! If that isn't a come-down! With that, a whole world crumbles. Everything you've ever believed in, every dream you've ever dreamed, the few principles you still clung to, it all comes undone, falls apart, crashes to earth. What good are flowers now, and butterflies? Sunshine? What's that?

Just imagine, Pimoe, a magnificent trout, still wriggling only the day before, as at one with the stream as the current itself, the muscle of the light, the intel-ligence of the water, its tender flesh accented by a spray of lemon, sprinkled with finely slivered almonds, diaphanous hosts toasted golden in butter, just you take a good whiff of that, but what's this? what can it be? that stench? Unholy God, it's cauliflower gratin! But that's pulling the old bait-and-switch on the newborn babe extending his lips toward the breast of the Virgin and its fresh, wholesome milk! It's beating that helpless, trusting innocent senseless! But how horrible! How unspeakable! What a sham! Be so kind as to remove this thing from my sight at once, Marthe, you seem to be forgetting that I left my boots on the doorstep. I'm not some swamp monster, I don't eat such muck! And I'd been promised ... But never mind, hear how it reeks! Like the laundry room of an army base the evening after maneuvers. Somewhere around here there's a gassy hyena, I just know it. Or is it cauliflower gratin? Oh sooner that, yes! Much sooner that hyena!

Much sooner the putrefaction of blessed souls or a black rat vomiting up a plague-ridden microbe. I'd been promised a trout amandine, I didn't make that up. And what happens? What does that tub of lard bring me, and pleased with herself to boot? Cauliflower gratin! A dish that disgusts me, no less than a live toad, don't want it, never eat it. I'd have to be force-fed with a funnel, clamped to the wall. I didn't hold back, Pimoe, I gave it to old lady Moindre right in the face, she went pale, stammering, But... but ... but ... But what, lardbutt? You mesmer-ize me with the shining silver of a trout and then you afflict me with a plateful of cauliflower! I hope you're not expecting me to give thanks to God for springing you from the void? Anybody would have hit the ceiling! Ask around, you'll see. Go poll that bargeman, or the reader! Imagine: you order a nice guinea fowl from the man at the rotisserie, he hands you a rutabaga—what do you say? Oh thank you, mister rotisserie man? Certainly not! You immediately curse him forever and for good, however fat he may be, and however jovial, one single idea now occupies your mind, the dream of thrusting that skewer into his blubber and grilling him over the fire, that's what you're thinking, that's the chorus you can't get out of your head. Do you understand me better now? Have you put yourself in my place? Can you picture that scene in all its numbing horror? Now you know what I've been through. Hunger. Frustration. Nausea. I don't like cauliflower gratin, I never did like it, for as long as I can remember, even back when I was in limbo, and when I was a lictor in Rome, and when I shod horses under Pépin the Short, and when I was a sea snail or a warbler, I didn't like it then either. That repulsion goes way back, it's written, it's rooted, it's the indelible hallmark of my being. Yuck! Oh, that slop, anything but that!

But, but, my dear, she dared stammer. My dear! Ladling on the irony and cynicism, the better to humiliate me. And yet something in her manner seemed at odds with those stinging words. She appeared to be genuinely hurt, even distraught. Then she wept. But how could she have gone so wrong? Mixing up trout amandine and cauliflower gratin really was exaggerating the legendary muddle-headedness of bargemen to the point of caricature! It's true that her mind sometimes seemed disturbingly clouded: unable to remember my first name, she insisted on calling me Albert, like her son, who as best I could determine had stormed out one day, slamming the door behind him, never to return, then died in rather mysterious circumstances, or so at least his parents were convinced until just recently, when new developments came to light and revived their hopes. After a few attempts to correct her, I'd given up, thinking the repetition of that cherished name must have brought her some measure of comfort. I wasn't about to spoil that small consolation for so attentive a hostess, with a son no doubt near my age, whose attic room I now occupied. As I thought back over all this, the truth finally dawned on me: that day Marthe had, in all innocence, cooked up her son Albert's favorite dish.

My suspicions were soon confirmed; in truth, I still had much to learn.

—Look! cried Pimoe. She's turning!

And it was true, our ant had just veered away so abruptly that we'd walked on well past her, caught up in our momentum, or in my story. Were it not for Pimoe's vigilance we might have lost sight of her, realizing our misstep too late, so difficult is it to summon up the past without losing your foothold in the present. It's one or the other. We can live in the moment, frivolous and open to all manner of adventures but deprived of memory, without temporality, or we can go through life locked in a constant battle with time, stuffed full of remorse and nostalgia, well aware of the century but hopeless with seconds, flailing ineffectually as they flit by, like a cow's tail amid a swarm of horseflies. Or of one single ant, since this one had very nearly escaped me—in which case I would have irremediably run aground in the third dimension of time, a future without milestones or shoreline, which bored me in advance, a tunnel of fog, a dreary prospect, elusive and endlessly renewed; my ant was the second I could delight in—that I could even, if I liked, crush between thumb and index finger—a second of which I made something, a stimulating second, in short, which did not pass by in vain. Had my life not taken a new direction under that ant's guidance? We'd turned a corner, my ant, Pimoe, my life, and I, and we were bound for another world.

And so—I shortened the reins of the ant, clenching them tightly, and returned to my tale without fear, henceforth, of losing myself in it—Pimoe, dare I confess, I was stunned when, between two sobs, still rubbing my head (she was rubbing my head!) Marthe stammered out: But my child, my child, you were so fond of cauliflower gratin when you were a boy, and you always asked for seconds, and you scraped the dish, and you never wanted any other kind of birthday cake, what can have happened that you now look on it with such horror? There was a silence, then a long whistling shriek followed by a deafening crash: that was me falling to earth, from the asteroid belt into the Moindres' dining room.

Wha? wha? wha? croaked the Prince, suddenly become a frog. Blaise transformed into Albert Moindre. But only for me was the change so abrupt. I finally realized that Paul and Marthe had taken me for him all along, for Albert, the prodigal son now returned, that they'd welcomed me into their home on those terms, with an emotion all the deeper in that they thought he was dead, having been informed by the fluvial police of the discovery of a body upstream, unrecognizable to be sure, horrifically mutilated by the barges' propellers, dismembered, diced—at this point in their report, Marthe had fainted—but which, so near their cottage, could only be his. I had materialized before these bereaved parents like a ghost, back from the great beyond. Blinded by their sorrow, through that veil of tears, they thought they were seeing their son, missing for so long that he would of course have changed a little—it's the opposite that would be extraordinary, in fact, such that the less I resembled Albert the more assured their illusion.

It all fell apart thanks to a dish of cauliflower gratin—that will tell you the damage it can do—which I would have done better to hold my nose and choke down. If I'd known ... If I'd known, I still wouldn't have managed to conceal my rage at seeing my trout slip through my fingers and regain the clear waters, undulating, its flanks intact, mirrors of my unsatisfied hunger and rage; and the squirrels on the banks shelling almonds!

Then I interrupted my story once again, showing a consummate gift for the narrative art that I didn't realize I was endowed with (you can't have it all: the cops on your tail and a consummate gift for the narrative art—oh yes you can!), leaving room for digression, strategic pauses, teasing delays aimed solely at keeping Pimoe hanging on my every word, at binding her to my every step, which is to say also to my ant's, which for her part did not allow herself to be distracted by the story of my ill-starred life and coolly pushed on, now entering a narrow street, or rather galloping over the sidewalk, leather boots and polished helmet, one with her steed, bareback on the beast—just look at her go!

We held on for dear life behind her. Pimoe sometimes went off—would I ever see her again?—to seek something for our sustenance, and to my amazement she always came back, with a basket of hard-boiled eggs, sausage, cheese, a coffee-filled thermos. I left her in my turn for a few hours when afternoon neared its end. In her apartment I found a change of clothes waiting, cleaned and pressed. I took a shower—how wonderful are the banal necessities of existence, when the plumbing's working! Then I slipped between Pimoe's sheets for a restorative nap. On my return, I found that my two friends had tranquilly moved onward, stoutly putting a good thirty or forty yards of asphalt behind them. I congratulated them. Pimoe filled me in on the events that had transpired in my absence. A snooping cat had drawn near, and she'd had to stamp her foot to shoo it away. A passerby's heel had come perilously close to our ant as she lingered for a few minutes on a tangerine peel. Then Pimoe urged me to return to my tale. My story interested her; that was a new thing for me, that too, suddenly it wasn't just the police.

And so—Pimoe, you're very kind, are you sure I'm not boring you? Well, all right, then (she'd smiled at me as one does at a child making ready to recite his poem)—and so, to enlighten the Moindres, I briskly laid out my identity: Blaise, my name is Blaise. Before my eyes, their benevolent faces flushed with rage. Oh yes, things had changed. Marthe sank into a chair. Paul picked up a poker from the fireplace. But then ... but then ... he bleated. A bit brief, but it at least augured a future, unlike the but ... but ... I'd heard up to now, which I thought final and definitive. But then you're an imposter, a usurper! But then you're a murderer! But then you killed Albert! For, no matter what we might innocently believe, the future does not promise us only frolics and festivities. I retreated, not into the past, too late for that now, but toward the half-open window. Paul Moindre advanced on me, brandishing the poker; a vigorous old man, and I'd gone to fat. Murderer! he rasped. Which, Pimoe, I vigorously denied, I assure you, I never killed a soul. That corpse dredged up from the water could have been anyone's. I was the victim of an unfortunate confluence of circumstances. This was all a simple misunderstanding. I was sorry about their son. Pimoe, I went so far as to offer my condolences. If there's anything I can do, I added.

My good wishes were not well received. Marthe sniffled. Paul roared. The gratin was probably cold. Reaching the window, I threw open the sash, leapt outside, and here I am, Pimoe, I've just barely got my breath back. I ran alongside the canal until I finally left it in the dust, no easy thing, a punishing sprint, the two of us neck and neck until at long last I broke away. As for what came next, I can guess. Paul and Marthe called the police, accused me of their son Albert's murder, the theft of his identity, of his rights and privileges as heir to the levers of the lock, an enviable station that had clearly motivated my act—and I imagine that Paul, through his grief and his rage, couldn't help but see that laudable ambition as an attenuating circumstance, in some way he might even have understood my act and to some degree thought it justified: were he not so intimately involved in the matter, I wouldn't have found a better lawyer to plead my case.

You must realize, Mesdames and Messieurs, that you have before you a man still young, of obscure origins, born to his sorrow in a region scandalously forgotten by the network of canals that are the veins and nerves of our fair land, a boy who in that arid desert conceived the noblest vocation there is, a desire more imperious than any thirst: I speak of the dream of becoming a lockkeeper. A lockkeeper or nothing, Mesdames and Messieurs of the jury, and no doubt he sought to stifle that fervor, that lofty ambition, he struggled, have no doubt, but it was too much for him when chance, whose irony is well known to us all, placed in his path a renegade from that profession, a degenerate son born with a lock lever in his little hand, but who spat on his privileges. Imagine for a moment the confrontation between one who had everything and one who had nothing. He who had everything showed no gratitude to God or his father, he spurned his good fortune, he trampled his dynastic responsibilities underfoot, he pissed the blood of his forbears onto the ferns lining his road to ruin. Was my client to tolerate that? How not to understand and excuse his act? How not to hail it? All at once, as if by some miracle, he had been offered the opportunity to live out his passion. He had only to push aside an interloper, that cynical, dissolute wastrel who looked with such scorn on the highest human aspirations to the rank and position of lockkeeper. But no, Pimoe, I'll grant you, there's no point even thinking of that anymore. Paul Moindre does not have the credentials to serve as my defender, should I one day find myself standing before a judge. His ignorance of the law, no less than his lack of eloquence, disqualify him out of hand from honorably playing that role. Now you know all. I'm wanted for the murder of Albert Moindre. The police are after me. Officially they only want a statement, but I'm no fool, I know all about those ploys, those deceptive euphemisms of the judicial lexicon. If they catch me they'll lock me away, and then farewell precious freedom. Farewell Pimoe, farewell my ant. Farewell this glorious life of entomological wandering. No companion but a spider that sets out its silken traps in the four corners of the cell where I languish, further restricting my movements, perhaps finding human justice too indulgent, and inflicting this double punishment on me in the name of all Creation, of the great machine of the world in which I have abdicated my right to a place.

Thus did I relate my tragic story for Pimoe's edification, even, with a certain grim relish, laying out the likely next steps in hopes I might see her one day appear during visiting hours with a net bag of oranges, when there occurred a perfectly incongruous event, which may well be thought difficult to believe. I nonetheless affirm its veracity, and let me add that I did not undertake this account for the purpose of glorifying lies, as novelists do, with a blitheness all the more reprehensible in that they are later studied in schools, deceiving the simple souls of children with their fantasies, and let us not be surprised to learn that in those souls all the mendacity of this world consequently takes root.

We were maintaining a brisk pace, the ant before us, Pimoe and I behind, neither accelerating nor slowing to any appreciable degree. The asphalt sidewalk was more rugged than the square's polished paving stones, but our trio cared little for that, and pushed on at its own speed toward a goal known to the ant alone, which I was moreover in no hurry to reach. And here we glimpsed a silhouette or a shadow, a shape shall we say, to remain as vague and thus as precise as it was, slipping in between two cars parked by the curb. As I turned to Pimoe, asking: What's that?, she turned to me, asking: What's that? The touching accord of two souls in love. And with one single voice we answered: I don't know.

It was an animal. It had fur and four legs. But it wasn't a dog. It was a furred, four-legged animal much longer than a dog. Let me reiterate, this was all taking place in a large French city whose name I prefer not to divulge, for obvious reasons (we haven't yet reached the end of this adventure, and the police could show up at any moment). Consequently, it could be neither livestock nor denizen of our woodlands, neither cow nor deer. It was nosing around among the cars, not especially furtive, and soon we saw it and it was a ...—In these climes, Pimoe, astonishing! —At our latitude, Blaise, you must be joking! —In the middle of town, Pimoe, impossible! —How could it have got here, Blaise, just think! —Mad God in heaven! it was a tamandua. Yes, Pimoe, yes, Blaise, a tamandua. A tamandua in the flesh and bristly fur, excessively prolonged by that grotesque snout on one end, and on the other excessively prolonged by that ridiculous tail, which together distinguish it and indeed designate it for general hilarity. The tamandua inspires laughter. It's one of those animals you can't quite believe in. One of those clowns of creation. An odd bird that walks on its pant legs. Nonetheless, Pimoe seemed to know a thing or two on the subject. Adopting a professorial tone, she gave me a little impromptu lesson in natural history.

The tamandua, she said—and I was glad of the stroke of good fortune that allowed me to hear her speak that word tamandua; ask yourself if you've ever had the pleasure of hearing the one you love speak the word tamandua, and if, as is more than likely, the answer is no, then by all means encourage him or her to do so, for one day, inevitably, it will be too late, never once, very likely, in all your time together, will the word tamandua have breached the barrier of his or her teeth to wing its way toward your ear, and then you'll be sorry, oh so bitterly sorry, there's not that much joy to be had in this life, let us fill it up with these small pleasures, these loving attentions, let us delight in these simple joys, it's not nothing, and I speak from experience, to suddenly hear the one you love, whom you think you know down to the backs of his or her knees, to hear him or her utter an unwonted word, and particularly the word tamandua, particularly if it's spoken with good reason, if, against all expectations, it comes along just when it's needed, if it calls a spade a spade, and so try, that's a piece of advice I've taken to giving everyone I meet, try to bring about the situation that will induce your beloved to utter the word tamandua, you'll thank me for it, it will bring you a new thrill of a rare quality (the word tapir does not have the same effect), even if obviously, and I wish this for you—I do not jealously guard my pleasures for myself: that's just the kind of man I am—the emotion is purer still when it takes you by surprise, when nothing foretold it, in short when, from out of nowhere, the tamandua bursts onto the scene—is, continued Pimoe, a solitary mammal of South America, whose keen sense of smell allows it to move with precision through the sultry, odiferous atmosphere of the jungle. The tamandua spends the greater part of its day sleeping, curled up beneath its generous tail, which it drapes over itself like a sheet. The remainder of its time it devotes to the search for food. Its tubular snout insinuates itself into tree trunks and under leaves, whereupon it thrusts out its tongue, a sticky strand of spaghetti to which its terrified prey is held fast. Such are the placid, fearsome ways of the lesser anteater.

—The lesser what?

—The lesser anteater.

—Such are the placid . . .

— . . . fearsome ways of the lesser anteater, that's right.

— . . .placid, fearsome ways of the lesser. . . Pimoe?

—Anteater, for God's sake!

—Take cover!

Oblivious to the danger—this same amazing, unerring instinct drives snails, in groups of twelve, into the alveolae of the dish designed to receive them—the gallant

ant never slowed, still speeding toward the formicidal monster that was even now licking its orifice, or should I say its meatus, having sensed the presence of an ant in the environs, which means high times ahead for a formicidivore, no less than fruit for a fructivore, lox for a locavore, trout for a troutivore.

But really, where had that anteater come from? Was there in this city some private park untended by the team of gardeners charged with the maintenance of our green spaces, sheltering since time immemorial and unbeknownst to all a miraculously untouched wild fauna? It didn't seem likely. Perhaps, then, the police, let down by their dogs or tipped off about my strategy by a shadowy informant—here I cast a dark glance at Pimoe, a base and shameful suspicion, founded only in my contemptibility—had deployed this auxiliary, unusual but ideally suited to the mission at hand? I was about to settle on this latter hypothesis when Pimoe drew my attention to a poster on a nearby wall: THIS WEEK IN YOUR TOWN, THE LUZATTO CIRCUS AND ITS EXOTIC MENAGERIE. And so all was explained. This tamandua had escaped. The creature I'd taken for a henchman of the forces of order was, on the contrary, a fugitive like myself, the target of an active manhunt. This commonality of our fates shook my resolve to do battle. I took pity on the beast. It was probably hungry.

I have known, Pimoe, in the first days of my flight and until our miraculous encounter, I have known the torments of hunger. Our stomach is not the rude feedbag we take it for, it has its emotions, it aches even more painfully than the heart. I plucked still-green ears of corn, wild berries of varying degrees of toxicity, I devoured the eggs of blackbird and chaffinch, I poached with no great success (no rabbit was ever caught in the snares of my dragging shoelaces). Pimoe, my mouth watered as I gazed at my thigh, my bulging calf! I know all too well what this tamandua's going through.

The beast continued its advance throughout this aside, but still drew no closer—a wonder made possible, let me be allowed to point out, by a cunning dramatic montage. That's a basic principle of successful narration, without which the plot would bolt forward disastrously; every story would become impossible, and the world would appear in novels as it is in reality, a burning theater, a free-for-all impervious to description.

Nevertheless, the threat was growing more immediate; it was time to take action. I would have to pick a side without further delay, one or the other, the ant or its eater. It's an uncomfortable thing, touring the throes of indecision in a state of emergency, no less than the void of the heavens spiraling wildly beneath a stuck parachute. However, two arguments conceived in that maelstrom made up my mind in favor of the ant. For one thing, I was reluctant to change camps, lest I pass for a traitor in Pimoe's eyes. For another, Pimoe had had time to deepen my acquaintance with the alimentary habits of the tamandua, which, she confided to me in a whisper, must ingest a minimum of thirty thousand ants each day to really feel full. In sum, if it happened to suck up ours, the question of its next meal would remain entirely unresolved, only a little—imperceptibly—less pressing.

We know more or less how to take on an alligator, a boa, even a lion, but how does one combat a tamandua? A creature of a hundred and thirty pounds at least, Pimoe estimated, its feet armed with fierce claws. Should I wait till it charges? Will it charge? Or would I do better to strike before it attacks? Before it pounces? Do tamanduas pounce? I'd interposed myself between it and the ant. A few yards of pavement still lay between us. If someone had told me I would one day find myself battling a tamandua! If someone had told me that, I would at least have put in some training, worked on my technique. Do I seize the beast by that sort of long flexible snout? And then what? Or should I attempt to strangle it? I didn't have the faintest idea. Is that creature powerful? Is the whip of its tongue really so adhesive that it might hold me fast? Can the orifice of that sort of long flexible snout dilate enough to admit a man of my stature? No, it can't, can it? impossible to imagine that inhaler of ants and termites making one single mouthful of a strapper like me! It would be less surprising to see it sucking at a tea cup, in a circle of fellow lip-pursers. All the same, let's take no chances, rubber can be amazingly elastic. Mouths open wide under the impulse of anger: perhaps the crocodile was born with a piercing little cry that swelled and swelled until the corners of its mouth ripped open—and it's not over yet! At least I suppose not: it's still got a lot of body to split.

Then the tamandua halted and cocked its head to one side. I saw a gleam in its eye. Now it had spotted the ant de visu, between my legs. I stepped forward, arms outstretched, resolved to put up the best fight I could in the strange mêlée to come. To my amazement, the tamandua didn't make a move. I sensed an utter lack of interest in my presence. My gesticulations left it cold as ice beneath that black-and-tan coat. It's a bit irritating to matter so little, but my *amour-propre* had long since grown used to these mortifications, usually inflicted by creatures more gracious and graceful than this. Fine with me, I said to myself, go ahead, live your life, you don't know what kind of man I am, no idea what you're missing, go on and marry one of those convertible pretty boys, all swagger and sneer, you'll be sorry when he cheats on you with another woman, then another, maybe then you'll remember me, but it'll be too late, I'll be far away. At last the tamandua started forward again, but cautiously, on the pads of its feet; it circled around and fell into line behind me, next to Pimoe.

We've long known that the chimpanzee and the dolphin are deep thinkers; what, then, of the tamandua!? It has all the air of the most perfect dope, an idiotic, inelegant monster, clumsy, coarse-furred, and above all that head that's all snout, like an elephant with its ears on its trunk, an aberration of nature. And yet, appearances to the contrary, the tamandua is gifted with a nimble, perceptive intelligence. He's a clever one, is the tamandua. And especially this one, I couldn't help thinking, though obviously I had no grounds for comparison. Will the unpredictable twists and turns of existence once again place a tamandua on my path one fine day? The likelihood is slim. I do not write it off. I've learned to be very wary of that. If so, some light would be shed on that question—was the tamandua I met today unusually intelligent?—and there are times when I wish for nothing more. Rather than inflame its hunger by downing that single ant, it chose to follow after her, like Pimoe and me, albeit for very different reasons, assuming as it did that the ant would sooner or later lead it to the anthill where a sumptuous feast, and the prospect of a full belly, awaited. Now we were three tailing the ant, and I was beginning to fear that our little group might draw attention, all the more so because a tamandua is an oddity in an urban environment. On the other hand, I told myself, that beast would not fail to monopolize the interest of the crowd to my detriment, and thus to my benefit, since going unnoticed was my most ardent desire (that and meeting a second tamandua one fine day, though this latter wish was less fond than the other).

The tamandua and I forged a tacit alliance, insofar at least as our interests coincided. There would be plenty of time to settle our little quarrel later. The hour of the showdown would come, there was no hurry. In the meantime, the tamandua's keen nose was a considerable asset: we were now in no danger of losing track of the ant. Pimoe and I could take our eyes off her for a few moments to look at each other face to face, and better yet close our eyes and kiss. It was wonderful. And suddenly I understood why love had so long eluded me. I needed a tamandua. A tamandua to look after the details that escape our control in those moments of bliss, to survey the surroundings as I abandoned myself to the raptures of love. A tamandua on the lookout for alarms and alerts and the dogged pursuit of investigations in progress. For my part, I silently vowed to use all my experience and logistical sense to help it shake off its pursuers.

Who would not be filled with joy at reaching even a tacit accord with a tamandua? We inhabit this world alongside mongooses, pumas, kiwis, crickets, spider monkeys, and we will die without undertaking the slightest commerce with them, while at the same time we weary of recognizing in those of our own kind our eternal face endlessly multiplied for the sole purpose of simultaneously expressing every possible form of anxiety and befuddlement. Nothing moves me like earning an animal's trust. Is that not love at its purest, free of the specious aims of the species?

I assumed that the guards of the Luzatto Circus's menagerie had by now discovered the disappearance. For, indeed, if in an ordinary existence the absence of a tamandua is never experienced as such, and even less put into words by the one who nonetheless experiences it, an absence which for that reason causes no pain, as would, for example, a bite or a bereavement, perhaps despite the disastrous consequences that ensue and which he cannot explain, precisely because he lacks all awareness of their cause, no less than he lacks that tamandua—and no doubt the same hypothesis might be ventured with respect to other beasts, such as the orangutan, though this would have to be carefully considered (one could write a book on the subject)—its absence will on the other hand soon be perceived if it takes place in the context of a less banal way of life, in which the tamandua once occupied a very real and even preeminent place, as everyday companion and family breadwinner: suddenly, no more tamandua where there was one a few minutes before—that, in my opinion, one will note very quickly, it's more flagrant.

To be sure, at first sight, the situations seem identical: in both cases, no tamandua.

But in the first case we find a state that could be termed natural, however deplorable; this is how it's always been, we made do without, the question never even came up. Whereas, in the second case the tamandua played a role of primary importance, it couldn't be ignored, its sudden disappearance thus leaves a clear, well-defined emptiness, a tamandua-shaped void.

In order to slightly refine this quick comparative analysis, let us add that, in the first case, where the absence of the tamandua was in a sense a building-block of their lived reality, of its precarious, more or less tolerable stability, there was not so much as a longing for something different. Those who experience it were not forever saying to themselves: Oh, if only I had a tamandua! The absence of the tamandua, even as it was one of the most obvious characteristics of their world or their day-to-day life, was not a thing to be remarked on. A simple inability to see the big picture? Perhaps, I say, for we might well nevertheless find it surprising: the lack of a tamandua is plain as day, after all! Where there is no tamandua, there is no tamandua! Where there is no tamandua, one can clearly see there is no tamandua! I'm not dreaming, I'm not making this up: no tamandua, no tamandua. Could it be the similar absence of the mongoose or spider monkey that's blinding us to the tamandua's absence? Are we really that easily distracted? Dismayed or distraught by the absence of the mongoose and the spider monkey, you see, my mind was on other things, and I saw nothing of the absence of the tamandua. If I saw nothing of it, you'll retort, then that means I did indeed perceive it. Sophistry! That's my answer to you. Picking nits so you can split their hairs. You're overthinking this, people! The fact that you've seen nothing in no way implies that you don't perceive clearly and precisely the absence of each individual thing.

In the second case, that of the guards of Luzatto Circus's exotic menagerie, the tamandua's absence was of an abrupt nature, precipitous, rendering it more easily perceived. There was a break, a rupture, a discontinuity. Suddenly nothing was the same. Particularly because—another nuance that sensitive souls will already have grasped, which I thus point out here for the oafs among you—contrarily to the first case, in which we are aggrieved in theory but not actually pained by the absence of any tamandua, every tamandua, the Luzattos were bemoaning the absence of their particular tamandua, of that tamandua among all tamanduas, their beloved little tamandua, named Fluss or Chipie. The others were absent as well, all the others, but the Luzattos cared little for that, and besides, even had those others been there beside them, this one would still have been lacking, would alone have been lacking, and cruelly.

The entire circus must have been out searching for it. Not only the menagerie guards, but the performers as well, let us recall, Lorenzo, Stefano, Pietro, Oneto, Claudio, Giorgio, Aldo, Ermanno, Leonardo, Francisco, Luciano, Silvio, Calo, Dominico, and Giaquinto, the whole pyramid of Luzatto brothers, but also Pupi Luzatto, the father, Giuseppe Luzatto, the flea-trainer uncle, Polo Luzatto, the clown uncle, Perla Luzatto, the lion-taming cousin, Massimo Luzatto, the magician cousin, Rolando and Nanni Luzatto, the twin acrobat cousins and their aerial spouses Rosella and Antonella, the nephew Nino Luzatto and his monkey, the niece Nina Luzatto and her dogs, finally the horsewoman, great-niece Clara Luzatto, no doubt every last one of them was after that tamandua, unknowingly adding to the numbers of the police already scattered throughout the city, things were heating up. We'd have to play it close to the vest, and redouble our vigilance.

—More than you think, added Pimoe in a tiny little voice.

—What do you mean?

Whereupon Pimoe launched into her life story: that's what you get, sometimes, for asking a simple question. Some people, to make a point, think themselves obliged to go back to the beginning and set off from there; sometimes, before finally naming the shop where they've just bought a hat, they begin with the first protoplasm to divide itself in the murky waters of the geological ages, then the animalcule that first hoisted itself onto the muddy shore, not without skidding back a few times, which later grew complex enough to feel the discomfort of walking bare-headed in the rain, for it is a fact that we are not born with hats on our heads, and that any improvement in our living conditions came at the expense of great efforts. Our patience as listeners is sorely tried for such a meager reward: the name and address of a haberdasher. Pimoe had that flaw, but I loved Pimoe's flaws as well, no less than the undulating line of her body, no less than the curls gathered into a topknot on the crown of her head.

Before giving her the floor, an update, perhaps, on our ant: she was scurrying ever onward, evidently oblivious to the presence of her most fearsome predator behind her; she was running along her tightrope, without haste or letup, guided by a superior instinct, a valiant soldier ever undeterred from her mission.

I loved another man before you, Pimoe told me. And to be sure, it was a cruel confession, as much as the yataghan in the sadist's hand, and I the pink baby he slices up, but at the same time I fully suspected that such a beautiful young woman could not have kept herself entirely untouched in hopes of meeting me one day. I ask of no one a temperance equal to my own, my moral rigor having successfully tamed my inhibitions and timidity enough to keep carnal temptation permanently at arm's length.

He was strong, she went on, intelligent, charming, and thoughtful. I can see why you wearied of him, Pimoe, but are you telling me all this to highlight my virtues by comparison? She gave me a sad smile, sad but so lovely that I was ready to twist her arms behind her back just to someday see it again. His many charms hid as many faults, she said, but obviously, I only discovered that later. I let him into my life. The more space he took up, the more fulfilled I felt. His possessiveness didn't trouble me—I wanted to be his. One day I lost an eyelash; he spotted it at once, he felt he'd been robbed, dispossessed, despoiled, I saw his gaze darken and realized that my wishes had come true beyond my wildest dreams: I no longer belonged to myself. He demanded that I explain every little thing I did, even my glances. You could safely have substituted his loving attentions for the electric barbed wire that confines savage bulls or the double wall of a high-security prison. I was a captive of his passion. I was supposed to exist only for him. Who would want to be loved like that, Blaise, apart perhaps from your trout amandine? I ran away. One evening I drugged his wine, and when he was sound asleep I threw my clothes into a bag and left. I covered my tracks. I burned all my bridges. I moved to another town. To this day, I fear I might see him pop up on every street corner. I'm sure he's searching for me. Then I saw you, Blaise, and I knew I should put myself under your protection.

Pimoe fell silent. I took her hand. One more reason to keep looking over our shoulders. No question about it: we were a highly sought-after couple.

—If he saw us this way, he'd kill us.

—Dear Pimoe, as long as we trust the ant to choose our path, we're in no danger.

Such was indeed my wager. And that wager was founded on a theory that had thus far coincided neatly with the facts. The thing to do was to rely entirely, blindly, and without question on our ant's decisions, in short to place our fate in her hands. She would never suspect the importance she'd suddenly acquired in our eyes, and so she would never misuse it (we didn't want to be led around by the nose, a caravan of porters or sherpas trailing behind her). By walking the way of the ant, I rightly supposed that we would steer clear of the routes taken by our fellows, which is how, in its cruel objectivity, biology forces us to classify cops, clowns, and jealous lovers. We now had, without quite understanding what they were, the preoccupations of ants. We confidently assigned all our rights and privileges to her who was henceforth our guide, thereby ripping ourselves away from the ranks of men: while the tamandua, let us note, stuck to its species' rudimentary logic, Pimoe and I had thrown off the shackles of ours. This choice, improbable and even unimaginable, left us next to invisible, no less than an ant in mid-city. I found in this other felicities that will perhaps be judged shameful or scandalous, even debased and degenerate, which will give you a sense of their intensity and of the joys they afforded me, body and soul.

I'm willing to try to explain myself on that point, though my goal is not self-justification, in any case I care precious little about appearing to my best advantage. At birth, I found myself automatically if not by force enlisted into the human community, when a she-wolf or a sow would have just as willingly clasped me to her teat; I was never allowed to choose. Early on I felt the sorrow of having been thus brutally separated from those loving, nourishing mothers, and at the same time forever cut off from the many possible lives that lay open to me. I am not unaware of the qualities of men, they're ingenious, industrious, dominant, I was never given my share of those qualities, though I think myself endowed with unexploited aptitudes that would have made of me a very comely wolf or a first-rate piglet. I was in any case meant to be some other animal, I'm convinced of it. The schemes and enthusiasms of men leave me cold, I never see myself in the choices they favor; their ambitious works, their vast undertakings arouse in me no passion. I sometimes enter museums, where man stockpiles the best of himself in the form of musty old collections; my yawns soon close my eyes. This weariness came over me very young. I was bored among children my own age; like sitting through a never-ending Mass among my brothers. Their bouncing balls were projectiles.

And if I possess a firm jaw and two rows of teeth, it's so that my mouth will never let slip the hurrahs and olés to which most human conversation is limited. Never was my enthusiasm aroused by the prospect of successively striking the poses recommended to nobly incarnate the ages of life; I was bored with all that in advance, and I lent myself to the task with a patent bad faith that left those around me ill at ease. I was an unconvincing child, a dubious adolescent, a faulty adult. I played my role so badly that I was taken for a traitor or a schemer. I applied myself all the same, taught myself the requisite customs and practices, but always as if I were trying to learn the folk dances of some foreign land. Once a week, Wednesday evenings, an hour of Icelandic quadrille, why not? But never again to move in any other way, no thanks. Even my language, my mother tongue, was as if dead in my mouth, a still-born tongue, wheezing, crotchety, archaic—people pulled long faces when I spoke to them, as if I myself were a trumpeting elephant. Words seemed to me better used to name things that didn't exist, and I couldn't see the point of duplicating a self-evident reality with that spittle-soaked echo. I spoke strictly at cross purposes; people thought me incoherent. I was then taken for a drunkard, a madman, a defective. Outraged common sense knitted straitjackets for my use. Meanwhile, I launched my sentences into space, I cast them into deserts, into voids, they grew antennae, fluorescent tentacles that grasped nothing, and I followed after, escaping the gravity of all earthbound ideas. Who would ever want coffee or spirits filtered through a white beard? And yet such is the wisdom we're offered. I pushed away that chalice with horror. We know how I turned out.

One further confession, to my shame as always. These inabilities, these refusals produced no usable energy, inspired me to no vitriol or revolt. Rather, I fell into a sort of melancholy inertia, sterile and sniveling. My spite lacked enthusiasm. Overturning everything, toppling everything, that could wait, some other time, first I needed a bench on which to sit and then stretch out, as I've said, and so the day will go by, then the night. I awoke the next morning and shook myself off. But how to shake up the world! In my unfruitful reveries, I mused on the stout leather handles of yesteryear's suitcases, and told myself that this is what we would somehow have to find a way to do: locate some solid ground, and anchor to it—or graft, relying on the organic properties of leather?—that stout handle; then at last, yes, perhaps we could hoist the world high and give it a good shaking up. Such projects sometimes occurred to me. I pursued them no further, outstretched on my bench, I turned them over lazily in my head, I grew drunk on their imagined audacity; never for a moment did I seek to devise solutions for the niggling technical difficulties that might compromise their realization, and even less to break ground for those labors in the mud and ice of this world. On the contrary, I naively aspired to find a place in this world, my psyche's complexion forever exposing me to its rebuffs; I cherished the idea that I might fully succeed by the exercise of some modest activity linked to the control of its flux, a cog, if you like, a mere cog, but an essential one: overseer of a railway station, air-traffic controller, or lockkeeper, with an instinctive preference for the latter, as the lockkeeper executes orders he receives from the higher-ups of fluvial navigation, he has no say in the matter, and yet his every move is as decisive as the sorcerer's commanding the rain: their influence can only be compared to the moon's on the tides. After a lifetime of wandering and senseless speculations, I had, with the Moindres, at long last found the chance to seize hold of the lever that would allow me to weigh, gently but firmly, on the course of things. We now know what befell me there.

And how I finally found myself on this sidewalk, in the company of a woman and a tamandua, pursued by the police, a vindictive lover, and the entire staff of the Luzatto circus, following with measured gait in the footsteps of an ant, hoping to vanish into the landscape along with her, now firmly resolved to walk out on it all, to lead my life in accordance with non-human laws and logics, looking forward to better times ahead, and it was then that the child appeared.

I surely had much to learn from an ant, if only how to carry sixty times my own weight: it took all my strength just to drag myself out of bed. And then how to blaze my own trail, no matter the terrain, dismayed by neither hills nor swamps. And to know neither boredom nor idleness nor doubt nor hesitation, and it was then, as I was saying, that the child appeared.

Because this is the thing: the ant scarcely exists, and yet she fears nothing—should be crushed by the mere thought of the enormity of the world looking down on her, and yet, no. A vigor that withstands every trial, abashed by no humiliation. Six feet, but not one for perplexedly scratching her forehead. Moving onward, always and everywhere—who will block her path, if the elephant can't? Who among you thinks yourself so heroically posed, on so grandiose a scale, that the ant will not find your weak spot? If your superb assurance cracks between your toes, that's where the ant will get through. Everything that is not concrete is a breech for the teeny tiny little ant. Insinuates herself, trickles through better than water—do ants seep? Nothing of the sort! They bead up, on every available surface. And it was then that the child appeared.

A bit like the ant, in fact, suddenly there unforetold, neither silhouette on the horizon nor cloud of dust, nor pounding hooves, as if she knew how to slip through the stitches of the sheer fabric of days sewn one to the next, as if she were not a prisoner of that cloth, unlike every other creature, and were no less at home on the wrong side than on the right; as she wished, and whenever she saw fit, she could say enough of all this, disappear, then miraculously appear once again.

He had appeared, and so now he was there, a little boy of three, four, or five, I've always had a hard time estimating the age of these newborns—does one go by the rate at which snot flows from their nostrils? Then he must have been five. Sniffled in vain. A fine child's face with birdlike eyes, lively and round, and tousled hair. It was the tamandua that interested him, of course. He pointed at it with his index finger; his silent mouth formed an oh that swelled and swelled without ever coming unstuck from his lips, as soap bubbles sometimes do. I'd been doing my best to keep the anteater out of sight, pulling a flap of my coat before it like a curtain whenever we met a passerby, but the child had seen it from afar, and, no doubt eluding his mother's surveillance, he'd approached, irresistibly drawn.

—That, he said simply, pointing at the animal.

And indeed, what more was there to say?

Even in its natal forest, the tamandua is a curious sight—very likely the cause of the marmoset's high spirits—and when, in order to drink, it kisses its own reflection with its snout, there really is something to laugh at: suddenly one understands what the parrot is mocking. But, in the modern Western city, for a tyke whose knowledge of the animal kingdom is limited to pigeons and poodles, the tamandua constitutes such an astonishment that it justifies forgetting his mother, whom he's been seeing every day for the past five years, in different getups, it's true—but that old trick doesn't work anymore, he recognizes her all the same—there, to start with, is a good reason to stray from her, take a little distance: a tamandua! What mommy could hope to compete, no matter how pretty? And so comes the first desertion, the first decampment, there is after all more to life than cleaning your room and coloring in empty shapes. There is also the tamandua.

—That, the child said again.

Yes, let's go have a look at that. That's worth a detour. Mommy's very sweet, but she doesn't have a snout like that. I can look at mommy's nose anytime, evidently mine's much the same, so much the worse, so much the better, whatever, it's a nose, it sniffles, you blow it. Whereas that tamandua snout, that's something else, at long last something else, what a weird thing! That's what they call a tube, isn't it? I don't even know who mommy is anymore. What's a mommy? Do I have to have been born to a mommy, now frantic with worry? And running this way and that in the distance—I can still see her from here, but she's fading fast—desperately questioning the bystanders, alerting the gendarmes, who are ruling nothing out, an accident, a kidnapping, when in fact all it is, is I'm captivated by that tamandua, and I believe I have every reason. What was I supposed to do? Cling to my mother's skirts and disdainfully avert my eyes from that phenomenon? What kind of life will I have if at my age I'm already turning up my nose at such wonderments? I'll become that incurious bespectacled nobody soon enough. I'm still just a child, and I'm sorry, but when a child sees a tamandua, you can't ask him to clean his room or write his first name in cursive. When a child sees a tamandua, he doesn't waste a moment, he makes a beeline straight for it. Have you completely forgotten your old amazements? Apparently so! So you claim that when you were five and a tamandua happened to pass by you scarcely gave it one weary, scornful glance? Go ask your aged mother, she'll refresh your memory. She very clearly recalls the many times you dropped her hand to follow a tamandua. When a child sees a tamandua, he follows it, that's how it is, it's a law, it would be absurd to object on the grounds of who knows what rigid pedagogical principles, absurd and dangerous: what will become of a child closeted away to keep him from following the tamandua? How will he turn out? Just where do you suppose cretins come from? How do they become so complete? Worse, there is alas every reason to fear that he will one day reproduce, it is alas likely that he will reproduce those detestable ways, that brutishness, and that his own children in turn will systematically find themselves deprived of tamanduas. A family curse settles in, a burdensome inheritance passed down from generation to generation, a suicidal, tragic reflex, to be perpetuated to the end of time.

In short, we now had a panicky mother on our tail as well. We nonetheless made no change to our itinerary. The ant led and we followed. We pressed on as quickly as her top speed would allow, never straying from our path. And of course I need only say that to see the ant immediately turn away—but it was only a sidestep, hardly a detour, undertaken to hoist onto her back a grain of rice longer and wider than herself, concealing her from our aerial gaze. I was a little disappointed. So she'd wandered so far from her sisters, risking her life in the vast human wasteland, simply to search for provisions! I'd imagined a more daring incursion into enemy territory, into unknown worlds, for reconnaissance and conquest. I was prepared to betray my own kind (my own kind!), to press my experience into service for the success of that raid. I had valuable information to offer on the ways and customs of these land's masters, their soft spots, the chinks in their armor. I would have been a stalwart and trustworthy ally, in exchange for a modest position in the new regime. Still, perhaps this apparent supply mission was a red herring, intended simply as a front for less above-ground activities? Why deny ants a sense of strategy? They traverse the centuries just as we do, they survive cataclysms, earthquakes, destructions, they must not be entirely bereft of such talents. Their society's organization has gone unchanged since the beginning, whereas ours has to be constantly reformed and adapted to ensure our survival. One ancient civilization still survives in the ruins of Rome and beneath the scattered stones of the Aztec temples. And while we struggle to come up with twelve pairs of wooden clogs to keep our folklore alive, ants perpetuate their traditions with such constancy that they seem neither quaint nor obsolete.

Or else—another hypothesis—that grain of rice was meant to serve as a ready source of sustenance for our ant, which would nibble chunks or slices of it all through her journey, thus sparing herself the distraction of searching for nourishment. But whether warrior disguised as a housewife or provident, well-prepared traveler, that ant had successfully found, in the immensity of a city little known for its production of cereals, the very grain of rice she required. To fully grasp the inerrancy of her instinct, the best thing would be to try the experiment for yourself. Go ahead. Go out into the street and start looking for a grain of rice. The playing field is uneven, though: we stand head and shoulders over the ant, and can thus scan a much broader area. Oddly, this advantage would not appear to be doing you much good. I'm waiting for you to bring back a grain of rice picked up from the pavement, and I don't see you coming. You can find a great many things in the city, supply precedes demand, motivates it, creates it, your every move is a response to some stimulus, but outside the world of commerce, what do you find? Nothing of any value! Not so much as a grain of rice! You spend the day searching in vain, darkness falls and you go on, with the aid of a flashlight, a lantern, your blindly groping hands, still nothing. And the next day? Back to it, scuttling like a crab from side to side, squatting, you caress every smooth surface, finger every crevice, with one nail you scratch at the concrete crust: nothing, nothing, nothing! Something as modest, as derisory as a mere grain of rice, and our formidable senses, no more than our phenomenal brains, have no idea how to detect it: they'd have an easier time discovering three new exoplanets. Rice is something we find in a paddy or a supermarket, never anywhere else. That's one of the limits of our endlessly boastful genius, no doubt the most visible, the one we most often run up against. We could join forces, form little squads, divide the city into sectors and assign one to each, we could mobilize the army, we'd still come back downcast and empty-handed. A cruel blow to our pride. Christopher Columbus's caravel would have exhausted the seven seas in vain, we can't see the tiny detail, the precious detail that ensures the worth of the whole.

But the ant can: our ant had discovered it straightaway. Should we put this down to a mere stroke of luck? Or had she set her course for that grain of rice from the start of her odyssey? Was that her goal? But if so, would she not have turned back the moment she got her mitts on that treasure? She showed no such intention. She sped ever onward; more astonishingly still, we soon found that her new burden in no way slowed her progress. She paid it so little mind that we wondered if she'd forgotten she was even carrying it.

For us, on the other hand, that grain of rice changed the situation entirely. Habituated to following a tiny black form, our eyes now had to track a tiny white form (so the grain of rice had been cooked), scarcely more sizeable than the other, and this was nothing less than a sea-change in our way of seeing the world. When the surface beneath us was dark—fresh asphalt, wet sidewalk—that new state of affairs suited us neatly and eased our task; but as soon as the ground grew lighter everything became much more complicated. Another cause for concern: would the tamandua's sense of smell, only middlingly interested in cereals, not be so put off that it would wander away, lose the trail? We were soon reassured on that score, however, and so our anxiety was forced to find another raison d'être: pigeons. Pigeons abounded in the area, and a grain of rice waddling over the paving stones would constitute too rare a windfall to long elude their search and sweep, less disorganized than it seems. They did in fact seem to be massing around us. Should one of them manage to snatch up that grain of rice, it would no doubt at the same time inflict grievous damage on our ant, assuming, and on this point there was every reason for concern, that it didn't swallow her outright. Not bothering to wait for the order, the child shouldered the task of dispersing them. Whenever one came a little too close, he spread his arms, produced an engine-like sound with his lips, and raced toward it. The bird flew away, and the biplane broke the dogfight, no point going on.

—Charlie.

In response to Pimoe, who was asking him his first name.

To be sure, we now formed a group still more easily spotted, thanks to its size or the space it took up, and at the same time still more banal, less likely to stand out, nothing more, it would seem, than an exemplary little family out for a stroll: the father, the mother, the child, the pet, which from afar could easily have passed for a dog, a rather strange dog no doubt, but there are so many breeds, and so many possible associations and combinations of those breeds, that we are regularly confronted with canine calves or reptiles, never-before-seen specimens to which we pay only an amused sort of attention, soon drawn to other spectacles. We each found what we needed in this fortuitous alliance. The police were looking for a lone man, Pimoe's jealous lover a lone Pimoe, Charlie's tearful mother a lone Charlie, and the Luzattos a lone tamandua. Together, we frustrated their vigilance, we became as if invisible, our individual, distinct, easily identified personalities opportunely dissolved in the group.

I had only to congratulate myself on my intuition. Friend, when misfortune strikes, when hard times befall you, entrust your fate to an ant. An ant always knows where to go, and her well chosen path will serve you far better than any endless wandering. May I tattoo this axiom on your forehead? HE WHO WALKS BEHIND AN ANT WILL NEVER AGAIN BE CALLED A VAGABOND. At long last you have a goal, even if you don't know what it is. What matters is that you will draw strength from the ant's tenacity. You'll be galvanized by her glorious ardor. And in your loins, in your once faltering legs, there will be her drive. No more doubt, no more procrastination. Forward! From here on you will cleave the waves. On reflection, it's best to know nothing of the goal—but hasten toward it, that's what matters. Does an arrow flying through the air know if it will end up buried in a heart or an apple? What does it care? What does it matter? It flies through the air, whistling.

As was I, under my breath, happy as never before, escorted by Pimoe and Charlie, making our way in the company of a tamandua, guided by a fleet-footed and resolute ant. Where were we going? We were going, that was all that mattered. And leaving the old world behind, though without making a great show of our exit: with a simple kick of the heel. It was rather the world that was rolling into the distance, behind our backs.

Here, however, I must document another encounter that could well have turned out badly, which is to say have diverted us from our route and led us to our doom (the police, the lover, the Luzattos, the mommy). It was little Charlie who first caught sight of the temptress.

—That, he said simply, pointing at a windowsill just level with his eyes. That, in Charlie's language, ordinarily designating a tamandua, I felt a shiver of anxiety run through me. For if I had come to terms with the idea that I would henceforth be accompanied by this anteater, if I was even able to fully appreciate the advantages of that chance alliance, I immediately envisaged the complications a second tamandua would bring with it. That much harder to go unnoticed. And why exactly should we always be the ones to suffer the consequences of the Luzattos' negligence and ineptitude? Really, how hard can it be to lock a cage? When you're lucky enough to own a couple of tamanduas, I believe it's your duty to look after them. Otherwise you shouldn't have saddled yourself with the things in the first place. It should be quite clear when you welcome them into your home that this is a new obligation you've taken on. It's a simple question of personal responsibility. I was beginning to suspect the Luzattos of surreptitiously taking steps to get rid of them. A swat on the rump and off you go, you're free.

How now to remain discreet? A two-tamandua man is no mere face in the crowd; he stands out, head to toe, exposed to every gaze. Not to mention: would this newcomer be as patient as the other? Would it not pose an immediate threat to our ant? How would those two get along? We all know how couples are. And might the first, seeing the ant as its game, its own private hunting reserve, and anticipating the possible intentions of the second, not prefer in the end to sacrifice its quarry without further ado?

But it must be that in the mouth of a child a word can have more than one meaning, depending on tone or inflection, which is incidentally what makes that language so very difficult to learn, and no doubt explains why we abandon it when we grow up, before we've even fully mastered it. For this time Charlie's *that* did not denote a tamandua. I suspected as much, let me say in passing, not that I mean to boast, I simply thought it unlikely that so sluggish and low-slung a beast could have hoisted itself onto a windowsill—and if it had, we would surely have seen it without having to cluster around the sill as we did, having implicitly adopted the principle to neglect nothing that aroused the interest of one of our number: we were all involved, by the very fact of our being here. Our survival depended on our solidarity.

It was another ant.

It was another ant, but this one with wings. A winged ant, an aberrant and monstrous creature, if you want my opinion, no less than a flying fox or indeed a flying fish. When you claim to be alien to your species, and set out to exploit the characteristic advantages of another, you're forced to adopt attributes that were originally lacking and which, even once taken on, integrated into your being by graft or mimetic mutation, will never lose that forced or artificial appearance, like a deep-sea diver's suit or a mountaineer's gear extracted from a knapsack. A curious perversion for an ant, this yearning to fly, and to join the insectivorous sparrow in the heavens! But that was what pleased me about this one at once. Was I too not at odds with my fellows, a runaway from the human race? And if I chose to abandon my ant so as to follow this renegade, could I not hope that I too might take to the skies, might she not teach me to soar, might I thus not extract myself once and for all from the physical laws holding me prisoner to my state? Already I could feel a promising quiver in my legs, my blood pumping through my veins as if to top up my fuel tank, and I stood on tiptoe, my body outstretched, in rocket mode.

I was about to confide my new intentions to Pimoe, I would invite her to join me, and Charlie would tag along as well. The time had come to take wing. Let our pursuers comb through the dust in search of our footprints ... Imagine the look on the face of the cop tracking the bird: *Say, chief, did you know our man had three toes?* ... Just then the tamandua's purple tongue burst from its sheath, snagged the insect, and instantaneously wrapped back around the bobbin of bone set into its larynx, or so at least I imagine, and with this all my plans came crashing to earth. I looked at it, put out, and its round eye answered exactly this: sorry, but winged ants don't cotton to hangers-on, you've got to take what you can get and be done with it.

What would be the point of protesting? The matter was closed. I hoped at least that this modest snack would allow the tamandua to soldier on a little longer without sustenance, sparing our ant the consequences of a craving as sudden as it was irrepressible on the part of her traditional predator, for the moment muzzled by its strategy (a cork would have done even better).

But:

—Bravo! Encore!

Applauded Charlie, seeing the tamandua's lasso-quick tongue seize the flying ant and disappear, sucked down at once, to his eye every bit like a noodle.

Encore! But was that little innocent not simply encouraging the beast to now set its sights on our ant? I pulled him close to shut him up, more brutally than I intended, and the child began to cry. With a certain pique, Pimoe extracted him from my embrace and set about comforting him, stroking his hair. I realized for the first time that this little Charlie truly was in our hands—mine rather rough, Pimoe's far softer—and that I now might well be considered a kidnapper. I would inevitably be accused of taking him hostage to ensure my getaway.

To which, at my trial, I will retort that in that case every couple who conceives a child should be tried for the same crime (*murmurs in the courtroom; a few stifled cries of indignation*). In the meantime, I thought it best not to linger before this window: an immobile crowd always ends up attracting attention, especially, perhaps, when it includes a sizable tamandua. Set them in motion, and that same crowd always seems about to dissolve or to scatter, and if its cohesion nonetheless guaranteed, in my opinion, the invisibility of each one of us, our individual movements within it had the advantage of blurring the lines and muddling the vision of the enemy so keen to destroy us. Besides, during that pause, the ant, unconcerned as ever by our dithering, had gone on ahead. We had some ground to make up. We could in fact no longer see her. Pressed into service, the tamandua transformed itself into a living radar site—though it more closely resembled a vacuum cleaner, its nose, which is to say also its mouth, glued to the cobblestones, nodding its inexpressive little head, snuffling loudly, while the broom of its tail swept right and left. We followed it on tiptoe, taking care not to dirty its clean floor. Soon it had discovered, not her tracks—the ant's foot leaves no visible dent in asphalt, even with the added weight of a grain of rice—but the ant herself, just as she was about to cross a heavily-traveled avenue. All at once we found ourselves plunged into an urban hell.

And it was in no way certain that we could all manage, like the ant, to fit into the tread of the tire that would run us over, then blithely resume our trek once the juggernaut had passed by. There was reason to fear that a part or the whole of our group would be crushed, which would draw a crowd and an influx of policemen, before the city road crews came along with their hoses and turned on the waterworks, to which would be added the tears of the mommy, the lover, the assembled Luzattos; and what about me, who'll cry for me?

Wisely, we decided to make for a crosswalk, once again relying on the tamandua's nose to locate our ant on reaching the opposite shore. But the tamandua had other plans, and followed her into the rushing automotive torrent. Now, what does a motorist do when he suddenly sees a tamandua before him? He simultaneously slams on his brakes (which squeal) and leans on his horn (which honks), while the terrified tamandua emits its own piercing plaint, all the more grating and dissonant in that the beast rarely finds a moment to exercise its voice—the tamandua is naturally taciturn, and from the sound of the thing it's all too clear there's an untalented beginner pinching its vocal cords. Nonetheless, it never lost the trail. The first car skidded crosswise, mid-avenue. And was consequently struck by two others, one tailing it, one approaching in the opposite lane. There followed on both sides a chain of collisions whose echo—a lovely sound effect, musical, marked "decrescendo"—grew ever fainter, though never fading entirely, at such length that, having autodidactically pursued my intellectual development to some considerable length, thanks to which I was not unaware of the rotundity of the earth, I found myself wondering if the two crashes, left and right, might have in a sense met up on the other side of the world—whereupon the last two vehicles in both dented rows, seeking to disengage themselves by desperately shifting into reverse, rear-ended each other. And then, at long last, silence.

We made use of that break in the traffic to follow the tamandua through the cars' smoking remains. The confusion suited us nicely. Variously bruised and battered, the motorists were too busy cursing each other to pay us any mind, and the paramedics were having some difficulty making their way through: we were far away when they arrived on the scene of the original collision, and the incoherent claims of the drivers, who blamed all this on a tapir, were given short shrift by the gendarmes, here demonstrating an atypical sagacity.

Now we were out of the city center. The ant went on, unwavering. Contrarily to what I'd supposed, she never allowed herself a brief rest for a nibble of her Chinese dinner. By turns—with the exception of the tamandua, which seemed to feel no need for sleep—we went off to restore our strength at Pimoe's, Pimoe taking Charlie along with her and at the same time seeing to the matter of provisions. How many more days this escapade lasted I can't say. Night fell earlier; the temperature dropped. Summer came to an abrupt end. The autumn rains washed it away. But the snow fell thick and fast, and one morning springtime took us by surprise. Ground down by the dog days of summer, we weren't sorry to see the first leaves turn yellow. Then the wind carried them off. Paralyzed by the cold of winter, we were moved to discover the first daffodils, peddled in bouquets on the street corners. Etcetera. Charlie was now a handsome young man, the tamandua was going gray, and the ant reached the wall that surrounds the big cemetery.

And began to scale it, most inconveniently for us. Not much of a climber, the tamandua, able only to raise its trunk, for surely the time has come to dare to call that unlikely, flexible, prehensile tubular snout a trunk. There is a word that designates such a thing very clearly, and like it or not, that word is trunk. What earthly purpose, we can only wonder, does the word trunk serve if it is inappropriate or inaccurate in this case? Must an elephant eternally appear in the wake of the word trunk? Or an oak tree? Which we're supposed to do what with, exactly? In spite of it all, trunk is the *mot juste* here. In all honesty, I see no other possibility. An un-likely, flexible, prehensile tubular snout is ideally summarized in the word trunk. Any circumlocution would only slow us down, just when everything's picking up speed, just when the tale is about to break free of the ant's glacial pace and race at long last to a conclusion.

We were little nimbler than the tamandua when it came to scaling that nearly nine-foot-high wall. I gave Charlie a boost; he hoisted himself onto the top, then dropped over the side. When, in turn, albeit one step at a time, the ant began her descent, Charlie was ordered to keep an eye on her while we hastened toward the entryway designed for us bipeds, whether standing, walking, or reclining between four planks, and the quadrupeds that sometimes accompany us, once black horses hitched to the hearses, today tamanduas.

Off we went, and we were back at Charlie's side before the ant even reached the ground.

I was taking my time, you understand, letting them make their tedious detour on their useless long legs. Once they were all lined up in a neat row behind me, I resumed my trek. Or the last few yards of it, anyway, up to the dark crypt whose masonry we've eaten through on one side, home to our colony since Queen Doryla's escape from the Luzatto Circus' exotic insectariums, two years ago. Guided by instinct, she came to this place, and in this regularly-restocked larder, beneath this protective slab, she laid her eggs. Here we so prospered that today we number twelve million, and there are no longer enough dead to satisfy our voracious appetite. Are we not army ants, fearsome of mandible? Back in our homeland, we devour a buffalo at every meal. A few hours and he's stripped to the bone—his tragic moo still rocks his carcass. Now I can drop the grain of rice I'd picked up, not as a garnish for our next feast—we never touch such bloodless fare—but only to better deceive my prey: thus accoutered, I seemed to them even more harmless than before, like one of our inoffensive vegetarian cousins.

Mission accomplished.

I give you, dear sisters, the fresh meat you so love: three choice cuts of human and a tamandua, this latter to satisfy our thirst for vengeance along with our hunger. Likely soon to be followed—entirely of their own accord, so subtle, so intricate is the trap I devised for them—by a lover, a mommy, the entire fraternity of Luzatto brothers, and a squad of policemen, among them, inevitably, a few stout, well marbled hulks to make up for the lack of buffaloes.

My sisters are swarming all around the crypt. The alert has been sounded. Deep inside, Doryla orders the attack. We're girded for battle, our body is nothing but armor. The entire colony pours over our bewildered guests, we have the element of surprise on our side, not to mention our speed, our numbers, we give them a generous spray of acid, blessings upon you, lambs of God! We burn their eyes. They fall to their knees; toppled to one side, the tamandua frantically wriggles its legs. The assault's second wave covers them completely. We undress them with our mandibles, the tight garment of tender flesh gives way at the armholes, we know just how to rip out the stitches. This is grade-A prime, little sisters, savor it well! Melts in your mouth, oh my God! A touch more

(An old man went by, towed by his walker. It was a carbon-fiber walker, ultralight, designed like a ship's prow, with three wheels whose soft rubber tires had been tested on a Formula 1 circuit, an aerodynamic walker, a walker built for speed, meant to shatter records, an ironic walker, impossible to keep up with, humiliating, the last word in modern technology and ignominy.)

What to cling to now? The rim of the gratinée pan, I suppose? That boat that contains the heaving sea and the shipwreck!

Oh! how it churns!

Be so kind, Mademoiselle, as to consider the situation coolly. Let's let the dish go cold—that won't make it any more appetizing, but it will be less fluid at least, less unstable, and it won't burn our tongues. Let us now gingerly venture out onto its lumpy surface, weighing as little as we can. You wish you could pull on a pair of stout, thick-soled shoes before setting out. Buffalo leather, rhinoceros hide. Your wish cannot be granted. For one thing, that hardened surface remains treacherous and unpredictable: you won't get far. For another, if the experience is to have any value, we must advance on our bare feet, depending on those sensitive antennae to enlighten us, our eye having seen far too much of the thing and grown jaded—one wonders if anything will ever disgust it again.

Here we go, Mademoiselle, be brave.

Would you like me to hold your arm?

First observation: ouch.

Better to walk over thorns, over broken glass!

No better training ground for the fakir.

It's painful, it's thorny, barbed, jagged. You skin yourself against

---

pungent, the tamandua lends a little spice to the meal, which might otherwise have proven just a little cloying for our tastes. But what a wonderful change from the over-aged fodder we've been forced to get used to! Because it's another thing entirely when the blood is still pumping, stirred and enflamed by terror, as by passion. These bodies have long been steeping in Sentiment, in Ideas, the wine and onion of our marinade. What a delight for the palate! So toothsome! Oh, how perfectly you have impregnated yourself with your dreams! You're spoiling us! Perhaps you're a little dismayed by our appetite; take it, at least, as the compliment it is.

And my sincere hope is that Blaise heard my words of thanks as I gnawed on his ear.

it. You wound yourself on it. Now you're hurting all over, you're aggravated, unhappy. Your feet are bleeding. But did you come here to seek anything other than that confirmation?

Did I not give you fair warning?

After so many others, will it now be you who turns my best intentions against me?

I was a charming boy. Life tested me, and yet I remained, I swear, a charming young man, thoughtful and polite. Never was any old lady forced to complain of my rudeness. I was like a relic from the good old days.

It was then that I was unwittingly enlisted as a bully. With my every minuscule movement of hand or arm, a head came forward to take a nasty blow. I couldn't move without flattening a nose or blackening an eye. Similarly, the moment I uttered a word, however harmless, however banal, the one person on earth it might hurt came running to hear it. If I said cow, for example, there suddenly appeared before me, outraged and sobbing, the man deprived of his virility by Bossie's mighty kick. If I said *child*, a barren couple burst into tears. And if I said *chair*, a bankrupt furniture maker threw himself under a train. Mademoiselle, I said *plume, cotton, flake*, and there ensued cries, sorrows, vexations, lifelong hatreds.

And so I made my way through this world, charming boy that I was, amiable, sensitive, mannerly to a fault, sowing ruin and desolation wherever I went. Extended in hopes of reconciliation, my hand split yet another lip. Behind me, howls and keening.

As you shall see, my murder may have been but one more unexpected consequence of my exemplary conduct, in every way obedient to the Kantian categorical imperative.

There was no violence in me. I knew nothing of evil, until it appeared to me in the toxic, concentrated form of cauliflower gratin, so venomous that twelve vipers in the bag of candy into which the child dips his dimpled hand truly are mere licorice whips in comparison. No doubt my innocence deserved some sort of comeuppance—but to be dealt the cruelest of all retributions right there on the spot! Here we are, the plat du jour for the fine apple-cheeked lad whose round face wanted to see in itself a mirror for the whole world. Suddenly a grimace splits it in two. Now you can read on it every sad story of separation, of love lost. Bereavement is thus the law. It precedes every union, bulldozes its foundation, works from the beginning toward its ruin. Potato and cauliflower, forced together in spurious union, like an odd and an end, only to be put asunder by the four teeth of a fork—how, henceforth, to believe in human creations? Landslides, burials, submersions, all those promises will be kept. What edifices will be left standing, what monuments? Here, then, is what our civilization is built on, destined from the start for archeology's groping probes: it takes a lot of foresight to be thinking ahead to that when you're just laying the first stone!

What solid affections could one then possibly imagine, sealed by that glue of béchamel and cheese? Hard to believe our loves could ever fall apart!

I thought I held Anne, Florence, Méline, Susan in my arms: embraces so tight that I pawed only my own shoulder blades. Will you tell me why those girls never let themselves be caught? They weren't always so elusive—had I not glimpsed Émile, Franck, Thierry, and Wilhelm on their arm?

Look at the man before you.

Is he so hideous?

Mademoiselle?

Oh, I've always known my appearance alone would never elicit the emotions propitious to coupling. I never left it at that. I spent a fortune on finery. My gaze smoldered with passion. Nothing worked. I might as well have been a dead fish. I might with the same success have set out to seduce a she-fox, a titmouse.

Can you explain this to me?

Mademoiselle?

Am I really that ugly?

Do you think I talk too much?

But that's just it, that can't be it, because I remained perfectly mute in those women's presence. They couldn't get a word out of me. Not one word. The most perfect reserve. Often, in fact, I observed them from the shelter of a tree trunk or a corner cupboard. Could anyone be less importunate? Tell me, you whom I am importuning? And above all tell me why they remained so distant, so indifferent? My attempts at invisibility and even inexistence left them utterly unmoved. And yet I disincarnated myself with perfect silence and distance. A real gentleman. I never got fresh, always stayed frozen. And yet my attentions were never repaid, can you believe it, I met with only their disdain![27]

---

27 For, no matter what he may say, the author does sometimes find consolation in books. Thirty years on, he can still rattle off the credo of the goatherd Eugenio, who, in Chapter LI of *Don Quixote*, regales that pitiful but valiant knight with the sad tale of Leandra, in love with a rogue who took advantage of her devotion to rob her blind, and the woe of the man who truly loved her: *For my part, I follow a simpler path, and I believe a far wiser one, that of cursing the fickleness of women, their inconstancy, their duplicity, their false promises, their broken vows, in short the little taste and tact they display in their thoughts and affections.* That was a balm, an unguent the author applied to his wounds, he drowned his sorrows in that nectar, he sweetened his bitter shame with that honey. All to no avail. That shame was his constant companion: he thought of decking it out in a dress, stockings, titillating underthings. He pulled it onto his knees and caressed its stiff hair for hours on end. It wasn't very pretty, and it weighed a ton. It took a miracle—which certainly wasn't in the plans for his existence, wholly devoted, out of pride or spite, to the labor of writing—to avenge him at one stroke of that shame. He would eventually get his share of grace, youth, beauty, and curly hair that blows in the wind, and shoulders round and golden as brioches. Now and again, though—it's not easy, overcoming old habits—he still intones the goatherd's proud, pitiful profession of faith, but at such times he's not thinking of women, or rather he is, from the blind spot of his writing desk: he's thinking of women readers. He blames them for his books' meager sales. His ironic and even sarcastic prose, little given to narrative, is not to their taste. All generalizations are flawed, he knows that, and he will blush as he accepts the honeyed praise that will not fail to be lavished on him by a few stubborn, refined souls who will be rightly offended by this ham-handed sexual stereotyping. As a precaution, then, to cover his tail, the author will specify that his conclusions are founded in a very different observation: apart from the blind and the amblyopic, men do not read at all, neither ironic and even sarcastic works of prose little given to narrative nor anything else; they've become cold, efficient machines, devoted functionaries of the status quo, engrossed in their tasks, taking delight only in the fluid meshing of game plans and gears—a purring engine, a smoothly passed ball—incapable of meditation and solitude, fiercely anti-intellectual, a lost cause for literature. Their interest awakens only when it is generated by their principal. (And because they never step forward to lend a hand, but leave the chore of tackling all literary production to their helpmates, it is women who must see to the reading of bad books as well as good.)

(Who would have thought it? Shopping had become an act of war. People pressed their avid noses to the windows of army surplus stores. The daintiest young women now wore multipocketed khaki fatigues with dull brown or gray patterns imitating blotches of mud, dust, or dried blood, ostensibly designed as camouflage in the maquis, but which in truth they wore to be seen: rebellious, unsubmissive, independent. We might have been overjoyed to see the sense of the uniform thus perverted into its opposite. But fashion cohabited happily with that symbol and its humiliating values: obedience, conformity, and subjection.)

Then I met her: I naturally sat down at her table and she listened as I spoke, which is to say that I whined and complained as she listened, patiently, perhaps even with an indulgence I should have taken as a warning.

But innocence is a quality I've kept from my days back in limbo. Not even the callused hands of the crone who ushered me into this world and then immediately gave me a spanking could slap any sense into me. Very likely I took her for a fairy godmother, giving me the gift of endurance, girding me against the cruel blows of fate.

She listened to me, and for once my plaint did not crack the walls of my room, it nestled lovingly in the hollow of a prettily formed pink ear, whose sinuous, waxy conduit seemed made to welcome endless digressions, since every new object I spied served to broaden that plaint, to expand it, and to justify it.

Perhaps I wasn't giving things a chance. I could feel only their sharp corners. That ear had none, and to my sorrow I once again took a part for the whole. I believed that that roundness, that softness, that gentleness surely extended to her entire person.

Her pointed knees were concealed by her skirt, her elbows by her puffy sleeves, her fingernails and teeth were all smiles, the former even as they drummed on the false marble tabletop.

Above all, I had forgotten what aggressive, bristling, irascible forms our flexible brain can take in the grip of a twisted or malevolent idea.

(We were always surprised to see such small men emerging from the big-

gest, most luxurious cars.)[28]

At that time I was working as a clerk for a bailiff. I drew up the papers for foreclosures and evictions, never finding all the joy that punitive, vengeful enterprise seems to promise. Because the most important thing of all was still missing: I couldn't choose my victims. I did sometimes enact secret reprisals by drafting eviction papers to be served on one of my enemies—scornful women, condescending bureaucrats, impostors of every stripe—who generally had no idea of the place they held in my life, but those documents, though scrupulously by the book and faithful to the letter of the law, led to no concrete action. I lacked the power to make them a reality. Were they in short anything other than literature, and not bad for that matter, a bolt of cold fury composed upon a solitary stool, perfectly classical in their concision, completely ineffectual?

---

28 The author is not possessed of a driver's license, he does not own a mobile phone, as he's already said, and has never knotted a tie around his neck—not even in jest. All these refusals aim in some vague way to complicate his relationships with others, and thus, no doubt, also to limit them, to restrain them. It would be interesting to know the reasons for this reflex, how it developed, why it persists despite the ease and self-assurance earned from the passage of time, from the author's finally successful integration into a structured and even standardized existence, equipped with all the essentials, why he continues to prefer the park's long alleyway devoid of all human presence. His companion, his friends, even some of his publishers have come to seek him out in the depths of his lair, where, to be sure, fearful, angry, ridiculously proud, he was awaiting them. Is it vanity? Perhaps shame? Or mere cowardice? The author will admit to anything, but don't be taken in, when he seems to belittle himself, it's only because he believes his page makes a sufficient show of strength, simultaneously avenging him and turning the admission of weakness back into an advantage. In some contexts the beard of the bearded lady is her greatest charm; she curls it, she perfumes it, she adorns it with pretty ribbons. Then that beard makes her fortune. But here's the thing: whatever the strength of your writing, or more precisely the strength you think writing gives you, that strength will crumple like a little child's fists against the cellar door when it encounters the first obstacle on its path, which is to say the impossibility of leading your enemy—or at least the opposing force you want to vanquish or bend—onto that field of battle, for neither God nor fate nor illness nor death nor love will be led there. There will be no combat on the terrain where you had some kind of chance. At the very most, you will manage to turn that strength back against yourself and reduce yourself to tatters.

What do you want? It made me feel better.

I seized the properties of the pope, I evicted kings, presidents, and ministers from their palaces.

Not that I forgot my immediate circle. I saw to my neighbors. They were by far the most ill-served of all. I hung their hats and the roofs over their heads on my coathooks. Everything they owned became mine. Then I might have got a little drunk on my power. I also took their wives. I evicted their noisy children.

That game-filled forest was now mine.

Into my sack went the mountain.

Mine were the patents on the tire and the match.

Fire? Mine.

I helped myself.

Those were the most wonderful few months of my life. Sitting at that old desk in that grimy office, the world was my oyster. My elbows and knees showed beneath my clothes, I'd lost a great deal of weight, but my face was aglow. I appropriated the country around me as I sat scarcely moving in a pool of lamplight that grew to encompass the planet, whose inhabitants I now expelled into interstellar space—good luck getting your deposit back! I was determined to see this through to the end, to be the last man standing on earth, so for once I could take pleasure in solitude on my own initiative, and on my own terms: the solitude others imposed on me was less glorious, I wandered aimlessly inside it, I smacked into its walls.[29]

---

29 A very tidy distinction, typical of a character's observation. As for the author, he will probably never know if the solitude to which his timidity confined him at a very young age determined his vocation as a writer—what else was there to do, in those days at least, when an inhibited adolescent couldn't take refuge in the virtual worlds of the internet, what else was there to do but write?—or if it was precisely to write that he sought out that solitude, encouraging, by a tactic as twisted as it was calculated, the timidity and inhibition that ensured it, sparing him the company of friends whose games and obsessions little interested him, and the endless hunt for girls, desperate, frustrating, crowned with meager catches—minnows, immediately tossed back into the stream—to which most adolescences are limited. Shyness as an underhanded, socially acceptable form of withdrawal, not free of arrogance, that could well be: I take shelter behind the red screen of my blood, like a suicide, no one will come all this way looking for me. The shy child is not as helpless as people believe. He learns to know himself before he becomes mixed

Alas, that bold undertaking took up all my time, and I somewhat neglected (which is to say completely ignored) my official duties. Obviously I'd included my boss Bailiff Montségur among the very first evictees, but he was unmoved by my measures. It must be said that he was heavy as an ox, and even imagination faltered at the very thought of launching him into the heavenly void; even imagination, usually so mighty that it can lend a hand to faith and move mountains—it lugs the stones while faith takes on the surrounding emptiness—would have needed a winch. Not an image or an idealized simulacrum of a winch, but a real one, one that creaks, such as raises the fish-clogged nets on a tuna boat's prow.

Eventually Montségur looked into my papers and flew into a wild rage. His heavy hand landed on my shoulder and seized me by the collar, whereupon I felt his foot collide with my backside and picked myself up off the sidewalk as best I could, with no help from my defeated imagination, bruised and contused on every side, like a tomato fallen from the greengrocer's display, which nevertheless, however woeful its lot, must surely take comfort, or so at least I'd like to believe, in the thought that it has escaped the tedious company of the cauliflower.[30]

---

up with others. People immediately try to assimilate him to the group, mingle him with the gang—he retracts, he delights in the time that is his own, in no hurry to take on the role assigned him by his age, a well-integrated little creature, enslaved to social interactions, a role he's supposed to seize on and never let go of again. Something in him resists, refuses to give in, to give himself over, and since he can't storm out like an old bull, sign his letter of resignation and slam the door to this world, lacking the necessary forcefulness and assurance, besides which he has nothing to break off with, being engaged in nothing, bound by nothing, he spontaneously devises this stratagem: he will be shy, too busy biting his nails to exchange the handshakes that bind you forever to others. This little creature, evasive, apathetic, laconic, whose discomfort unsettles, who quickly discourages every attempt to approach and to tame him, is in fact full of a disdain and a haughtiness he's wise enough never to put to the test of reality. His solitude is a kingdom. He rules over it without rival, and for good reason. He has only to blush a little to keep others at a distance—his blood is boiling oil, molten lead, pitch, his entire head a red-hot cannonball. Then he will one day have to leave this scarlet paradise of childish self-love. A whole other story. Not easy. Habits have been formed, the habit of writing very possibly among them.

30 Such is indeed the place now reserved for the scrivener. The writer was of

(A guide raised her umbrella, and, like moths around a lamp, a throng
of tourists hovered around her, consenting to move in one solid block, in a

---

course always a loner by nature, but he long built, on the margins of society—to which for that reason he found himself consigned—bold literary constructions condemned at first to the incomprehension and censure of a society he defied, in anticipation of the new freedom to come, the beauty of tomorrow, in a language that made his contemporaries tremble and blush, the revelation of their narrow-mindedness being his very goal. He was a reprobate; he was feared; no one wanted to see or hear him. Today, the indifference he inspires is at best tinged with a vaguely amused pity. His sibylline logorrhea is tolerated as might be a madman's or a drunkard's. He speaks a language that has lost its hold over the real world, as impenetrable for non-readers as that of Montaigne or Du Bellay in the original. His vitriol spices up the world's insipidity to the same degree that a sugar cube dunked in the Atlantic alters the salinity of the seven seas. What's happening to literature is what happened to painting: no one gives a damn. It has no more reason to be. The talent is still there—just as you would surely find some excellent stage-coach drivers, if you wanted to go to the pointless trouble—but the written word has had its day: Mallarmé's *disabled bauble of reverberant vacuity*. Surely there's no lack of masterpieces, but no one gives a damn, that's the thing, what do we care about masterpieces? The very idea of the masterpiece seems faintly ridiculous to-day, as outmoded as the codpiece. It no longer belongs to this world. Are there not already monuments enough to keep us bored for all eternity? The writer is a sort of ghost who sometimes finds a few readers, ghosts themselves, who cannot recognize, lest they dissolve completely, that the castle they haunt is uninhabited, or at best converted into a museum, that their culture has become a chimera with no future, that the world wants nothing more to do with it—could not possibly care less—and is preparing to do without it entirely, that the schoolboy's yawn is an abyss into which all books disappear, that the new brain, still as capable to be sure, has developed other aptitudes, incompatible with reading, circuits of thought in which the heavy-freighted train of language derails. How still to believe that the circumstances propitious for the birth of a reader of Mallarmé or Blanchot might ever again come about? Literature no longer bites, no longer grips, no longer grabs—or still grips a little, grabs a little, like a shipwreck victim to the railing; but it's too heavy, it's worn out its welcome, feet crush its fingers. No longer does literature invade the real world like a hammered spike; rather, it begs to hold on to its place, it strives to take up as little room as possible. Its time has come and gone, all its attempts to adapt and make nice with its age work against it, hasten its death throes; any violence, revolt, and irony it had left fade in those bows and curtseys. How to go on believing in it? The author stubbornly keeps at it, he's too far in to give up, now more or less incapable of any other trade, but his literature is without illusions, sabotaged, suicidal. His homemade bomb fizzles in his hands, a dud bottle rocket. He writes as people immolate themselves when their goose is already cooked. And needless to say, he will refuse to grant that his desperately clear-sighted analysis of the situation betrays only his own weariness.

swarm, even if their wings might be singed, even if they had to abandon a perhaps hard-won freedom, obeying the injunction to look this way, then that way, happy to find in the stony vestiges proof that mankind had once lived and that a history had indeed unfolded in which he was the central character, the hero, reduced though he now be to an extra, forming with his fellows a group of photographers and visitors led along with a stick by a middle-aged windbag, nodding their heads where their horses once reared, as if the actors were suddenly interrupting the play to appraise the set and open an antique shop stocked with their own furniture.)

I know, I know: the cauliflower, before it is tragically reduced to a gratin, is not all that intolerable; its firm bulges are as pregnant with promise as an egg or a coconut. One should be able to extract great and good things from it, and indeed, its raw little bouquets lend themselves to the long, loud, thoughtful mastication of the sage or the bovine, the source of the noblest ideas, the boldest inventions, and the tenderest meat. I like to think that the recipe for trout amandine was created by a meditative cook absent-mindedly nibbling a cauliflower.

It's cooking, first of all, that's fatal to cauliflower, robbing it of its essential quality, its curvaceous density, to make of it that vegetal sponge engorged with dirty water. See how its color changes, from snowy white to urinous yellow: I call that a failed experiment. The ingredients then desperately thrown into the pot by the sorcerer's apprentice only make matters worse. The fiasco is complete, and the only decent and honorable thing to do would be to admit it and dump that sickening magma into the garbage—surely the electric toilet was not invented solely for the bastard pups of our flighty Frisette!—and then put a bullet in your brain. Instead of which, here is our little chemist as pleased with himself as if he'd transmuted lead into gold, convinced that he holds here his ticket to glory and has earned humankind's undying gratitude—and I can only throw up my hands and lay down my arms, in hopes of becoming a quadruped, for he does indeed reap that gratitude from his fellows!

So away from this place! Gallop off, far from him and from them! Nothing's holding me back, except trout amandine. Neither the leopard nor the horse ever eats it—so their lot isn't so enviable either.

Trout amandine, I know it well, oh I'm painfully aware of it, is my soft spot. That's how I can be captured and held. I weaken. I melt along with the tender mouthful. I'll take orders from anyone. A smile emblazons a crack into my morose face. I've been known to laugh. To sing! I've been known to dance! I have kissed the ground.[31]

---

31 *On a misunderstanding concerning my books* is the title of the author's contribution to an unpublished survey on the subject of irony, which he thinks it fitting to offer here *in extenso: There is not one ounce of irony in my books. Everything is stamped with the seal of truth, sincerity, and emotion. Allow me to say that I find it highly irritating, and even insulting, to be approached for this survey, as if I were one of those wiseasses who aim to seem smarter than they are by insinuating that their platitudes conceal dark abysses, or that they're yukking it up in the basement as we sit bored to tears in their living room, and even then they don't really think what they claim, in fact they think just the opposite, or the opposite of the opposite; and we're left spinning our wheels in that black snow, and if they say to us "good day," we must understand that their intention is to disturb our sleep ... Forgive me, but I am a simpler man than that, I like a firm, cordial handshake, a few heartfelt words, a brisk stinging cold in the winter, and the long summer sunsets. When I say white I mean white, when I say cat I mean cat, and when I say white cat I'm not talking about a mole. I despise allusion, ellipsis, double-entendre, antiphrasis; even euphemism and litotes are for me dissimulations as perverse as they are wearisome. Such things are a cover for a moth-eaten soul. I want a literature without hidden traps, without affectations, recording reality with a cold eye, like light itself. I want all that is written to have none but a literal meaning, like Larousse's definition of the chair, seat with a back and no arms, and when I plop down on it I don't want to find myself sitting on nettles. Irony burns only weeds, said Jules Renard. Let it begin by burning these! There is a repellent moral ugliness in irony; it's a form of cowardice trying to pass itself off as refinement. Sorry, I won't play along. You are completely mistaken about me. And if I sometimes dispense a little oil from my oilcan to give my sentences a bit more cohesion or tenderness, I save all my vinegar for my salads. I dip my asparagus into that vinegar, and my pen only into the beautiful black ink that shares in our sufferings and sorrows. The ironist would be nobody's fool, not his own, not other people's, not of words or the letters that make them up: he covers himself on all sides. He's a slippery eel, a perverse bastard who abuses the naiveté of young girls and the trusting innocence of his readers. You're supposed to read between the lines, you're not supposed to take his words at face value! Yes, but the thing is that I bought a book, and I'd like to be able to read what it says, in black and white. What would people think of an ironic baker who, in exchange for your little coin, rather than the promised baguette, pulls the old bait-and-switch and throws a custard pie in your face? And what am I supposed to do with a book in which everything that glitters is a lure, every tasty morsel mere bait? Not without reason do readers in love with the noblest sentiments—which, as everyone knows, are to be found in the hearts of surgeons who run their own clinics and the cleated shoe that launches good solid*

I am at peace with the world. I find good reasons for the existence of the nettle, the tarantula, I understand the need for evil, the lessons of sorrow—ah, what can you do, sometimes you've just got to have a war, in certain very specific contexts there are sound arguments for child slavery—I become magnanimous, infinitely benevolent.

I also like filet of trout in maltaise sauce with toasted nuts, but its effect on my outlook is not as decisive as trout amandine's. Deep inside me, a trace of dissatisfaction lingers. I remain repelled by a great many things. Trout amandine, on the other hand, brings me a bliss that I know only in its company, still troubled, alas, only by the never entirely banished threat of cauliflower gratin, which, as I've learned from experience, can at any moment, like an avalanche into a peaceful valley, land on the table in lumpy masses, sometimes even—O height of misfortune, unnamable heresy!—as a side-dish for trout amandine (yes, there are indeed such misguided cooks), and I must confess that the violence of my rage then surpasses the intensity of my pleasure by a thousand lengths, that all trout amandine's many virtues are one by one silenced and refuted by cauliflower gratin's potent counter-arguments—the trout says *finesse, tenderness,* the gratin answers *splatch* and then *splatch* and carries the day. The debate is over. The trout lies on its side, knocked flat. No negotiation is possible. A little flower

---

kicks down the middle—turn away in horror from those cold slabs of formal cynicism, which in the end attract only the complicitous snickers of misanthropic loners, morbid and repugnant, whose life is a succession of failures, of sexual fiascos, of letdowns and debacles. For the ironist, every emotion is suspect; he thinks himself expected to put on his act before the most profound or pathetic scenes of the human condition, those so wrenching that only our tears are pure enough to baptize the brow of the newborn, bathe the feet of the lover, or quench the thirst of the dying man. Ironist, take a good, hard look at yourself. Your dry smile is as false as that of the carp hooked by the fisherman, you need water, what's truly tormenting you is your insensitivity, your indifference, you're a man of paper, bloodless and two-dimensional, incapable of sympathy and knowing no tender caress but the wedgie and the Indian burn! And me, you take me for one of those sad specimens, thank you very much! You've understood nothing of my work! I write with my heart on my sleeve, sitting there like a little tamed tree frog. My skin is pink, my eyes are clear. Some people will find the look on my face a little simpering and inane. Better that than the horrid rictus of irony, that mask of Voltaire further hollowed out by Léautaud, soon to have no more cheeks at all. Not me, that's not me, to think otherwise is to misjudge me entirely. That anyone might think that of me plunges me into despair.

withers beneath ashes. Nothing remains of the intimate candlelit dinner but a puddle of wax. Your trout's backbone suddenly seems to have taken up arms for the cauliflower: it's the same yellowish loupe-like translucence that rolls up its eyes and elucidates nothing, the same tentacular, bristling complication. That comb is the ideal spoon with which to sip the hair soup stagnating in your bowl. The very flesh of the fish seems to you strangely fibrous and friendly with silt, the golden almonds bear a disturbing resemblance to little slices of gratinéed potatoes.

This is the proof that all delicacy is one day derided, defiled, corrupted.

This is the end of all hope.

(Then the crowd of history-and-culture-mad tourists dispersed. Shopping ho!)

There is nevertheless a moment, if you know how to seize it, before the threat of cauliflower gratin becomes a physical fact—most often, as is only right, but not always, not exclusively, in the form of a cauliflower gratin—a moment when trout amandine seems a possible alternative, it doesn't last long, you have to be there at the very moment that window opens, so you can rest your arms on the sill—as for climbing out to permanently take your place in the world it reveals, don't get your hopes up, that window's too far off the ground, you'd break your neck if you jumped; alas, we truly are imprisoned in this tower, itself most often concealed by the clouds of steam pouring from its *meurtrières*, and when those clouds finally thin or part, we can only stare into the inaccessible distance, whence deliverance might one day come, and as a matter of fact …

As a matter of fact, there's an army heading this way right now!

An army whose front ranks are now coming into view.

And that army's surrounding the tower.

All those obtuse helmeted heads, storming the tower: oh no!

An army of cauliflowers!

And nothing to defend ourselves with but sacks of potatoes, buckets of boiling béchamel.

Which is simply playing into the enemy's surprised and delighted hands.

Thus, even fairy tales end unhappily ever after in the sunlit land of lucid awareness.

But I swear to you, Mademoiselle, I kept the faith as long as I could, drawing on all the power of my imagination, all the earnestness of my will. There were such things as rivers. There were such things as almond trees. From their meeting could come delight and a new world order. I did what I could to encourage it; in the branches of the almond tree, I built a cozy little nest for the trout. Or else I cut down the fruit-laden tree at its roots, set it alight, and cast it into the stream.

Nothing came of these interventions.

I knew just what was needed, just what steps must be taken to make this world a better place for us all. My input was not welcomed. My opinions were thought irrelevant, my acts futile; I had no mastery over anything.[32] I was expected to finish my cauliflower gratin, period—and no leaving the table until I cleaned my plate.

Then they heaped on another ladleful.

Since I seemed to like it so much.

It was more than I could bear. I was doing justice to everything I most despised.

But that, Mademoiselle, is how we struggle in cages and traps, clutching chamois cloths, feather dusters, and ceiling mops in our fists.

More! More!

And indeed, we have two cheeks and two buttocks, to taste of our punishment twice.

Could I be suspected of a secret affection for cauliflower gratin?

Meaning that my anger is merely an extravagant lyrical variation on the proverb *To punish well is to love well*? Because only my unbounded anger could fully express my secret hunger for cauliflower gratin?

Unable to admit to that craving, I defile what I adore—that blas-

---

32 Recognizing himself here beneath the traits of his character, the author is seriously considering taking himself to court.

phemous rage betrays only the ardency of my faith?[33]

That's how you've come to see me, isn't it? A hypocrite who, at nightfall, a cape drawn over his face, steals into smoky cellars where a few would-be sophisticates and actually-are tubs of lard, naked save

---

[33] Might the same be true of the animosities claimed by the author, who will surely be the only one to take his character at his word? He does not doubt that people will try to tease out the sense of his allegory; it will be translated, recast in plainer language, clearer terms, and he will be credited with intentions nobler than those here asserted—because really, a whole book against cauliflower gratin, what a ridiculous conceit, it's not credible, not for a second. Or else, despite what he says, his character really has escaped his grasp, and bad luck, that character was no Ahab, no Rastignac, no Raskolnikov. And a character who escapes escapes like a Freudian slip, like an *acte manqué*. So this is the best the author could unwittingly loose on the world: a maniacal little monster with a stunted, narrow mind, a habit of droning on about nothing, the appetite of a sparrow. No, the reader will surely prefer to see all this as an allegory, and will struggle to decipher it: that cauliflower gratin can only be a metaphor for the good old-fashioned novel still stewing in the kitchens of our literature. Not at all, he will answer himself, its meaning must be broader than that, and deeper: cauliflower gratin stands for the quagmire in which our lives are stranded, held back by the mediocrity of human ambitions, by the boredom we exude for lack of imagination, because we're driven only by the urge to further our own interests, our own comfort, because we aspire to satisfy only those desires closest our bodies, to appease the crudest appetites, a primitive, undiscriminating hunger; once that's been sated, digesting becomes our sole occupation, toward which all our forces are bent, to make room for the evening meal. No, no, no, oh no, he will correct himself, it goes further than that, a great deal further: cauliflower gratin represents our very condition, life in its essence, the world in its cruel indifference—we struggle with a mortal body in a perilous jungle, all our noble efforts, our courage, our valor can't keep us from dying in the end (often even long before), difficulty is reborn as we overcome it, trouble is always directly ahead of us, the work done still to be done; no progress is possible—apart from growing old. Then the reader will put forward other hypotheses, and he will not be wrong. Is a reader ever wrong? The author, friend to the prolific, divinely-named Polysemia, will obviously not render a verdict. Perhaps he is settling his scores with a minuscule demon, an obscure enemy he alone knows. Perhaps he despises celery remoulade and has rather deftly transposed his loathing, giving it a more trivial motivation; which would make of his book an ironic satire that lies about its object the better to destroy it, sparing itself a tiresome, sterile debate over its premise. Perhaps he himself doesn't know what it's about, and intoxicates himself with his outrage as one might with pure form, a literary ecstasy with no other aim than to affirm a possible life in language, freed of all the contingences and physical laws that make of us simple corks bobbing in the current. Or perhaps…

the napkin tied around their loins, indulge until dawn in vile orgies, rolling and tromping with porcine grunts through basins brimming with cauliflower gratin, guzzling and devouring, unashamed to graze on each other's armpits if tempting morsels happen to be hiding there. And then, in the early morning light, they pull on their strictly-tailored suits, drape themselves in their rumpled, dour dignity, and all day long publicly affect the deepest hatred for their secret vice.

Really, is that what you think? You find my loathing for cauliflower gratin overblown, disproportionate, almost deranged, and so, to your mind, it is either the sign of a serious mental disorder or, more likely—since in every other way I strike you as a logical, coherent, not to mention tiresome man—a cover for my secret turpitude, as well as a means of never straying too far from the object of my passion: through trickery and intrigue, through perverse machinations, I transform my amorous obsession into hatred, for bellowing my hatred in its face still means clinging to it, still means seeing it—its scaly skin, its flabby flesh—still means inhaling its cloying, captivating scent, and the blows with which I pummel it, crater it, those too mean touching it, sinking in my hands, the violence that tenderness abhors offering me at long last a true full-body union, a clinch that brings the whole being to spasms of bliss, not just its most delicate sphincter. So profound is my love for cauliflower gratin that I must embrace it to a pulp, feeling the object of my love where it is least resistant, beneath its scaly skin, in the folds of its flabby flesh: touching its most intimate depths! Enough of superficial caresses, of simpering sentiment and silly candlelit idylls, clenched fists and insults would offer me access to its quivering heart: I strike it so as to know it utterly undone, pitiful, and then to offer it my rescue and consolation—all the while putting on a devious act, shielded by the honorable façade confirmed, in the eyes of the world, by my averred predilection for trout amandine, that fodder for fussy gastronomers, so called because they keep their telescopes trained on their navels, that vastly overrated fish that hasn't seen the inside of a flowing stream for ages, but swaps oily bubbles with the carp in sewers and industrial lagoons, gorging itself on heavy metals as if conscientiously arming itself to duel the fork and knife of its predator, stunned to find it so resistant.

(From a transparent plastic sleeve, a man was extracting bank statements, mortgage certificates, administrative correspondence. He anxiously shuffled those attestations of his social existence, as if one were still missing, an ontological certification, for example, an official document, duly stamped, confirming his status as a living being.)

Now, my dear young lady, I don't mean to be disagreeable, but allow me to inform you that you are out of your puny little mind. Forgive me, but I believe you're letting yourself be carried away by your deductions, deep into a tunnel so narrow that not even a ferret could find you.

Sometimes I wonder if you're even listening to me.

I wonder if you're carefully weighing the sense of my words.

Would you like me to raise my voice?

Because you really have to be pretty goddamn obtuse, if not stunningly unjust, to hear in my words a paean to cauliflower gratin! Go hail your sovereign with such poetry, and see if he showers you with gold.

Of all human inventions, cauliflower gratin is the most unjustifiable, the most depressing, the most destructive—have I made myself clear at long last? Alas, I don't believe irony enters into that vulgar recipe, unappealing as a witch's gruel: if you find any wit in there, it can only be half a newt, dumped in along with its eye. No double meaning, save to repeat in a graver tone what has already been said outright—just as cauliflower gratin's false bottom, what a real estate agent would call a full basement, is crammed to the rafters with still more cauliflower. No point digging into it: the archeologist not put off by mud will bring up only the remnants and residues of earlier gratins, whose crude archaism is proof enough that there's been no progress since, that man very early learned all there was to know of it. And immediately dropped it, like a hot potato, never to take it up anew. Contrarily to his natural impulse in every domain, just this once he saw no point in improving or at least amending that crude prototype. As if he thought there were no room for improvement. Which I am willing to grant, Mademoiselle, yes I am. That there was nothing to be salvaged I am in fact fully convinced. And I will concede, too, that it was beyond our competence, or our incompetence, which also has its limits, to make that mess any worse. Rarely, no doubt, does an idea find its definitive form at the moment of its birth, with no tweaks required; such was the case with cauliflower gratin. One would perhaps have liked to see man suddenly stand up, or at least recoil in dismay, and renounce that unfortunate discovery of his own accord. He was after all quite capable of consigning the pillory, the guillotine, and the bludgeon to his attic.

For that matter, it is not impossible that he sought to do just that.

The gratin held fast, with its gift of sticking to whatever it touches, to the point of molecular bonding. No one knows if it eats away at those surfaces or takes root in them; but no, it interweaves with them, like lichen, it infuses them, like a dead leaf—nothing that flies is ever beyond its reach: the seagull ends up pathetically mired in it. No beyond, no way out, not even for the eye alone. For those are indeed cauliflower gratin vapors rising laboriously into the heavens, like a morbidly obese tenant climbing to his mansard rooms, who pauses breathlessly on each step, who stagnates on every landing for an hour or two, eventually forming that blanket of puffy clouds that stall our dreams, our prayers, and our rockets. We instinctively raise our eyes to seek help, to beg for assistance, and that's the only azure and light we discover, that's the only hope hanging over our heads: still more cauliflower!

(Paid by humanitarian agencies to drain the pensions of vulnerable old ladies, young men in gaily colored jackets were energetically accosting the passersby, deploying, for all their earnest anti-globalist faces, complete with dreadlocks and piercings, the methods of the most cynical market capitalism: a sales pitch carefully tailored to its prey, the establishment of an authority over that prey with slick words and smooth talk, drawing on the power of language to manipulate their victims into a sense of guilt and a sort of urge to buy. And oh, the sad, defeated faces of those who ended up signing a pledge to get out of their clutches!)

And then, and then.

And then I went away.[34]

That's right, Mademoiselle, I who sit here before you, I've seen dawn break over Irfûr, over the pink frost of the Emplâtre valley, when the humped budiles' guttural rutting wrenches you from the deep sleep you fell into when your glass of razou capsized and you gently slid off the two-footed stool that the old men can sit on all day long with scarcely a wobble, peeling fat water onions, which they chew slowly and thoughtfully while the women, wrapped in spotless yellow drapery, embroider flowered fields on featherbeds stuffed with curcula down, curculas being eaten as mere chicks, skewered on the fine blades of the spinglets that, once sated, the men wipe clean under their armpits before picking fights for any reason that comes to mind, for the simple pleasure of the brawl, unless, that is, they unsheathe their flutes—made from *twelve*, a reed that grows abundantly on the banks of the little runnels and that can also be woven into chairs, necklaces, curtains, hats, tents that in summertime form cool villages

---

34 Whereas the author would never do such a thing, would never react in such a way. He is not unaware of the beauty of this world, which he can contemplate for hours at a time from his windowsill. The view is nothing to sneeze at, opening as it does onto the heavens as well, the star-speckled universe. But he has a passion for the sedentary life, awaking early each morning in the same bed, the limpid brook flowing in unstanchable rivulets through pipes judiciously distributed along the walls, the old couch, broken down like an old horse that's been around the block more than once. His wandering thought twists its yarn of sentences in his skull, refuses to let itself be distracted by the spectacle of this profuse world, its unceasing solicitations, its extravagant richness—how to absorb all those jolts? And yet he has traveled, reluctantly, gripped by a profound unease. His foot has trod the soil of four of the five continents, always hesitant, as if venturing onto a footbridge of rotting planks suspended over the void. How to absorb all those jolts without falling to pieces, how to remain yourself when your every move is a false start? How to casually insinuate your gray existence into the crowd of saris and boubous? He relies on the same rationalization to explain his complete lack of aptitude for languages. Not one word of English after fifteen years' study! My mind will have nothing to do with it, he claims, for fear that my style might lose its acuity, tempted by the nuances of synonymy in other tongues, and that its concern for precision might thus paradoxically precipitate it into a Babelian babble and confusion. Yet another sophism, the widow Nisard would retort, one more ruse in the guise of an excuse. And what does it cost you to confess to something you can't go to jail for?

beneath the blazing sun—and, along with their erstwhile opponents, perform a sweet, crystalline duo that will echo off the towering vertical walls of the nearby Mi-Kun, the color of a long beet, of which it is said here that with every revolution of the earth its peak pierces a new crater on the moon, and go on echoing until the next day, whereupon it will be the flies that launch into their routine in the mountainous cirques, and their buzzing will grow ever louder, slowly becoming vibrations, then palpable tremors, which displace—and here arise more occasions for duels and disputes—the wooden pieces on the board used for the game of *bou*, to which people here passionately devote themselves from childhood on, laying offerings of game and fruit on the sacred stone to gain the backup of the gods, but not hesitating to poison those foods when victory slips through their fingers or the fishing is bad, the entire local economy relying on that activity, which the locals practice by heaving huge cakes of salt into the runnels with levers; the poisoned fish float to the surface and are then clubbed unconscious and hauled to land by means of long poles fitted with a transverse paddle, not unlike our croupier's rakes, and it's a heart-wrenching sight, for the most common fish in these runnels is the *krujåc* (etymologically, the fish that speaks), which argues in vain for its very real incomestibility and the defenseless alevins it's leaving behind in the depths, and its pleading tone will bring tears to your eyes, but it is nonetheless captured like the others—its barbels are woven into chairs, necklaces, curtains, hats, tents that in summertime form cool villages beneath the blazing sun, and its gigantic single eye is used to make jewels, cushion ornaments, and aphrodisiac unguents—and sold in the marketplace, hung by the lip with its uncles and brothers on hooks suspended from a rod, still wriggling feebly, and thus fanning the merchants sweating in their woolen bonnets—if you've never felt the summer heat on the Onthracia plateau, you have no right to complain of the discomfort of high temperatures—as you gaze into the vast, endless landscape overlooking this little square of gray sand: the poplars like halberdiers flanking the glistening parade of the river as it snakes through the gold-tinged stubble fields, as black gorse covers the plain straight to the horizon, as a flock of starlings suddenly takes flight like a column of smoke, as the budiles resume their rutting, their husky brays punctuated by the tinkle of their rhythmically shaking sonnatels, as the air fills with the fresh scents of nocturnal mint and plaited lupine (used to make chairs, necklaces, curtains, hats, and even tents, which in summertime form cool villages beneath the blazing sun), as tranquility descends from the heavens with the shadow of night, as the moon lights its cigarette by the last flames of the setting sun, yes Mademoiselle, and then I came back.[35]

---

35 The author calls his character to heel. Get back here. Nevertheless, he himself did once set off on a journey with another of his creatures, a few years ago, to Africa, to Mali. More precisely, he made that voyage *as a character* (his emphasis), a tactic conceived to help him overcome his fear of the unknown. And so that character, saddled with the gaudy sobriquet *Red Ear,* consequently and contrarily to all the others, went on living after the journey and the book had come to an end. He can thus reappear in these footnotes without incongruity, to serve as a foil for this book's fictive character, to counterbalance him with the living figure of a being of flesh and blood. Here then, in its proper place, is the *Supplement to the Voyage of Red Ear.*

It's a small town famed for its white, round little anise candies, a hilly town, deserted this Sunday, famed for its fresh, aromatic little anise candies, a gray town on this overcast Sunday, whose sweet, exquisite little anise candies are enjoyed even in distant lands, and indeed one can scarcely imagine anything but the wondrous sight of an avalanche of those white, round, fresh little anise candies cascading through those hilly streets, bouncing merrily over the cobblestones, that might distract the citizens and occasional visitors from the seductive temptation of suicide. Nevertheless, the passing stranger who has the idea or reflex to look up, seeking some way out of this pit of despair before the gathering black clouds seal it off forever, will perhaps encounter the fixed gaze of a man standing at his windowpane, and the existence of that life in this dead town will intrigue him enough that he forgets for a few moments the ambient gloom.

That man is Red Ear, the explorer, back from Africa, who now and forevermore observes the world from his bedroom window.

And immediately backs away, realizing he's been spotted. He really must buy a tulle curtain, he keeps telling himself, behind which he would be invisible from the street, or at least reduced to a blur, and thereby relieved of the weight and encumbrance of his body, with no concomitant slackening of his vigilance, which would on the contrary only grow keener, once rid of that self-consciousness forever forced on him by others, the passersby, those unfortunately inspired to raise their heads when they're under his window. Behind that tulle curtain, a light, liberating shroud, he would see without being seen as the world modestly goes about its business in those hilly little streets, without him, back from Africa, now withdrawn into that room, on the third floor of the family house he inherited, still redolent with the smells of his childhood, long since gone stale, old egg, old garlic, old dust.

But Red Ear thrives in that mud, in that stench, among the cockroaches, his hidden sisters, which inherited the house along with him, in joint ownership.

But in order to buy that curtain he'd have to go out again, venture into the streets, deal with a shopkeeper so as to deal no more with this world, and not forget to ask about the rod, because everything goes together in these things: the curtain, the rod, you can't have one without the other; the curtain without the rod is the heavens collapsed onto a devastated field, a landscape of ruins and fog peopled by dim spectral forms, while the rod without the curtain skewers you like a chicken behind the glass of the rotisserie. It would seem, then, that the prerequisite for withdrawing from the world is to expose yourself to it in the most visible and ridiculous manner, a curtain rod under your arm, and that no withdrawal or isolation is possible without that prior public humiliation.

If I at least had the curtain, I could roll myself up in it, Red Ear tells himself, cursing his lack of foresight.

Still living up to his African nickname beneath this leaden sky, in the boredom of November and the house where he was born, now his once more. He gently wiggles his big white feet in his rope-soled sandals—a pointless sport: the blood never drains from his ears. A tagged dog, recognizable in any pack, returned to his masters. To the doghouse. The old homestead welcomes him into its shadows, into the junkshop of memories. He sits in his father's armchair: the illusion is complete. It's him. The same man. Procreation is an absurd repetition. The role is handed down from father to son. That wooden armchair could well be the off-spring of his father's. A chip off the old block. Red Ear revels in this immobility. He moves less than ever in his father's body, and that suits him perfectly.

His only fear is that he might consequently have to be born again.

Red Ear has thus chosen immobility, which is to say going so fast that you're already back. He's packed his bags: stores of canned and frozen foods. If he rations himself, he can hold out for six years, by his calculations. He won't even have to raise wild goats. Fully aware of the threat, as a man who has braved every peril, he exposes himself to the danger of scurvy. Such is the life of the conquistadors. A risk you have to take. He's seen worse. At least he knows he's protected from tempests, from shipwrecks, from pirate cannons. He's also disconnected his doorbell. Sometimes a salesman knocks on his door, himself sounding the three blows of the call to battle-stations. Well barricaded inside, Red Ear doesn't even jump. He stoically ensures that the door to his room is locked tight. He wedges the back of a chair under the knob.

Then crawls under his bed.

His arms stick close by his body. His hand has to be there to mop his brow, light his cigarette. His feet never leave each other's side. He makes little use of them. They seize the occasion to rub elbows a bit. Get to know each other. In Africa they were always apart. Each going its own way. Often, now, they take off their sandals. They like being together, two lovers interlacing digits. Red Ear can gaze at them for hours, deeply moved. What are they saying to each other? They're reminiscing about the ocher dust of the footpaths, the flat, burning hot stones on the bank of the Niger, the merry leaps they made in the circle of dancers. They've put all that behind them. Now they would gladly let themselves be cast in bronze, they wouldn't stomp off in a huff, they'd be perfectly happy on marble soles.

Cozily closed up in his house, Red Ear does not intend to expose the statue of the explorer to the four winds, nor to the insults of the pigeons.

But he has the joy of finding his reflection in the glass when night falls, a rendezvous he would never miss, at any price. That appearance fills him with delight every time. The night of the ages swallows up the façade of the antiquarian across the street, and suddenly there he is, open and innocent, like an archangel. His fat face replaces those of the many passersby glimpsed in the course of the day, which ended up coalescing into one single scowl. Whereas he always wears a benevolent smile. And a fresh rush of blood empurples his ears. He prefers nights without moon or stars, nothing to hamper his pure contemplation. So he doesn't flee all company, as we might have thought.

He seeks out his own with the insistence of an intrusive bore.

So much for the character, and so much for the plot. The setting is a room papered with little pink flowers, long since withered. But the damp has encouraged the germination of enough molds and mildews to make an exuberant springtime all the same. Red Ear stands out against that verdant background, like a pheasant. You can't miss him. Sometimes he wanders into the house's other rooms, but those expeditions have grown rarer and rarer. They bring only disappointment, nothing worth the rigors of the voyage. He has little taste now for rising at dawn. Dragging heavy trunks mile after mile has lost all its charm. Of the path under my feet and the heavens above, I know only the mudpuddle I'm mired in, Red Ear concludes.

It's an illusion to believe that one's being espouses the distance and duration of the voyage.

Red Ear has burned all his bridges. Now he stands atop his column. The paint on his ceiling is flaking, sketching out an intricate network of lines, ramifications, atlas enough for the immobile traveler. There are Indians on the banks of those rivers, savage tribes with unknown customs and odd ways, the tarantula and the ocelot their foes. Those trails head into salt deserts where thirst worries it won't find any pepper. Those roads lead to bustling capitals, those little paths vanish into snowy expanses, any point on the earth can be reached by those dirt paths wending their way over taigas, pampas, savannahs, steppes, hedged pastures …

I've got to get that repainted, Red Ear tells himself.

Is there then no peace to be found at home? Noise comes up from the street as well. The town is livelier during the week. Sometimes a potential customer enters the antique dealer's. Sometimes that potential is realized, and he emerges with a side table, an ox yoke, a bust of Napoleon. Nonetheless, many of the objects on display have been there at least since Red Ear first pressed his nose to his window, that top hat, that rocking horse, that clock, exhibited there perhaps from the beginning, brand-new at the time, never finding a taker. The townspeople's comings and

Having failed to find in my travels the distraction I sought. Everywhere I went, cauliflower gratin recalled itself to my mind. It was cauliflower gratin awaiting me in the peat bogs of Khanzar, in the shifting dunes of the desert of Tumb, in the drool of the reveling crab of the Far Empire, in the spume on the shores of the inland sea of Irthruria. It poured down the slopes of the Mongwi, it gathered in the sky over Townville. It was cauliflower gratin that emanated from the woolly, steaming fur of the rutting budiles, as if born like an instant offspring of their filthy hindquarters' thrusts, and the ritual crucifixions of overweight eunuchs in the Loche valley evoked, once again and as always, that same vile crucifer: everywhere its ghost was watching for me, sometimes a sour smell, a limp blow, a stubborn, pernicious unease—there it was.

Meanwhile, the delicate counterweight of trout amandine was most often nowhere to be seen in all my travels, as if I could eat it only from my own plate. For I know my plate's ways, its environs, I know every road leading to it. A virtual double wall—virtual, but for that reason ideal, insurmountable—forbids all access. Atop it two sentinels make their vigilant rounds, pacing in opposite directions. I've armed them with machine guns and grenades. They have orders to shoot on sight. Greengrocers' trucks and carts are meticulously searched before they can deliver their loads. Nothing gets waved through. Sacks of rice are punctured with a bayonet, soups are strained and analyzed.

---

goings are a wearying distraction. Where are they bound? And why in divergent directions? Rare are those who wander aimlessly. Most have places to go. They hurry along. But often those hurrying along the day before are hurrying along again the next day at the same time. Going nowhere.

Is Red Ear the only one who's reached his goal?

If you've just got to go home again, why leave? Red Ear basks in his own warm but discreet presence. Anyone else would only further encumber him in this modest room. As for him, he moves about in it effortlessly, never colliding with himself or getting in his way. Sometimes he's not sure he's there himself, so open and clear is the space before him. His father's armchair, a bed, and an armoire are furniture enough for one who has spent a part of his life in Africa. A sink bolted to the wall also serves as laundry and bathtub. And the watering hole where this wild beast comes to drink. The scurvy rations are piled up in the hallway, next to the door. That's where Red Ear takes his meals, sitting at a little table. He owns a pot and a hotplate, a dish and a handful of silverware.

Cloistered at home, every exit bolted, Red Ear flees himself no longer.

And in spite of all that, Mademoiselle, can you believe it, the barricades have sometimes been breached, most often by ruse, by false promises, and a dumptruck has loosed its load of cauliflower gratin onto my plate. Someone had corrupted my men, perhaps plied them with strong drink, even concealed the trough and its contents beneath the grapefruit or melons of the hors-d'oeuvre.

Happily, such misadventures are rare nowadays. I doubled the watch, I trained my dogs to sniff out that poison behind the cloak of perfume—and then take the miscreants by the throat. Some of them never rise again. I know just where to bury them, and in what. You don't have to look far. You don't even have to dig. You just lay out the body, and in it sinks. There, perhaps, is a suitable outlet for cauliflower gratin, in spite of its horrors, one that would greatly ease the working conditions of gravediggers: just peel back the browned skin on the surface—but using the blade of a stout shovel, all the same—then drop it and tamp it back into place like a lid (for the occupation will remain an arduous one, reserved for the most hardened souls and stomachs).

I'm just throwing out that idea. I have no illusions. I can already hear the hue and cry. In any case, now no one can claim I do nothing but carp, and never offer solutions.

Still, those cemeteries. Imagine them in the moonlight. Then choose to reserve the dark earth for our crops and our gardens.

Speaking of which, you're still waiting for me to get to the murder. Patience, I'm coming to that.

Anyway, all things considered and despite the occasional mishap, my plate is rarely befouled, and remains for me a clearing in the tangled, swampy forest of crucifers.

For trout amandine, too, it makes a safe harbor.

Every flick of that spangled fish's tail leads to it, from the roe and the milt onward, and if it braids the silver strand of its swim to the current of the glimmering stream, it's because my plate lies at the far end, white and clean; it's the target of that arrow that never misses the heart, the moon aimed for by that rocket. Split open, the trout applies its two profiles to it, as if on a glorious medallion.

For it was my plate spun from china clay; for that trout was it kilned and then stamped all around the rim with a slender band of gold.

My plate was awaiting the trout to deserve the name of holy host.

(There were few old men, and countless old women. The disparity was becoming flagrant, disturbing. Hard to know how to explain this imbalance, this longevity of women so insolently greater than men's, now that the latter rarely died in the mines, now that the former worked in the same professions and indulged in the same risky, hedonistic pastimes. A suspicion was growing, which no one dared put into words: women overcame their husbands. They wore them out. They killed them over a slow flame.)

I couldn't just stand idly by. My thoughts turned to armed rebellion.

The rule I'd established in my plate, a modest dominion governed by harmony and order, could perhaps, I thought, be extended to the world around me. Rather than going through life eternally besieged, selfishly encamped in my stronghold, why not radiate out from it, and, like Rome, widen my circle of influence?

It was time to drive cauliflower gratin over the horizon.

Kick it out.

Push it back to the sea.

I embarked on a study of the great military campaigns of history. I read *The Art of War*. I wearied my imagination with marches and countermarches, roused at the crack of dawn by a bugle. I gave myself a crew cut. I too took to shopping for clothes at the army surplus.[36]

---

36 With the repeal of obligatory military service, a whole slice of popular oral literature has vanished—but literature is clearly the last thing on our leaders' minds when they're making ill-conceived decisions such as this! The tales of military service our uncles served up at dinner between the cheese and the pear (at the author's house, the cheese preceded the pear) will soon be as obsolete as the fireside chat. Which is why, the author having belonged to the last generation of lucky conscripts, he will now step into the opening his character is innocently giving him—much obliged, son, I'll take it from here—to tell the tale of his own military service, so as to edify a youth short on points of reference, deprived of that precious rite of passage, that mainstay of a social bond that we now see irremediably unraveling. Come back with me, then, to October 1987. A month earlier, the author published his first book, *Dying Gives Me a Cold*. Life is beginning—his

words are finally appearing in print. But he is now inducted, not far from Saumur. And there, lads, hold on to your hats: the quartermaster issues him his kit. Soon there will be precious few of you who can boast of so savage a feat of derring-do: the quartermaster issues him his kit. The author, who has not opened his mouth since his arrival at the base, refuses to take it and sits down in a hallway with *Don Quixote*. Prodding has no effect. We'll deal with this tomorrow, when the Captain's here. The Captain! He joins his fellow disciples in the barracks. He's assigned a bed and a locker. He lies down on his back. Then comes lights out. And here a miracle occurs. Brushing the ground, his hand encounters a small, hard object: a rough shard of glass, hardly sharp at all, but enough, all the same, to plant an audacious idea in the vigilant soldier's fevered brain. Incredible, that gift for improvisation you acquire in the heat of a campaign, when the enemy's swarming all around and the ammunition's run out. The night is long when you're facing that peril. The author does not sleep. There will be bloodshed at dawn. A few minutes before reveille, the valiant warrior gingerly slashes his left wrist, not cutting the veins but clenching his teeth. The blood begins to flow, and he spreads it as far and wide as he can, stains his sheets with it. By God, things are heating up! Then he feigns semi-consciousness. The lights go on. From the next bed comes a cry, and everyone assumes battle stations. The hero is carried off, letting a weak moan filter through his lips: *Don't worry about me, try to save yourselves*. A real slice of the military life. The wound is superficial; still, it was a close call, the shell just missed him, and the chief of staff thinks it best to entrust the casualty to the army hospital, psychiatric division, for observation. The quartermaster issues him his kit: a pair of pale blue pyjamas, a white terrycloth bathrobe, stained, unspeakable—that uniform has seen its share of sweat and tears, if not blood—and a pair of brown corduroy slippers two sizes too small. His not to reason why; this time he accepts the costume. Thus garbed, he'll have no trouble perfecting his social misfit act: finally a true-to-life character. His hospital mates are half genuinely suicidal, half malingerers. Not easy to tell them apart. The author's neighbor has nonetheless tacked up a photo of his grandfather on his deathbed, and day after day his mother brings him a bag filled with his impressive collection of fossils and minerals: that one's not leaving anything to chance. Less ambitious, the author still stubbornly refuses to speak. Not one word escapes his lips. Meanwhile, the psychiatrist overseeing his case has caught wind of the reviews of his book, now beginning to appear in the press. He has some difficulty reconciling the specter shuffling through the halls with the promising young writer hailed by the critics for his vivacious humor. He's seen a great many things, but this case intrigues him. *Dying Gives Me a Cold, really* ... What's that supposed to mean? Don't you have to be a little bit off to come up with such nonsense? A discharge board meets once a week, their task to decide the fate of the patients in their care. If they see through his simulation, the author will be found guilty of disobedience and sentenced to six months in prison, after which, like it or not, he'll still have to do his military service. The psychiatrist hesitates, stalls, lets three weeks go by without reaching a decision. An amazing coincidence: another patient has also published a book,

But mine was a lonely struggle, closer to guerilla warfare. The army is on the side of the gratin: they gratinée on a major scale. Besides, their equipment was ill-suited to my plan of attack.

Rather, I chose a snowplow.

Oh what a beautiful device! what a powerful machine!

What a vehicle!

Its sharp edge scraping the bottom of the dish, the blade clears a straight, tidy path we could walk barefoot, a path that can only lead to another world, this one inhabitable—no more will our innocence be ceaselessly humiliated and wronged.

Yes, Mademoiselle, I naively dreamed of exile in the wonderful land of Utopia. A clement and hospitable land, unwelcoming only to the crucifer, whose sprout withers like the owl's chick in a hundred-watt bulb, like the baby viper in the breast of the mongoose, like the stringy son of the jellyfish on the burning hot beach pebble. There is nothing in the wonderful land of Utopia that we don't already know, only the selection is more exacting, less indulgent: cauliflower gratin is not cooked there.

And I was rolling that dream around in my poor head, pierced on either side, incapable of holding it in, for, contrary to popular opinion, the orifices of our sensory organs are just as liable—even more!—to

---

Bubu, a horrible yellow book that he keeps compulsively clutched to his chest. That one really does seem in bad shape. He mumbles incessantly, walks from one wall to the other, smacks into it, presses against it, pushes off with his buttocks and sets off again. Is La Pensée Universelle a serious publishing house? the psychiatrist asks the author, evidently unaware that it's a notorious vanity press. The author refuses to make common cause with the doctor against that companion in sorrow, who, he thinks, expresses the absurdity of his situation better than he himself ever could. Besides, it could be a trap. The psychiatrist is trying to test his reason. The author maintains his silence; it is after all in silence that universal thought flourishes most abundantly. Finally, after three weeks, the psychiatrist summons him to his office. He intimates that he's seen through his act, but that he is nonetheless not the stereotypical brute that the author, in his immaturity, in his ignorance, in his pathetic arrogance, most likely sees in all military folk—and to prove it he releases him, returns him to civilian life, to what he hopes are the grateful arms of literature, with the shameful rank of *P4*, thanks to which he will never find work in the civil service. He'll survive. *P4*—but the ear of the author, red with shame like the nose of the clown, hears in that label only a riddle: What is *P4?* P is for pansy.

leak as they are to capture and record external phenomena. Through those holes we discharge our loveliest notions, they drain out of us, to be immediately absorbed by the sponge of reality—only then can our head, now empty again, be invaded, stuffed, crammed with reality's sinister visions: thus, in my snowplow's rear-view mirror, I looked back at the inescapable hell through which I thought I'd cleared a path for our frolics and, by way of avalanches, slippages, gangrenous proliferation, saw it taking shape anew.

Quick as a ship's foaming wake, the trail I'd blazed was disintegrating behind my back.

The back never was a good guardian for our conquests. Blind and mute, it never keeps a close eye on them. Although fitted with arms like everyone else, it can only fold its hands over its belly and let things take their course. Most often it chooses to flee. In truth, I suspect it of betraying us, of working behind the scenes to undo us. It pushes us toward the grave, where it's no doubt hoping for a nice lie-down. At its hands, everything we've so patiently, tirelessly, enthusiastically built suffers the same sad fate as it inflicts on the tomato and the apple, bite into them though we did as if into life itself, marveling at their wholesomeness, their sweetness, it corrupts all of that, makes of it an object of ridicule, turns it into turds, little turds that it expels and sows with tedious labors or nauseating ease, and not without delighting in the one as much as the other, not without a sort of abject pride, perceptible in the rictus of our sphincters, and there, in the end, is all that remains of our passage.

We embrace the world, our arms and faces open, we caress bodies, furs, pelts, we breathe deep of the fresh air of the mountains, the sea, we make our way through the green and the blue, our sexes vibrate like antennae—everywhere are springs, hives, gold, beds of sand or snow—we ardently partake of all that to be part of it, we intervene gently and thoughtfully, we clear brush, we shape stones; gifted with science and music, our fingers sift through raw materials, currents, vital principles, sort seeds and chicks—and behind our backs, in the end, all that simply falls back to earth—all that passion, that ingenuous ingenuity, that good will, our back can only counter it all with a skeptical sneer—turds, it says, it can only say, guano, excrement, droppings, it repeats, for we can grant it this: it's got a rich vocabulary, as power-less, unproductive, cowardly people often do, it's even got a name for the pharaonic endeavors of the sun-spangled child: caca.

(A distance had settled in between the spouses. They were drifting apart. The ravages of time, we diagnosed, with a touch of fatalism. Then suddenly, miraculously, they came together again ...)

I'd met her, and she pegged me at once as an easy mark and an ideal victim for her sadistic fantasy.

Had I not naively bared my soul to her concerning my immoderate fondness for trout amandine?

Had I not above all confessed—and thereby handed her the club with which to bash me—my deep loathing for cauliflower? And particularly cauliflower gratin—and thereby invited her to drown me in the muck.

At that moment, I'm sure, her plan was decided, and over the many years she spent by my side, I'm sure, she took an endlessly protracted pleasure in perfecting the details, in forever putting off the moment of action.

I was thus her dupe and her plaything all along.

Since that's where it ended up, that's where it was headed from the start.

I who placed all my faith in her, I who had no idea what was coming!

Thus, the enemy pursued me into my most private moments: it inhabited my safe harbor.

I loved her.

(... It's a miracle, suddenly they were together again, side by side, two become one, just like the best of the good old days, but this time beneath an umbrella.)

I've tried everything.

Behind me the cauliflower is growing back, a flood of béchamel sauce spreading far and wide, beneath the baking sun.

And once again I'm surrounded.

Once again left, with disgust my sole companion.

There is only the trout, so rare. And rarer still strewn with almonds.

Before me, behind me, and all around as well, cauliflower gratin.

As pervasive as kelp in the ocean, larches on the Alpine foothill, moon rocks on the moon.

And since I'd turned my eyes to the heavens, I cried out to God, it was worth a try.

After all, I know a guy who gets rid of burns and warts just by laying on his hands. I didn't really believe in that either at first.

But it works.

My prayer rose up.

Oh God!

My God![37]

---

37 *To be closer to God*, the author replied in his first job interview, when asked by the parish priest why he aspired to be a choirboy. Excellent answer: the lad was hired on the spot. Oh, it's true! in his tender youth, the author was a genuine Bible boy, the mildest lamb of God, that insatiable ogre who devours his prey alive. Born into an irreproachable Catholic family—his uncle Jean would be one of the four White Fathers assassinated by the GIA at Tizi-Ouzou on December 27th, 1994, and that uncle was a prince of a man, good-hearted, playful, even mischievous, and he was slain by a twenty-year-old kid who would be killed by the Algerian army a few months later, and that good-hearted uncle, playful, even mischievous, compassionate, would have mourned that death more than his own, that senseless mess, that deadly madness, that mindlessness, he who exercised his ministry with modesty, with none of the evangelical fanaticism of the first missionaries, simply being there, and staying there when the threat came down on him, doing his part as a public scribe for the neighborhood people who gave him their paperwork to fill out and who expressed to the family their shame, their anger, their grief when he was shot down like a dog, that day when for the first time, the one and only time, the faith of his brother—the author's father—wavered, later to grow stronger again, but now wavered as it never had when the adolescent author, newly subscribed to the *Atheist Bulletin*, read him passages from *The Antichrist* or, with some venom, spat what he thought to be irrefutable arguments in his face: So what about the first soul? When does the first soul date from? Are we to believe that the son of some rough prehominid suddenly found himself endowed with a soul? There's one father who would have been even more horrified by his offspring than you! Or else: What about a father who lives a saintly, sinless Christian existence, and so earns his salvation, what happens to him if his son's a blasphemer and leads a dissolute life that condemns him to Hell? What will Heaven be for the father, whose son is burning in Hell?—born into that

Come to the aid of your little Pierrots, your Hortenses, your Jeannes and Jeannettes. Ease their sorrows, since you're the only one who can do it! Open your magnanimous, munificent hand, then close it again on the ignoble crucifer, rip it out by the roots, pump away the béchamel, scour and scrub, O holy one! Be a father to us at long last, admit your mistakes and we will forgive them, enough of this, wipe it all away, O Papa!

Once again I fell silent, my eye watchful, my ear bent: nothing.

I fell to my knees—*splatch!*—landing in the gratin, inevitably. God loves poses of humility, of humiliation, he likes you to graze on his grass. He took care that the mightiest animals have curved, bent spines, heavy foreheads, their nostrils deep in the clover. I bent down as he wished, like the buffalo, like the elephant, lower than the ground.

Then like the walrus, I crawled.

God oh God, part the seas and drown cauliflower gratin, you have

---

irreproachable Catholic family, before he rebelled, before he read Nietzsche, or misread, mostly, though he never mixed up the order of the consonants in his name, which earned him good grades in philosophy class, before he admitted, above all, that he did not feel God's presence anywhere around him, and especially not within him, that he felt only a terrifying absence (for atheism is like wine, joyous for some, who draw from it delight by the bucketful, unbridled merriment, the intoxication of uninhibited freedom and joy, and sad for others, the author among them, who find in it only dereliction, a bitter awareness of the absurdity of our lot), even and especially in the course of those interminable Sunday masses, listening to the priest drone his desperately flat metaphors, the way, the light, the harvest, before he lost faith, then, or rather before he admitted to himself that he'd never really had it, that he only believed he believed, that he was the victim of a spell, of the influence of his family, his environment, that he had agreed with no reason to doubt it that God was God as milk was milk, a bird a bird, or a chair a seat with a back and no arms, before the revolt that so saddened and worried his parents, the author in his childhood was a devout little old lady of the sort you never see anymore. His ministry as a choirboy was short-lived, however; he got a few paper cones of sugared almonds at baptisms, a few handfuls of small change, immediately confiscated by the priest for the needs of the parish, he had a fit of uncontrollable laughter at a funeral, which earned him a supplementary sermon, then he fled the sacristy one day, gripped by panic, when he found himself serving at Mass all alone, and joined his parents in the front row of the church: at the end of the service, the priest brought him his shame-besmirched jacket, holding it by the collar. The consequences of that desertion went no further than that, he was granted holy clemency: he expiated his crime in confession.

that power! God oh God, may the mountains crumble onto cauliflower gratin, you have that power, may the boar and the bison tunnel
through it like termites in house frames until the whole thing col-
lapses, you can do that as well, it's child's play for you, God oh God,
do it for your Jeanjeans, for your Marguerites, your Bernadettes,
your little Blaises!

Do it for your Octavios, your Dinas, your Priscillas, your Isabelles!

God oh God, my God!

Deliver us from our daily cauliflower gratin!

I waited a while. You have to expect a little delay, for reflection
and reaction. So many measures to be taken, even when you have carte
blanche—such an ambitious reform! so vast! so decisive! absolute!

Even for the warts, it took a few days.

Still, after a few days they were gone.

I tried again. My prayer was too short. God was a stickler for
protocol.

I laid it on thicker.

Oh my God, creator of heaven and earth and all that goes into
cauliflower gratin, unharden your heart.

Will you let your Naths, your Matts, your Grégoires go on floun-
dering?

What will you do for Ernest, Violette, and Pandora?

And what for Albert?

And for Franz, and for Luce?

Nothing? Really, you'll do nothing?

Not even for Agathe and Suzie?

For Agathe and Suzie at least?[38]

---

38 Superstition? Residue of a religious faith that won't wash away? A coy little
wager cravenly palmed off on Blaise? The author can't resist quietly slipping the
names of his daughters Agathe and Suzie into this list. But also, when you're a
writer, how to renounce the two prettiest words in the French language? On reaching adulthood, as a matter of filial duty, Agathe and Suzie will burrow into the
tunnel of his books—dozens of titles by then—from which, years later, their sal-
low little faces will emerge, hollow-eyed, sneering, and desolate; poor little things,
now cursed with scoliosis and myopia, their youth left behind in that maze …
Consumed by remorse and regret, the author cannot advise them strongly enough
to reserve those pleasures for their old age.

At least don't abandon Agathe and Suzie!

God oh God!

For pity's sake!

My voice swelled, and I looked around for updrafts, hoping to heighten my prayer's chances of reaching its goal, of being heard up top, of finding the Ear of the Almighty in His celestial retreat.

No answer.

It was like asking the tiger to have fewer fangs, fewer claws, fewer black stripes on its orange fur, fewer roars. Nothing would come of my complaint. Not on the agenda. I might just as well have demanded an extra arm, my two hands struggling to describe and define in the air what the third would have grasped without effort: that's what prayer is, and it's swallowed up by the silence.

(Simply by those men's grave, lined faces, we could tell this was a serious matter. These guys held the fate of the world in their hands. Or not, on closer inspection: only two pétanque balls.)

How to live, given that, in society? How to be sociable? How to knowingly expose myself to the danger of seeing a dish of cauliflower gratin—careful, it's hot—land on my hosts' table? What to do then, if not empty my clip into them? As you see, Mademoiselle, one question leads to another, and before long we're counting the bodies. And I'm not even counting my own, which would thus have to be added to the list, my face flushed with black blood, my limbs stiff with terror. Could I accept invitations that might turn out so badly?

That's why I withdrew.

I retired.

I stopped leaving my house, scarcely a touch, scarcely a glance exchanged even with she who shared it.

Two parallel, sphinx-headed andirons: the delights of a happy home life.

Myself, furthermore, turned to the wall, toward the hearth's blackened back.

Sullen and distant as can be.

Others were such a threat!

Even with the most winsome face, the most cordial character, nothing guaranteed they weren't already devising the plan that would lure me into the ambush we now know so well. Any chance meeting with an amiable stranger might conceal a trap. I took my eyes off him for one second: there he was, hard at work in the kitchen!

The traitor!

I was about to confide in him. At long last spill my guts on a friendly shoulder. I'd bought two trouts and a little packet of slivered almonds. The butter was sizzling in my pan. I turned an attentive and understanding ear to his tales. If his nose ran, I took out my handkerchief. In me he'd found a brother, a father, a benevolent priest, an inventive and uninhibited lover. I would be his cat, his duck, his rat. I pushed the boundaries of friendship so far as to encroach into the lands of solitude and animosity. I was ready to fight him, if that's what he liked. Pick him up by the nose, hooking two fingers into his nostrils, if that's what he wanted.

And what did I get for my trouble, my thoughtfulness?

What trouble did he go to in return? How did he thoughtfully repay me?

By coldly picking out a couple of cauliflowers from the greengrocer's stand; by coldly removing their leaves in his kitchen; by coldly cutting up their little yellow bouquets, then coldly tossing them into boiling water!

There, Mademoiselle, is the truth about friendship.

There is the true face of the friend.

After all I've done for him!

He cuts me into pieces! He parboils me alive! Or almost—because I'm his real target. You can't fool me.[39]

---

39 Here, once again, the author is torn between an act of contrition and a self-serving defense. He flees all quarrel and conflict, and prefers to break things off at the first sign of discord, the moment the relationship threatens to sour. Several of his friends have paid the price for this preference, along with him, share and share alike. He is well aware of the theory of the partisans of perpetual psychodrama: the friend is that frank, loyal companion who nurtures you with wise counsel and keeps a close eye on you to make sure you don't go astray. If your jacket is in bad taste, he'll frankly and loyally tell you. Your nose is getting longer with age: he'll tell you. Soon it seems all his attentions aspire only to uncover your faults. He

The ingrate! As if I hadn't listened to him drone on night after night about Louise, and then Éloïse, as if that weren't my umbrella you see him carrying in the downpour, while the water cascades from my hair, as if I hadn't given him half of my fortune and unquestioningly dug a trench in my cellar for a long rolled-up rug he didn't know where to store, a pair of boots strangely poking out from one end, as if he weren't still of this world only by the grace of my left kidney and right lung!

A most bitter experience, believe you me.

Who can you trust after that?

Possessed by the demon of self-destruction, self-loathing, would that one day be me in the kitchen, emptying the pot of boiling water into a colander, draining that cursed cauliflower over the sink, carefully arranging its pestilential bouquets in a gratinée pan as if in a vase, pouring hot milk over the white roux, grating cheese into the wallpaper-paste sauce: and how hideous that floral motif! It's my childhood bedroom closing in on me, the doorway bricked up and covered with that same dismal paper, its spare pieces plastered to the bottom of my dresser drawers, so as to block off those last refuges or escape routes as well, forbidding me even the possibility of a withdrawal into myself, the shelter of a secret world, privacy, introversion, self-possession.

(It was frightening. We didn't like that music. We didn't like that literature. We didn't like that art. We didn't like that fashion, that mentality, that society. We didn't like that youth. We were beginning to cast the police loving glances when they brutalized one of those enormous, rubber-supple, dog-voiced louts, who suddenly seemed to us the real masters of

---

becomes difficult to distinguish from the enemy, though better informed about you and for that reason better equipped to cause you pain. For he knows all your sore spots, and he knows he need only touch one, very lightly, to bring the hurt raging back. The author wants no part of such friendship. He wants souls entirely won over to him, self-selected allies; he wants to be accompanied on his downhill slide if he chooses to barrel down merrily, and race to the bottom with a laugh, hand in hand with his friend. But you who come to him with a magnifying mirror and a bucket of cold water, do not hope for his gratitude; bring him flowers, cakes, don't spare the praise. Because that's what friendship means to him; if he wants a bumpy ride, he'll make do with the trot of his ill-tempered donkey and the uneven ground beneath his feet, which have never let him down.

this world, insolent, swaggering, violent, when they were in fact likely the most downtrodden of all, and even as we cried out for the revolution that would topple the system, we knew it could only come from them, we knew they alone had the necessary nerve, energy, and anger—the insolence, swagger, and violence—and we secretly feared the resulting upheavals even more, for we were afraid of them, their enormous rubber bodies, their dog-like voices, we were afraid of everything. We didn't like anything anymore.)

Can you imagine that?

Like I was consumed with the stuff.

Worse yet: I sensed that my arms, my hands, my fingers, ostensibly busy with utterly unrelated tasks, were in fact, from sunup to sundown, making the very moves required to brew up the poison that was killing me.

All day long, I labored over a cauliflower—my arms pulled it from the ground, my hands stripped off the leaves, my fingers broke it into bouquets, on and on, without surcease.

I thus—O height of irony—evoked the loathed cauliflower, I invoked it, convoked it; summoned up from the abyss, it took shape between my palms, I bore it wherever I went.

I must have had all the look of a man obsessed, a maniac.

The man who's never without his cauliflower!

The man who gratinées from dawn till dusk!

And even deep into the night. At night too, in his dreams.

That was me!

I didn't dare touch my face, take my head in my hands, I could feel suspicious rough spots beneath my fingers, grainy patches, an eczema that seemed the symptom of an illness nearing its final stages, when the allergy sympathizes with the allergen—and the beaten child becomes an abusive father.

A paradoxical effect of my idée fixe, I perpetuated the very abomination I claimed to flee, better than any other ever could.

—Now, there's an idea, children, I'll make us a cauliflower gratin for dinner! a woman cried out one day, running into me in the street with her two daughters, just when I was putting on my most innocent air, the hood of my parka pulled down over my brow, my perverse, disobedient hands thrust deep into my pockets.

These mortifications began to come thick and fast. I could no longer sit down in a restaurant: not even taking my order, the waiter inexorably brought me a dish of cauliflower gratin, and if I balked, he claimed I'd demanded precisely that dish, observing that the customer is of course always right, but they'd had to move heaven and earth back in the kitchen to satisfy me, adding with a touch of irritation that it was not the usual thing to fulfill such desires in a pizzeria, and not only were my protests uncalled-for, but it wouldn't kill me to show a little gratitude!

Here, then, is what even professional restaurateurs could read on my face!

In a market, I was pursued by a greengrocer convinced I had lifted a cauliflower from her stand, certain I was still hiding it under my jacket. Her harpy-like shrieks brought the crowd running. I was soon surrounded, a circle of furious, howling faces closing in on me, whereupon a wholesale butcher, a chevillard, herculean like all of them, seized me by the shoulder and brutally wrestled me to the ground. The greengrocer's hooked hands soon reduced my clothing to rags. Not surprisingly, nothing came of this search, but I was suspected of having ditched the cauliflower as I fled. They sniffed at me: you can still smell it! You can still smell it!

I was this close to being lynched.

Once again I holed up at home.

But don't go thinking I found any peace there.

Peace?

What on earth is that?

The contamination had spread to my domestic environment. It was now my own modest possessions being corrupted by that invasive force, down to my plump pillow, down to the eiderdown, and I awoke from my nightmare to an even worse reality that left me missing that nightmare like some magical dream.

Cauliflower gratin entered my house with the rising sun; it bubbled in the lightbulb; it dripped from all my faucets; it backed up from the plumbing; it spilled over the sideboards, the cupboards—no more soft rug to stretch out on!—I opened a cabinet, only to be submerged in the flood.

And the level was rising and rising.

The ceiling was coming closer.

It must have been then that my last resistance gave way, and I lost my footing.

You must admit, Mademoiselle, I'd displayed superhuman patience.

You must admit, I had stoically endured my lot, clinging tight as I could to the guardrail of logical thought to preserve some coherence for my mind, some cohesion for my body, disciplining my constantly irritated, sorely tested nerves, amid the relentless mockery, debasement, and humiliation of my good faith, my good will, my disposition to love the beautiful things and beings of the animal and vegetal worlds, save the crucifer reduced to a pap and gratinéed, with which I am unstoppably force-fed the moment I open my mouth, just to keep me quiet, I came to understand that, because my word is an accusation, because my song is off-key, because no one wants to hear what I have to say nor listen to my solutions, and people would rather see me suffocate, choke, and perish, as if I would let them do as they please and never fight back, but you little know me, and now it's time we got to the murder, well past time, my dear, let's get to the murder.

(And sometimes, too, inexplicably, a man who nonetheless seemed in full possession of his faculties and who for nearly thirty years had lived tranquilly alongside his spouse abruptly leapt on this latter as she sat beside him on a café terrace, and broke her neck.)[40]

---

40 With this the author claims to give his tale of suspense a surprise resolution, whereas we sometimes solve the mysteries concocted by the masters of that genre well before the last lines, thereby threatening the dominance of aged English ladies in that arena. He trusts that this twist will leave his reader agape, and, why not, stammering, *Wha ... wha ...* —even as he magisterially demonstrates *in fine* that he was firmly holding his character's reins all along, dropping them only so as to precipitate him into a crime, according to a carefully worked-out plan. The author will however readily concede that he takes less care with the end of his tales than with the beginning, believing that every end—including, then, the end of life—is a catastrophe before which, powerless, despairing, and paralyzed, we can only look on. It is true that this notion suffers from a certain paradoxical idealism, or perhaps negative idealism, for how can we ever know what's starting and what's ending: does BIG BANG not sound more like the end of it all than the beginning?

⑤ SELECTED DALKEY ARCHIVE TITLES

MICHAL AJVAZ, *The Golden Age,*
The Other City.

PIERRE ALBERT-BIROT, *Grabinoulor.*

YUZ ALESHKOVSKY, *Kangaroo.*

FELIPE ALFAU, *Chromos,*
Locos.

IVAN ÂNGELO, *The Celebration,*
The Tower of Glass.

ANTÓNIO LOBO ANTUNES,
Knowledge of Hell,
The Splendor of Portugal.

ALAIN MRIAS-MISSON, *Theatre of Incest.*

JOHN ASHBERY AND JAMES SCHUYLER,
A Nest of Ninnies.

ROBERT ASHLEY, *Perfect Lives.*

GABRIELA AVIGUR-ROTEM,
Heatwave and Crazy Birds.

DJUNA BARNES, *Ladies Almanack,*
Ryder.

JOHN BARTH, *Letters.*
Sabbatical.

DONALD BARTHELME, *The King,*
Paradise.

SVETISLAV BASARA, *Chinese Letter.*

MIQUEL BAUÇÀ, *The Siege in the Room.*

RENÉ BELLETTO, *Dying.*

MAREK BIEŃCZYK, *Transparency.*

ANDREI BITOV, *Pushkin House.*

ANDREJ BLATNIK, *You Do Understand.*

LOUIS PAUL BOON, *Chapel Road,*
My Little War.
Summer in Termuren.

ROGER BOYLAN, *Killoyle.*

IGNÁCIO DE LOYOLA BRANDÃO,
Anonymous Celebrity.
Zero.

BONNIE BREMSER, *Troia: Mexican*
Memoirs.

CHRISTINE BROOKE-ROSE,
Amalgamemnon.

BRIGID BROPHY, *In Transit.*

GERALD L. BRUNS,
Modern Poetry and the Idea of Language.

GABRIELLE BURTON, *Heartbreak Hotel.*

MICHEL BUTOR, *Degrees,*
Mobile.

G. CABRERA INFANTE,
Infante's Inferno,
Three Trapped Tigers.

JULIETA CAMPMPOS,
The Fear of Losing Eurydice.

ANNE CARSON, *Eros the Bittersweet.*

ORLY CASTEL-BLOOM, *Dolly City.*

LOUIS-FERDINAND CÉLINE,
Castle to Castle.
Conversations with Professor Y,
London Bridge,
Normance,
North,
Rigadoon.

MARIE CHAIX,
The Laurels of Lake Constance.

HUGO CHARTERIS, *The Tide Is Right.*

ERIC CHEVILLARD, *Demolishing Nisard.*

MARC CHOLODENKO, *Mordechai*
Schamz.

JOSHUA COHEN, *Witz.*

EMILY HOLMES COLEMAN,
The Shutter of Snow.

ROBERT COOVER, *A Night at the Movies.*

STANLEY CRAWFORD, *Log of the S.S,*
The Mrs Unguentine,
Some Instructions to My Wife.

RENÉ CREVEL, *Putting My Foot in It.*

RALPH CUSACK, *Cadenza.*

NICHOLAS DELBANCO,
The Count of Concord,
Sherbrookes.

NIGEL DENNIS, *Cards of Identity.*

PETER DIMOCK,
A Short Rhetoric for Leaving the Family.

ARIEL DORFMFMAN, *Konfidenz.*

SELECTED DALKEY ARCHIVE TITLES

COLEMAN DOWELL, *Island People,*
Too Much Flesh and Jabez.

ARKADII DRAGOMOSHCHENKO,
Dust.

RIKKI DUCORNET,
The Complete Butcher's Tales,
The Fountains of Neptune,
The Jade Cabinet,
Phosphor in Dreamland.

WILLIAM EASTLAKE, *The Bamboo Bed,*
Castle Keep,
Lyric of the Circle Heart.

JEAN ECHENOZ, *Chopin's Move.*

STANLEY ELKIN, *A Bad Man,*
Criers and Kibitzers, Kibitzers and Criers,
The Dick Gibson Show,
The Franchiser,
The Living End,
Mrs. Ted Bliss.

FRANÇOIS EMMMMANUEL,
Invitation to a Voyage.

SALVADOR ESPRIU,
Ariadne in the Grotesque Labyrinth.

LESLIE A. FIEDLER,
Love and Death in the American Novel.

JUAN FILLOY, *Op Oloop.*

ANDY FITCH, *Pop Poetics.*

GUSTAVE FLAUBERT,
Bouvard and Pécuchet.

KASS FLEISHER, *Talking out of School.*

FORD MADOX FORD,
The March of Literature.

JON FOSSE, *Aliss at the Fire,*
Melancholy.

MAX FRISCH, *I'm Not Stiller,*
Man in the Holocene.

CARLOS FUENTES, *Christopher Unborn,*
Distant Relations,
Terra Nostra,
Where the Air Is Clear.

TAKEHIKO FUKUNAGA,
Flowers of Grass.

WILLIAM GADDIS, J R, *The Recognitions.*

JANICE GALLOWAY, *Foreign Parts,*
The Trick Is to Keep Breathing.

WILLIAM H H. GASS,
Cartesian Sonata and Other Novellas,
Finding a Form,
A Temple of Texts,
The Tunnel,
Willie Masters' Lonesome Wife.

GÉRARD GAVARRY, *Hoppla! 1 2 3.*

ETIENNE GILSON,
The Arts of the Beautiful, Forms
and Substances in the Arts.

C. S S. GISCOMBE, *Giscome Road,*
Here.

DOUGLAS GLOVER,
Bad News of the Heart.

WITOLD GOMBROWICZ,
A Kind of Testament.

PAULO EMÍLIO SALES GOMES,
P's Three Women.

GEORGI GOSPODINOV, *Natural Novel.*

JUAN GOYTISOLO, *Count Julian,*
Juan the Landless,
Makbara,
Marks of Identity.

HENRY GREEN, *Back,*
Blindness,
Concluding,
Doting,
Nothing.

JACK GREEN, *Fire the Bastards!*

JIRˇIˊ GRUSˇA, *The Questionnaire.*

MELA HARTWIG,
Am I a Redundant Human Being?

JOHN HAWKES, *The Passion Artist,*
Whistlejacket.

ELIZABETH HEIGHWAY, ED.,
Contemporary Georgian Fiction.

ALEKSANDAR HEMON, ED.,
Best European Fiction.

FOR A FULL LIST OF PUBLICATIONS, VISIT: www.dalkeyarchive.com

⬒ SELECTED DALKEY ARCHIVE TITLES

AIDAN HIGGINS, *Balcony of Europe,*
Blind Man's Bluff,
Bornholm Night-Ferry,
Flotsam and Jetsam,
Langrishe, Go Down,
Scenes from a Receding Past.

KEIZO HINO, *Isle of Dreams.*

KAZUSHI HOSAKA, *Plainsong.*

ALDOUS HUXLEY, *Antic Hay,*
Crome Yellow,
Point Counter Point,
Those Barren Leaves,
Time Must Have a Stop.

NAOYUKI II, *The Shadow of a Blue Cat.*

GERT JONKE, *The Distant Sound,*
Geometric Regional Novel,
Homage to Czerny,
The System of Vienna.

JACQUES JOUET, *Mountain R,*
Savage,
Upstaged.

MIEKO KANAI, *The Word Book.*

YORAM KANIUK, *Life on Sandpaper.*

HUGH KENNER, Flaubert,
Joyce and Beckett: The Stoic Comedians,
Joyce's Voices.

DANILO KIŠ, *The Attic,*
Garden, Ashes,
The Lute and the Scars,
Psalm 44,
A Tomb for Boris Davidovich.

ANITA KONKKA, *A Fool's Paradise.*

GEORGE KONRÁD, *The City Builder.*

TADEUSZ KONWICKI,
A Minor Apocalypse,
The Polish Complex.

MENIS KOUMANDAREAS, *Koula.*

ELAINE KRAF, *The Princess of 72nd Street.*

JIM KRUSOE, *Iceland.*

AYŞE KULIN,
Farewell: A Mansion in Occupied Istanbul.

EMILIO LASCANO TEGUI,
On Elegance While Sleeping.

ERIC LAURRENT, *Do Not Touch.*

VIOLETTE LEDUC, *La Bâtarde.*

EDOUARD LEVÉ, *Autoportrait,*
Suicide.

MARIO LEVI, *Istanbul Was a Fairy Tale.*

DEBORAH LEVY, *Billy and Girl.*

JOSE´ LEZAMA LIMA, *Paradiso.*

ROSA LIKSOM, *Dark Paradise.*

OSMAN LINS,
Avalovara,
The Queen of the Prisons of Greece.

ALF MAC LOCHLAINN,
The Corpus in the Library,
Out of Focus.

RON LOEWINSOHN, *Magnetic Field(s).*

MINA LOY, *Stories and Essays of Mina Loy.*

D. KEITH MANO, *Take Five.*

MICHELINE AHARONIAN MARCOM,
The Mirror in the Well.

BEN MARCUS, *The Age of Wire and String.*

WALLACE MARKFIELD, *Teitelbaum's*
Window,
To an Early Grave.

DAVID MARKSON, *Reader's Block,*
Wittgenstein's Mistress.

CAROLE MASO, *AVA.*

LADISLAV MATEJKA &
KRYSTYNA POMORSKA, EDS.,
Readings in Russian Poetics: Formalist and
Structuralist Views.

HARRY MATHEWS, *Cigarettes,*
The Conversions,
The Human Country: New and Collected Stories,
The Journalist,
My Life in CIA,
Singular Pleasures,
The Sinking of the Odradek
Stadium,
Tlooth.

JOSEPH MCELROY,
Night Soul and Other Stories.

⬛ SELECTED DALKEY ARCHIVE TITLES

ABDELWAHAB MEDDEB, *Talismano.*

GERHARD MEIER, *Isle of the Dead.*

HERMAN MELVILLE, *The Confidence-Man.*

AMANDA MICHALOPOULOU, *I'd Like.*

STEVEN MILLHAUSER,
The Barnum Museum,
In the Penny Arcade.

RALPH J. MILLS, JR., *Essays on Poetry.*

MOMUS, *The Book of Jokes.*

CHRISTINE MONTALBETTI,
The Origin of Man,
Western.

OLIVE MOORE, *Spleen.*

NICHOLAS MOSLEY, *Accident,*
Assassins,
Catastrophe Practice,
Experience and Religion,
A Garden of Trees,
Hopeful Monsters,
Imago Bird,
Impossible Object,
Inventing God,
Judith,
Look at the Dark,
Natalie Natalia,
Serpent,
Time at War.

WARREN MOTTE, *Fables of the Novel: French Fiction since 1990,*
Fiction Now: The French Novel in the 21st Century,
Oulipo: A Primer of Potential Literature.

GERALD MURNANE, *Barley Patch,*
Inland.

YVES NAVARRE,
Our Share of Time,
Sweet Tooth.

DOROTHY NELSON, *In Night's City,*
Tar and Feathers.

ESHKOL NEVO, *Homesick.*

WILFRIDO D D. NOLLEDO,
But for the Lovers.

FLANN O'BRIEN, *At Swim-Two-Birds,*
The Best of Myles,
The Dalkey Archive,
The Hard Life,
The Poor Mouth,
The Third Policeman.

CLAUDE OLLIER, *The Mise-en-Scène,*
Wert and the Life Without End.

GIOVANNI ORELLI, *Walaschek's Dream.*

PATRIK OUŘEDNÍK, *Europeana,*
The Opportune Moment, 1855.

BORIS PAHOR, *Necropolis.*

FERNANDO DEL PASO,
News from the Empire,
Palinuro of Mexico.

ROBERT PINGET, *The Inquisitory,*
Mahu or The Material,
Trio.

MANUEL PUIG, *Betrayed by Rita Hayworth,*
The Buenos Aires Affair,
Heartbreak Tango.

RAYMYMOND QUENEAU, *The Last Days,*
Odile,
Pierrot Mon Ami,
Saint Glinglin.

ANN QUIN, *Berg,*
Passages,
Three,
Tripticks.

ISHMAEL REED, *The Free-Lance Pallbearers,*
The Last Days of Louisiana Red,
Ishmael Reed: The Plays,
Juice!,
Reckless Eyeballing,
The Terrible Threes,
The Terrible Twos,
Yellow Back Radio Broke-Down.

JASIA REICHARDT,
15 Journeys Warsaw to London.

NOËLLE REVAZ,
With the Animals.

JOÃO UBALDO RIBEIRO,
House of the Fortunate Buddhas.

JEAN RICARDOU, *Place Names*.

RAINER MARIA RILKE,
The Notebooks of Malte Laurids Brigge.

JULIÁN RÍOS, *The House of Ulysses*,
Larva: A Midsummer Night's Babel,
Poundemonium,
Procession of Shadows.

AUGUSTO ROA BASTOS, *I the Supreme*.

DANIËL ROBBERECHTS,
Arriving in Avignon.

JEAN ROLIN,
The Explosion of the Radiator Hose.

OLIVIER ROLIN, *Hotel Crystal*.

ALIX CLEO ROUBAUD, *Alix's Journal*.

JACQUES ROUBAUD,
*The Form of a City Changes Faster, Alas,
Than the Human Heart*,
The Great Fire of London,
Hortense in Exile,
Hortense Is Abducted,
The Loop,
Mathematics, *The Plurality of Worlds of Lewis*,
The Princess Hoppy,
Some Thing Black.

RAYMYMOND ROUSSEL,
Impressions of Africa.

VEDRANA RUDAN, *Night*.

STIG SÆTERBAKKEN, *Siamese*,
Self Control.

LYDIE SALVAYRE, *The Company of Ghosts*,
The Lecture,
The Power of Flies.

LUIS RAFAEL SÁNCHEZ,
Macho Camacho's Beat.

SEVERO SARDUY, *Cobra & Maitreya*.

NATHALIE SARRAUTE,
Do You Hear Them?,
Martereau,
The Planetarium.

ARNO SCHMIDT, *Collected Novellas*,
Collected Stories,
Nobodaddy's Children,
Two Novels.

ASAF SCHURR, *Motti*.

GAIL SCOTT, *My Paris*.

DAMION SEARLS, *What We Were Doing and
Where We Were Going*.

JUNE AKERS SEESE,
Is This What Other Women Feel Too?,
What Waiting Really Means.

BERNARD SHARE, *Inish*, *Transit*.

VIKTOR SHKLOVSKY, *Bowstring*,
Knight's Move,
A Sentimental Journey: Memoirs 1917–1922,
Energy of Delusion: A Book on Plot,
Literature and Cinematography,
Theory of Prose,
Third Factory,
Zoo, or Letters Not about Love.

PIERRE SINIAC, *The Collaborators*.

KJERSTI A. SKOMSVOLD,
The Faster I Walk, the Smaller I Am.

JOSEF ŠKVORECKÝ,
The Engineer of Human Souls.

GILBERT SORRENTINO,
Aberration of Starlight,
Blue Pastoral,
Crystal Vision,
Imaginative Qualities of Actual Things,
Mulligan Stew,
Pack of Lies,
Red the Fiend,
The Sky Changes,
Something Said,
Splendide-Hôtel,
Steelwork,
Under the Shadow.

W. M. SPACKMAN, *The Complete Fiction*.

ANDRZEJ STASIUK, *Dukla*,
Fado.

GERTRUDE STEIN, *The Making of Americans*,
A Novel of Thank You.

LARS SVENDSEN, *A Philosophy of Evil*.

PIOTR SZEWC, *Annihilation*.

GONÇALO M. TAVARES, *Jerusalem*,
Joseph Walser's Machine,
Learning to Pray in the Age of Technique.

LUCIAN DAN TEODOROVICI,
Our Circus Presents . . .

NIKANOR TERATOLOGEN,
Assisted Living.

STEFAN THEMERSON,
Hobson's Island,
The Mystery of the Sardine,
Tom Harris.

TAEKO TOMIOKA, *Building Waves.*

JOHN TOOMEY, *Sleepwalker.*

JEAN-PHILIPPPPE TOUSSAINT,
The Bathroom,
Camera,
Monsieur,
Reticence,
Running Away,
Self-Portrait Abroad,
Television,
The Truth about Marie.

DUMITRU TSEPENEAG,
Hotel Europa,
The Necessary Marriage,
Pigeon Post,
Vain Art of the Fugue.

ESTHER TUSQUETS,
Stranded.

DUBRAVKA UGRESIC,
Lend Me Your Character,
Thank You for Not Reading.

TOR ULVEN, *Replacement.*

MATI UNT,
Brecht at Night,
Diary of a Blood Donor,
Things in the Night.

ÁLVARO URIBE AND OLIVIA SEARS, EDS.,
Best of Contemporary Mexican Fiction.

ELOY URROZ, *Friction,*
The Obstacles.

LUISA VALENZUELA,
Dark Desires and the Others,
He Who Searches.

PAUL VERHAEGHEN,
Omega Minor.

AGLAJA VETERANYI,
Why the Child Is Cooking in the Polenta.

BORIS VIAN, *Heartsnatcher.*

LLORENÇ VILLALONGA, *The Dolls' Room.*

TOOMAS VINT, *An Unending Landscape.*

ORNELA VORPSI,
The Country Where No One Ever Dies.

AUSTRYN WAINHOUSE,
Hedyphagetica.

CURTIS WHITE,
America's Magic Mountain,
The Idea of Home,
Memories of My Father Watching TV,
Requiem.

DIANE WILLIAMS,
Excitability: Selected Stories, Romancer Erector.

DOUGLAS WOOLF,
Wall to Wall,
Ya! & John-Juan.

JAY WRIGHT,
Polynomials and Pollen,
The Presentable Art of Reading Absence.

PHILIP WYLIE, *Generation of Vipers.*

MARGUERITE YOUNG,
Angel in the Forest,
Miss MacIntosh, My Darling.

REYOUNG, *Unbabbling.*

VLADO Z̆ABOT, *The Succubus.*

ZORAN Z̆IVKOVIC̀, *Hidden Camera.*

LOUIS ZUKOFSKY, *Collected Fiction.*

VITOMIL ZUPAN, *Minuet for Guitar.*

SCOTT ZWIREN, *God Head.*